RUNNING FROM ME

RUNNING FROM ME

TAMARA MARTIN

THE HENRY MAYBERRY GROUP
Adelaide, South Australia

First published in Australia 2017 by The Henry Mayberry Group

www.thehenrymayberrygroup.com

Edited by Cathleen Ross

National Library of Australia Cataloguing-In-Publication data

Martin,Tamara, 1973-

The Fall of Jaz / Tamara Martin

1st ed.

ISBN: 978-0-6480250-4-7 (pbk.)

Cover Design: Kristyn McQuiggan, Drop Dead Designs

For Kelly

my partner in crime who's been leading me astray on wonderful adventures and fighting over Ryan Reynolds since we were fresh face twenty somethings.

For Carly

who understands the value of wine, movies, popcorn and Jamie Fraser

thanks for being so awesome

CHAPTER 1

He was born with his head between the legs of a whore and that's where he'd stayed. He couldn't help himself. He couldn't help who he was. It was in his blood. It's how she'd raised him, his mother, the whore, a mythological woman I'd never met. A woman I only knew through the letters she sent him, the ones he kept hidden in the false bottom of his jock drawer. Now it was all he knew, the default for how he coped with his life, the expectations, disappointments and every other inescapable emotion thrust upon his emotionally stunted brain.

I knew, deep down inside, he didn't feel the way other people did, that he was as restless and alone as I was, always afraid someone would see through the carefully constructed layers. I'd seen glimpses now and again of the broken little boy that lay beneath his charming, suave exterior before he'd clam up and shut down. No one was allowed in. We were the same that way. With our walls and our secrets. It's why we were so good together.

He'd told me once, after too much wine, he felt dead inside, that nothing made him feel whole but me. I suspected the hookers helped. It was the orgasms, the touch of another person that made him feel alive. I got it, the need to feel, to be seen, to be reminded you exist.

He'd tried his best and despite his extracurricular activities, he treated me well. If only he knew the truth about me, about who I was and what I'd done. But he couldn't know, no one could ever know. That's where we were different. I knew who he was and I'd chosen to accept him for who he was, the walls and the secrets kept us both safe, and it had been fine enough while it lasted. Now things had gone too far and it was time to leave.

Whether I liked it or not, I had to go somewhere too far for him to search or to even think to search because I knew he would. He'd feel obliged to make sure I was okay because he was a good man deep down and apparently, he loved me.

Leaving behind the few dresses I'd worn to garden parties at The Governor's house, pantsuits, skirt suits, summer dresses and gowns, I stuffed only the jeans I'd come with, a few t-shirts, runners and toiletries into my faded black duffle bag. I added in my camera, the only thing of value I owned and the few mementos that always seemed to come with me as I dragged them from pillar to post; a photograph of my parents whose faces I could barely remember anymore and a ceramic cat holding a bunch of daisies from a grandmother who'd passed through one Christmas, never to be seen or heard from again.

The battered copy of *War and Peace* I'd stolen from the old lady who'd been my unknowing saviour went in as did the heart necklace wrapped in tissue paper and stuffed inside an old orange sock, it was a gift, the necklace, not the sock, from Nick Perry, the only man I'd ever dated just because I'd fancied him. I'd been sixteen, he'd been twenty-three and had no idea who I was and fancying the pants off him was almost the end of everything. I've learnt so much since then. I never did anything now, just because. I'd learnt not to get too close, not to give away too many secrets or people start to piece together the puzzle or at least figure out there's a puzzle to be pieced and I couldn't let that happen.

I took my keys out of the hand-painted red bowl with tiny blue flowers around the rim that we'd picked up at the markets one weekend and now kept on the cupboard by the front door. I removed his house keys and dropped them back into the bowl. Hoisting my duffle bag onto my shoulder, I exited through the front door, making sure to pull it closed because it had a habit of sticking in the warm weather and because I cared enough.

After I'd seen the hooker coming out of our home that Saturday afternoon, it was the final straw. I mightn't have objected to his extracurricular activities but bringing them to bed I slept in was too much. I'd found the diamond ring hidden under that false bottom in his jock drawer that morning, so I'd already been planning to leave when I saw her, it was just a matter of timing.

Tossing my duffle bag into the back of my Jeep, I headed north. The car had been a gift of sorts from an old boyfriend. It had sat rotting in his backyard. He'd said if I could get it running, I could have it. So I did. It had needed some spark plugs, a clean-up, some oil and a patch on the soft top, but once I was done, it worked fine enough and I'd taken it with me not long after. It was unregistered and uninsured but seeing as I didn't have a license, anyway, what did it matter?

Stopping at a supermarket just before I exited suburbia, I filled the cooler bag squashed under the passenger seat with cold soft drink, chocolate and premade sandwiches, enough for lunch and dinner. I didn't need to waste time waiting for food to be cooked in some middle of nowhere roadhouse. I put a shopping bag with water, muesli bars, cheezles, chicken crimpys and a family bag of snakes and jelly babies in the passenger foot well, opening the bag of violet crumble bites and leaving it on the seat.

I left the bustling supermarket car park and headed for the highway and kept driving, the warm sun beating down on my bare arms, the music turned up loud. I drove until I was hungry for something more than junk food. I held off for as long as I could but eventually I had to pee. I followed the exit signs to a rest area nestled in the shade of tall trees. I stretched my legs, reaching up high to stretch the muscles crinking in my back and shoulders. It felt good.

I took my sandwich and a can of Coke to the picnic table furthest from the car park. It was quiet and far away from the small family that had driven in behind me. I took a deep breath, breathed in the shadows, let them absorb me for a little while. I felt comfort in the dark. As though it were a kindred spirit, a lone wolf who understood the loneliness that consumed me.

Always alone. Just me. Even when I wasn't alone, I was alone. I could never be me. I could never just breathe and relax, not even for a minute. But this loneliness was better than the alternative, I thought as I let the last of the Coke drip from the can into my mouth, feeling the cool, syrupy sweetness coat my tongue and my throat as a lone ant scurried across the table in search of a stray sandwich crumb.

I waited until I needed another bathroom break, I didn't want that Coke hitting my bladder a few minutes up the highway, then I was back on the road. I wanted to cover as much distance as possible. One never knew in these situations if the ones left behind would come searching. The further up the coast I got before sleep claimed my weary eyeballs, the better.

The sun was getting ready to end the day when I drove into the next rest stop for dinner. Unlike the comfort I'd felt in the shadows of the earlier woodland, there was no comfort here in the gloominess that reached out from these shadows, as though they held secrets I didn't want to know. Something about the place gave me the icks. I'd been looking after myself for so long now that I had come to trust my instincts. I'd planned to spend the night, get some sleep in the back of the Jeep but instead, I put my rubbish in the nearby bin and headed back to the highway. It could be dangerous to push myself, to drive too far in a day but it was better than being hacked to bits in some random rest stop. I'd spent too much of what was supposed to be my childhood dodging unsavoury sorts. I'd nearly lost everything because of one. I wasn't about to ignore my instincts now.

I went into Ballina to top up with petrol and get a coffee from the Macca's drive through and then continued on my journey. Nothing but me and the inky, lonely night to keep each other company as I drove through gloomy forests and along empty highways, the occasional truck driver casting a weary eye over the world from his perch the only other sign of life.

I was used to the long drives. I'd crisscrossed the country often enough on my own. I didn't know why I was worrying about the long drive now. I'd gotten soft and comfortable while being taken care of by Michael, that's why. It had been a while since I'd had to pack up and run. I was out of practice, too accustomed to being safe. I'd have to be more careful from now on. No more boyfriends for a start, they get too nosey, they care too much, they fall in love and want you to fill out paperwork, like marriage licenses, you have no ID for. But it had been nice. For a minute. To be like everyone else, to not have to be this person, live this life. It was nice for just a minute to forget I'd walked away from a dying man with his pants around his ankles. To forget that because of that man I'd never been to high school, could never travel, marry, have a home of my own. Maybe I could have gone to the police, but Peter had always told me the sort of things that'd happen to me if I was locked up and I'd chosen the lesser of two evils. Maybe I could never be me, maybe I could never get too close to anyone, maybe I'd run from who I am for the rest of my life, but I was free.

It was late as I drove into Noosa, or some part of it. I was struggling to keep my eyes open despite the copious amounts of caffeine and sugar I'd piled into my system. I pulled into an all-night service station for a wee break and asked the bored attendant if there was somewhere nearby I could rest for a couple of hours. He offered the carpark at the back of the building. He seemed nice and I'd developed a good sense of people over the years, so I gratefully accepted. I parked between the big green dumpster and an old brown Mazda, locked up and climbed into the back where I curled up under the picnic rug that lived on the back seat, my duffle bag under my head as a pillow and I was out like a light.

CHAPTER 2

Everything was stiff when I woke in the morning, the hot sun turning the Jeep into a sweaty sauna. I creaked like an old lady and my head pounded from the kink in my neck and the knots in my shoulder. I stretched as best I could and took some paracetamol with stale water from the bottle I'd left in the console without its lid. I went into the servo and ordered a coffee from the same guy as the night before who was somehow still able to manage a cheery greeting, then I went to the toilet where I brushed my teeth and hair, wiped away the sweat with a paper towel, put on deodorant and a clean t-shirt before returning to the counter. I also bought a newspaper and left, finding my way to the local shopping centre car park.

People were already beginning their day as I sipped my coffee and flipped through the paper to the 'for rent' section. It was old school but it was my only option, I had an old phone buried somewhere that just needed some money added to the account, but I'd left my smartphone behind seeing as Michael paid the bill but I didn't have ID to get a new one so the old prepaid purchased before they required ID would have to do. It didn't matter, old school rental hunting still worked and I needed a bed and I needed one soon, I couldn't keep sleeping in the car. I read through the listings, circling a few that sounded like my kind of places.

After filling my belly with a McMuffin, some hash browns, an OJ and another coffee, I sorted out the money on the old phone and called the numbers in the ads I'd circled.

Thankfully, two answered and both were free to meet. I'd try the ones that hadn't answered later if I needed to, but I hoped I wouldn't have to. I hated the search. I just wanted it over with so I could get on with things, so I could sleep, there was no need to be picky about it.

I followed the google map on my phone to the first house, which was a run down, single storey, cream rendered house with chipped paint and foggy windows and a big sweeping front lawn full of dying grass.

A scruffy surfer with salt-caked dreadlocks answered the door, shirtless, wearing nothing but board shorts, looking as though he'd just woken up.

'Hey. You Jilly?' he mumbled.

'I am,' I said, feeling my intuition shaking its head.

'Tal. Come in. Straight ahead,' he said, introducing himself and inviting me in with a big smile.

I felt his eyes sweep over me as I walked down the hallway ahead of him as he instructed and that intuition went from shaking its head to screaming, *hell no*.

'In here,' he said, angling a long, tanned arm into the open doorway on my right.

We walked into a large lounge room that stank of stale beer, feet, sweat and weed. It was surprisingly bright considering the dirty windows, which I wished they'd opened. There was an equally scruffy, shirtless man in board shorts lounging on a sagging, brown and orange striped velour couch. Beer bottles, burger wrappers and takeaway bags covered the battered coffee table. A pizza box not properly closed showed the crusts of a long-ago dinner in the process of fossilisation, shoved under the table. There was a big screen television and too many game consoles and equipment to count thrown into a snake pit of wires against the wall facing the couches.

'Sit, please,' he suggested.

I didn't want to sit. Food stains, sand and cat hair, despite no sign of a cat, covered the threadbare throws on the sofas, hiding who knew what underneath. I felt itchy and grubby just looking at them.

There were piles of sand on the equally filthy carpet, it looked as though someone had upended a shoe and not vacuumed in a really long time. Through the archway, the kitchen sink was overflowing with dirty dishes, the benches weighted down with beer bottles, pizza boxes and empty wrappers. My stomach turned. They didn't need a housemate, they needed a visit from Oprah's clean-up crew.

The man lazing on the couch watched me with a creepy grin and my spine tingled.

'Actually, no, thanks,' I smiled. 'I don't think this place is for me, but thanks anyway,' I said, turning to leave.

'But you haven't even looked around or seen the room,' Tal whined, surprised.

'I've seen enough,' I said, practically running down the hallway and across the lawn, desperate to get out of there as fast as I could.

I sped down the street and waited until I was around the corner and out of sight before stopping and laughing. I'd seen worse and they probably would have been just the right kind of unobservant housemates. But I'd lived with my hooker loving boyfriend in a swanky inner suburbs bungalow for the last eight months and going back to living in the slums with wasted bums wasn't high on my agenda. Guess I'd grown picky as well as pampered.

I'd enjoyed my taste of the high life and I could only hope the next appointment was better. The ad said it was a fully furnished room in a converted Queenslander with a pool. The rent was higher, but money wasn't really an issue. I'd earnt okay in Sydney and my expenses had been low while living with Michael and there was the family money I carried in bag marked dirty underwear in my duffle if I got desperate.

As soon as I parked in front of the Queenslander, I knew that it was better than the first house. I'd been doing this, living this nomadic life long enough that I could get a sense of a place, of the people who lived there, even from this far away. This house screamed comfort and happiness. I could use some of that. My heart screamed for it, a safe, quiet place to rest my head and recoup my energy.

Someone had converted the old Queenslander into a beautiful two-storey home. The conversion was seamless, the outside painted a cornflower blue with bright, white trim. Lush frangipanis filled the front garden, shading the house from the hot sun. Flowering hedges lined the drive, pinks and blues and purples intertwining as though in a dance choreographed by Mother Nature. I crossed my fingers as I walked up the driveway deciding which entrance they used, the original one at the top of the stairs or the one I could see at the top of the driveway leading to the converted downstairs area.

A perky, pint-sized girl with a bright blue bob popped out from behind one of the flowering shrubs like a fairy holding a handful of purple blooms with a big bright smile.

'Hey, you must be Jilly?' she said. 'I'm Sienna, we spoke on the phone,' she added, shuffling secateurs into the hand with the blooms and offering her now free hand to me.

'Hi, nice to meet you,' I said, taking her hand.

'Come on in,' she said, leading me to the doorway at the top of the driveway. 'We don't really use the other entrance,' she smiled, ushering me in.

The door opened onto a large open room with clean, inviting, poufy beige sofas. The whole room appeared devoid of pizza boxes and beer bottles. There were two closed doors on my right that I guessed were bedrooms, a corner I couldn't see around, which I suspected held wet areas and a staircase in front of me.

'We tend to flit between the two spaces,' Sienna said as she led me up the stairs. 'We're all friends so it's very informal.'

The stairs led to a small hallway, we turned right and walked the few steps into the comfortable lounge room. It was a little smaller than the one downstairs but just as well cared for, bright and cosy. The pair of sofas were a sky blue, an armchair was navy blue and white striped. There was a guy and girl sitting on one of the sofas that backed onto the small, debris free, dining room encased in windows. They looked up from their conversation when we entered with friendly smiles.

'This is Melanie but you can just call her Mel and that's Rick,' she said, introducing me to the couple. 'Guys, this is Jilly.'

'Hey,' they said in unison.

'Can I get you something, coffee, water, soft drink?' offered Sienna.

'No, I'm fine thanks.'

'Well, sit,' she smiled, indicating the armchair, so I sat.

'Are you new to town?' she asked.

'Yeah, just drove in this morning.'

'Nice. Where from?' asked Mel.

'Sydney,' I told them.

'You'll be wanting somewhere to sleep pretty soon then if you're planning to stick around, yeah?' asked Rick.

'I certainly am. Planning to stick around for a while, that is, so yeah, would be great to sort out somewhere to live as soon as I can.'

'What do you do for a job?' Rick asked.

'I'm a photographer. I usually sell my stuff at markets. I read there's a good one up this way. It's part of the reason I decided to move here. That and the lure of somewhere sunny but I always need a good market.'

'Oh, you'll love Eumundi, then, it's fantastic,' cooed Sienna. 'It's open Wednesdays and Sundays. I can go with you this week if you want to have a look,' she suggested. 'If you decide this is the place for you, that is.'

'That'd be great, thanks. What do you guys do? This isn't just a beautiful façade you have going on here, is it?'

Sienna giggled. 'Nah, we're all employed. I work at the Beach House. It's a cocktail bar on Hastings. I'm on the arvo shift today and I gig here and there with my band on the weekends,' she said.

'You're in a band?' I asked, thinking she might be the coolest person I'd met in a while.

'Don't be too impressed until you hear them,' Melanie chimed in, laughing.

'Hey!' exclaimed Sienna, not taking her seriously.

'I'm kidding, I'm kidding,' Mel defended. 'They're really good. You wait until you hear them,' she added proudly. 'I work on the front desk at a yoga retreat up in the hills. You timed your call perfectly, I'm going up there to catch up on some things and take a class this afternoon but you caught me before I left,' she smiled. 'Rick probably has the most sensible job, he's a fire fighter,' she said proudly.

'Impressive,' I said.

'Maybe. I still surf too much and we spend a lot of time on the job eating junk food and watching movies,' he grinned.

'Sounds pretty perfect to me,' I smiled.

'It's a pretty good deal,' he admitted with a satisfied smile.

'So, what do you think?' asked Sienna.

'You guys seem like you'd make fabulous housemates, the place looks great, much better than the last house I went to,' I said, telling them about the dirty surfer guys.

They laughed. 'I promise, we might not always behave like grownups but we clean up after ourselves,' Sienna said.

'Well, some of us do,' Mel giggled, nudging Rick.

'Hey, I'm housetrained,' he defended.

Mel snorted.

'Well, your room would be just down the hallway,' Sienna said, rolling her eyes at Mel and Rick. 'I'm up here as well. Mel and Rick are downstairs and there's a spare downstairs too which we like to keep just in case friends need a place to crash or my folks are in town or whatever.'

It sounded perfect. Almost too good to be true. 'What

happened to the last person?' I asked. It was always a good indicator as to what I was getting myself into.

'Ah,' smiled Sienna. 'That would be Mel. Rick moved in downstairs a while back and they've been shagging for ages, now they've finally decided to just occupy the one room, leaving us with a spare for you,' she smiled.

'Well, lucky for me.'

'Lucky all round, I say,' added Rick with a boyish grin that made Mel giggle like a schoolgirl.

They were sweet and I could feel they were nice people. I liked them. Some people are like that, you can just tell they're nice straight away. 'It's a great place from what I can see. Can I see the room?' I asked, crossing my fingers it was as perfect as them, as the rest of the house.

'Of course, come on through,' Sienna said, leading me down the hallway. 'That's me,' she said pointing to a door on the right. 'Bathroom straight ahead, and this is you,' she said, opening the door.

There was a big window overlooking the backyard and the pool. A double bed with simple, pale blue linen, two white bedsides, a small built in robe and a ceiling fan, which I'd read was necessary in these parts. I stepped into the room to get a feel for it but I didn't really need to, it was perfect and I got a great vibe from Sienna, Mel and Rick; this was my new home, I just had to hope they were as easy going as they seemed.

'Looks great to me,' I told Sienna. 'Let's do it. What do you need from me? The only reference I have is my ex, it didn't end well and I'd rather he didn't know where I was,' I lied, although I'm sure the note I'd left Michael left him mad as a snake, but he'd never be so mad I'd be afraid of him, I just needed the clean break.

I could have called on any number of ex roommates but it was always the same, I left when things needed official paperwork or people got too nosey so I'd rather no one knew where I was, it was easier that way. The last thing I needed was random people from my past on my doorstep asking questions.

'We tend to go more by feel anyway,' she smiled. 'I know, my brother is always on at me for being too trusting but what do you have if you don't have your heart and instincts to follow? How about four weeks deposit and the room's yours,' she said.

'Really?' I asked with a smile, amazed as I always was at how little information people asked of room renters but grateful all the same.

'Absolutely,' she giggled. 'Come back into the lounge and let's sort it out and have a cuppa.' I followed her back, thanking my lucky stars, hoping it wasn't too good to be true. 'We have ourselves a new housemate, folks,' Sienna announced.

'Excellent,' smiled Mel.

'Do you have any stuff you need me to bring up?' asked Rick.

'Nah, I'm good, thanks. I just have the one bag, I didn't bring much,' I said as Sienna went to put the kettle on.

'Really?' asked Mel in shock.

'Not everyone has as much stuff as you,' laughed Rick.

I smiled. I liked them already. Their friendly banter was contagious. 'I left what I didn't need with the ex, most of it was his anyway,' I shrugged as way of explanation.

'Ah,' they nodded. Mentions of a breakup usually explained things enough, people don't really like to pry, especially when you've just met. The fact I'd moved so far so quick they'd assume it was a bad break and best left alone.

Wrapping my hands around the hot cup of coffee Sienna gave

me, I took a comforting sip. It was good, real coffee not instant. It said a lot. 'So, what kind of music do you play?' I asked Sienna.

'It's kind of a folky, rock mix. It's hard to explain, you have to hear it. You'll have to come to a gig,' she suggested.

'I'd love to,' I said.

'We all converge on a gig when we can to show our support,' said Mel.

'That's great. How do you all know each other?' I asked, thinking they seemed pretty friendly, even for roommates.

'We've all grown up together for the most part,' said Sienna. 'Mel's mum and my mum go way back, so Mel moved in with us when she came to town. Rick's been friends with my brother, MD, since high school and when he graduated and got transferred back here he needed somewhere to stay and the folks had just gone travelling and left me the house, so I offered him the room downstairs.'

'This is your parent's house?'

'Yeah. I grew up here. Your room was my childhood bedroom. The folks went travelling a while back and handed the house over. They only come home for a week or so a year and stay downstairs, otherwise, it's just us.'

'Wow, that's some kind of life they have,' I said, thinking how nice it would be to do all that travelling with someone you loved and not having to look over your shoulder.

'They've worked hard for it. Most of it's towing a caravan behind the 4WD Dad bought when he sold the pubs he owned, but it makes them happy.'

'I could imagine,' I said. 'There's a lot of beautiful country to see,' I added.

'You sound like you've seen some of it?' asked Rick.

I nodded as I sipped my coffee. 'Yeah, I've moved a bit,' I said.

'Not one for putting down roots?' he asked.

I shrugged. 'I haven't found anywhere to stay yet. Maybe this will be it,' I lied, knowing that at some point, because there was always a point, I'd have to move on but I hoped that time was a long way off because suddenly I felt very weary.

'You sound like a gypsy,' Sienna smiled. 'I bet you'd get along great with my folks. I hope someday I get to live like a gypsy, playing music all over the world, that's my dream,' she said, wistfully.

'Everyone should get to live their dreams,' I said, hoping she was actually good.

'Someday,' she smiled, untucking her legs from underneath her. 'But right now, I have to go and get ready to make cocktails for the afternoon,' she smiled.

'Yeah, I should get going too if I want to do some work before my class starts,' smiled Mel. 'I'm going to catch up with Jess afterwards, so I'll probably see you all tomorrow,' she said with a wave.

Sienna returned in her beige Bermuda shorts and white polo shirt, 'Yeah, I gotta go, too. Will you be alright?' she asked.

'Yeah, of course. I think I'm just going to sleep for a week anyway,' I laughed.

'Yeah, I'm in desperate need of sleep, too, I just got off a shift,' said Rick. 'If you need anything, though, I'm downstairs,' he offered.

Then they were gone and it was just me. The room was quiet, empty without them but not lonely. I looked around the room, it was neat, well furnished, photos of smiling people reached out to me from the walls and the TV cabinet. They were of Sienna, Mel and an assortment of happy friends laughing and playing up to the camera at parties, on stage, at the beach. Sienna had claimed the space as her own and it was warm and fun and inviting, just like her.

The homeliness made me want to snuggle into bed and sleep. I knew I'd sleep here like I hadn't in a while and suddenly I needed to sleep more than I needed anything else. I went downstairs, outside into the warm sunshine, breathing in the melting pot of humidity. An assortment of smells hung in the air like cobwebs. The air was thick and warm, clean and good and it calmed me, nourished me.

I gathered up all the left-over travel food in the Jeep and put it back into the shopping bag, hooking it over my wrist and then slung my duffel bag over my shoulder. Back upstairs in my room, I put away my camera, tucking it into the corner of the wardrobe, put the battered copy of War and Peace on the bedside cupboard and lay down. I couldn't do another thing, I was dead tired and I needed to sleep.

CHAPTER 3

When I woke in the middle of the afternoon, the house was quiet. Peaceful. I was going to be happy here, I could feel it. This life I lived was lonely. I was always the outsider keeping everyone at an arm's distance. It was a necessity of who I was but sometimes it hurt. The loneliness, it ached, deep inside my belly where it was dark and black and empty. But there was so much love and happiness in this house. The light was already filling me, whether I wanted it to or not.

I showered and dressed in clean clothes before heading to the supermarket for supplies. I loaded up on groceries, ciders, because this seemed like a beer or cider kind of place, and a few snacks to keep me going. I took a peek at the local department store's self-serve photography centre and the art and craft supplies, as I printed my photographs in varying sizes then mounted them onto white cardboard for the buyer to frame as they chose. Satisfied the shop had everything I'd need, I headed home to cook an early dinner considering I'd slept through lunch and my stomach now protested, loudly.

I'd once shared a house with Tanh, a guy of Thai descent. Tanh made a mean stir-fry and had shown me how to make it, now it was one of my most cooked dishes, along with the Beef Korma I'd learnt from Indira in another house, and the eggplant parmigiana I'd learnt from Jason's girlfriend, Angela in another. I took pieces of the people I cared about whenever I moved on and as I went about putting together the stir-fry, I smiled thinking of Tanh. That'd been a great house, full of life and culture and music and laughter and I wondered what this new house would give me before I had to move on.

Laughter drifted up from downstairs by the pool. I stepped out onto the balcony and looked down, it was Rick and another guy having a beer, laughing familiarly, like old friends.

Rick looked up. 'Jilly, is that you? Come down and have a drink with us,' he called.

I grabbed a cider out of the fridge, turned the stove off and went down.

'Hey,' I greeted Rick before looking to his friend.

Rick was handsome; tall, tanned, slightly shaggy caramel coloured hair, cool blue eyes and an easy smile. His friend was ridiculously handsome. He had short, neat brown hair, serious, rich brown eyes, a deep tan, a serious face and a wicked smile. He was watching me with that wicked smile and a look in his eye I hadn't seen in a really long time.

'Jilly, this is MD,' he introduced.

'Ah, Sienna's brother?'

MD held his hand out. 'Indeed, I am,' he smiled. 'Nice to meet you,' he said, shaking my hand and raising an eyebrow as electricity sparked between us.

I gave a weak smile in return and took a long drink from my cider.

'So, Rick says you're new to our beautiful piece of paradise?' MD asked.

'Yep, just got in this morning,' I said.

'Wow, you don't waste any time, hey?' he smiled.

'It's a great place, I didn't want to miss out and I hate hotels,' I told him before Rick told him about my encounter with the beach bums and MD laughed, wholeheartedly, easily, his whole serious face lighting up.

'It wasn't funny,' I smiled, trying not to laugh myself because now I was somewhere nice and safe, it was pretty funny.

I listened as they told stories about great watering holes, the beach, surf breaks and the sort, interjecting their verbal tour of Noosa with stories of their visits. The day they fell out of their favourite pub unable to stand. The secret stretch of beach they'd found while trying to make out with some girls one summer in high school. The incomparable wave ridden by teenage boys that had become local legend.

They talked and they laughed as only old friends can and they drew me in to a world of sun and happiness and light and freedom. They made me ache to be a part of their stories, their world and I was suddenly sad that I never could be. I'd never be the cause of someone like MD's laughter, the kind that made his beautiful, rich eyes turn to pools of glistening, melted chocolate. I'd never make Rick splutter his beer over a memory because I could never be anywhere long enough. I could never be close enough to anyone to create those stories and memories that people looked back on with happy smiles. I would always be remembered as that girl that left unexpectedly, there one day, gone the next, no warning, no reason, just a random note that explained little. I would always be that nice girl who was a little weird because I could never let down my walls.

Beautiful men with wicked smiles would never lead me to secret beaches to kiss me because I could never date a man who thought that way. Men that kind were not for me. They cared too much. I'd only ever be an observer wishing to be more, no matter how much they drew me in. A rush of sadness washed over me, seeping into the crevices of my soul that had just dared to peek into the light.

'Jilly, are you alright?' asked MD, his face etched in concern.

I tried to smile. 'Sure, of course. Just hungry I think. I probably shouldn't have had this on an empty stomach,' I said, raising my empty cider bottle as though it were evidence, trying to make light of my abrupt solemnity. 'I'd better go eat. I've made a stir-fry, there's plenty if you guys are hungry,' I offered.

'Cheers,' said Rick. 'We'll just finish our drinks and come up,' he said.

'No worries. Nice to meet you,' I said to MD, not quite able to meet his eyes, knowing that what they held could never be for me and suddenly realising how much I wished they could be.

I'd lost most of my appetite and just spooned a little stir-fry into a bowl, dug around in a cupboard full of plastics until I found a suitable sized container for the rest and put it in the fridge. I zapped my small portion and forced myself to eat it.

The boys were still downstairs when I'd finished, soaking up the last of the evening's warmth, I suspected, their laughter drifting up on the breeze. I heard them coming up the stairs a little after I'd turned out my light, the fridge opening, the clatter of bowls and cutlery and hushed conversations. I blocked them out of my weary brain, focussed on other things. It'd been a big few days, my brain was still catching up and no matter how often I moved on, it never got easier, leaving behind people I cared about, lives that I enjoyed.

Michael would be wondering what had happened, right now. I'd left him a note but it didn't say much. It didn't say I'd known about the hookers. It didn't say I'd found the ring and I couldn't marry him. He was a good man aside from his hooker addiction. He'd been good to me and even though I didn't really fancy him as much as I should have, it made me sad to think I'd hurt him. But this was who I was, how it had to be, how I'd survived all this time and why I had to block out jovial laughter from beautifully sun kissed men.

I slept like the dead. Better than since... I couldn't remember when. I think it was here, this place, these people. It had a vibe, a something. Whatever it was, it was comforting. I hadn't felt much comfort since Mum and Dad died when I was eleven. My brother and I had lived with my Aunt and Uncle after that. They were barely adults themselves at the time, barely 25 and lived nothing like my parents. They'd drawn us into their world and that had been the end of my childhood. I'd been living on edge ever since. Then there was the shooting when I was thirteen and peace and comfort had become rare moments of pleasure, indulgences I couldn't afford.

There were no sounds of people in the house when I woke, so I assumed everyone had left to go about their day. I showered, dressed, had some cereal and took a magazine from the coffee table to sit by the pool and soak up some sun. Some R&R, that was exactly what I needed to settle into this new life, this new place, figure out who I was going to be here, what I was going to do. It had been a while since I'd had choices. The last few places had all melted in together. One group of housemates led to another group when the first disbanded and the second led to Michael, a colleague of one of my roommates. The cycle had gone on for a couple of years. The moving, the pretences, running into the same people over and over and keeping the walls up, remembering past conversations, stories, lies. It was exhausting. It was easier to start fresh, be anonymous. The longer you knew people, the harder it was not to get comfortable and spill your secrets.

I hadn't lain in the sun and enjoyed the warmth and relaxation without secretly being aware of every single movement and sound around me since I was a kid. Just lazing around without looking over my shoulder, expecting to be caught, wondering if my old life was coming for me, wondering what had happened to my brother and aunt, wondering if they were free. It was nice to breathe for a minute. This moment, this day, was easy and peaceful.

The vitamin D soaked into my skin. I breathed in great lungfuls of ocean air, tasting the salt that floated on the moisture laden air, feeling the goodness, letting it all fill me before closing my eyes to the brightness of the sun.

I was dozing off when I heard a car door slam in the distance and voices coming up the driveway, male voices.

'Oh, hey, Jilly,' called Rick coming into the backyard.

I lowered my sunglasses and got a good look at Rick and MD. They were shoeless, wearing nothing but board shorts, six-pack stomachs, damp, floppy hair and guilty, euphoric grins.

'Been surfing?' I asked, even though the question was clearly redundant seeing they were carrying their boards but I was at a loss for what else to say. The cat had snatched my tongue and pulverised my brain with its claws.

I couldn't recall ever seeing two more beautiful men, not in the flesh anyway. More so, I couldn't recall ever seeing something as beautiful as a blissful looking MD. His seriousness had vanished, he looked unguarded, relaxed and sexy as hell. It took all my strength not to groan as my eyes scanned his body. Then I realised I was staring. I looked from MD to Rick and they were both smirking. I coughed self-consciously and turned back to the magazine lying on my lap in a sad attempt to feign nonchalance.

'You been in?' asked MD kindly, nodding to the pool.

I smiled nervously and shook my head.

He winked and jumped in, spraying water all over my magazine.

Rick shook his head and went inside.

MD surfaced, swimming over to the edge in front of me. Water dripped from his dark hair, his eyes were molten and full of mischief. This was not good.

'How's the magazine? Any good?' he asked casually.

I shrugged. 'I only read a little and now it's all soggy,' I smiled, holding it up as proof.

He grinned mischievously. 'I'm sure there's better ways to fill a morning, anyway,' he smirked.

'Better than poorly informed Hollywood gossip?' I challenged with a raised eyebrow.

'Oh, way better,' he grinned.

'Well, I'll have to take your word for it, for now I'm sticking with the gossip,' I explained just to lay it all out there and make sure there was no miscommunication.

'Is that so?' he asked curiously.

'Indeed,' I added, afraid to look up from the soggy pages because I could feel his eyes on me and I wasn't sure I could maintain my resolve if I looked at him.

'You're pretty serious for a gypsy, you know,' he commented.

'Gypsy, huh?' I asked, unable to avoid looking at him.

'So I hear,' he added.

I shrugged.

'You're not?' he asked.

'Sometimes I am. I suppose,' I conceded

'Ah, a life of circumstance, not choice?'

'Something like that.'

'We might have more in common than you think,' he grinned.

'Is that so?'

'People are quick to put you in one box or another but no one's ever that black and white, are they? You sure you don't want to come in, cool off, while away your afternoon a little more productively?'

'MD, phone,' called Rick from the doorway, brandishing a black smartphone.

'Another time,' winked MD, climbing out of the pool.

I suppressed a groan as I watched water pour off him and the way the sun caught the droplets still clinging to his perfectly tanned, perfectly fit body, making them sparkle like diamonds as he took the phone and his serious face returned.

After he ended his call, he turned to me and said, 'Hey, thanks for the stir-fry last night, it was amazing. Beautiful and she can cook,' he winked and was gone.

I fanned myself with my soggy magazine. So much for relaxing. MD had just given me a lot to over analyse but embarrassingly, all I could think about was he'd called me beautiful and I felt my resolve crumbling around me. He's just a pretty face, I told myself, thinking after the last couple of days I was just feeling needy, my ego in need of stroking, that damn basic human nature we're gifted with. It had nothing to do with him seeing me, with connecting over our life circumstances. What would he know about it anyway, it was just a line, I told myself.

I was sitting on the balcony playing with my camera in the late afternoon sun, trying to see what usable shots I'd taken over the last couple of days when Sienna interrupted me.

'What are you smirking at?' she asked, looking over my shoulder.

'Nothing, just remembering something,' I said, embarrassed that MD's comment had shaken me the way it had, that still, even with the distraction of work, it was all I could think about. What was a man that darned handsome doing calling me beautiful, anyway? He'd totally shaken my equilibrium and I needed to clear him out of my head. I was in no position to fancy a man like him. He was too good, he saw people, saw me, in a way I couldn't explain. No, men like him were not for me. I needed the unobservant hooker loving type who understood walls and secrets and didn't pry.

'Ahuh,' Sienna smirked, unconvinced. She seemed to have that same way of seeing people MD had and it was unnerving. 'Mel's cooking dinner tonight, you around? Would be nice for us all to hang out,' she said.

'Yeah, I'm here,' I said. 'Sounds great.'

'Hmph,' she laughed. 'You say that now, wait until you see what she's cooking.'

'Why? What's she cooking?'

'I don't know, but it'll be some hippy concoction,' she laughed, going to change out of her work clothes.

Sienna, Rick and I were watching retro reruns on the telly when Mel arrived home in her own contented bubble of happiness, almost as though she floated.

'Too much time with the hippies, all that meditating and yoga has her in a perpetual state of happiness,' mumbled Sienna as we watched Mel float across the room and practically orgasm when she was finally in Rick's arms. 'Argh,' Sienna scoffed with a smile.

Mel called us from our corners of the house at seven fifteen. I was starving. I could smell all sorts of delicious smells that I hadn't quite been able to piece together. I sat down and Mel delivered our bowls of noodles, which looked pretty amazing.

'What is it?' asked Sienna, poking suspiciously at her food.

Mel smiled brightly. 'Noodles,' she advised as though Sienna was a child.

'They don't look like noodles,' she challenged.

'They're Zoodles,'

'They're what?'

'Zoodles. Zucchini noodles,' she grinned.

Sienna groaned. 'With?'

'Kale, sweet potato, veggies leftover from the retreat's garden and cashini butter,' she declared proudly.

'It looks amazing, Babe,' Rick praised.

I didn't recognise all of the ingredients, but they were just vegetables, how bad could it be? Cashini butter was new for me but the way I lived, jumping from share house to share house, I had become accustomed to strange and wonderful new foods. I had found some great meals that way and I hadn't been disappointed yet, so I happily dug in. It was creamy and nutty and you knew instantly it was good for you and there were more vegetables in the bowl than I'd eaten in months.

'You're not a hippy too, are you?' asked Sienna laughing at me eating the noodles like a starved person.

I shrugged. 'I like good food, this tastes good,' I smiled, slurping up a stray noodle.

Rick laughed, 'You'll fit in around here just fine,' he said, shovelling a big fork full into his mouth.

'You only love it because you get to eat pizza at the station,' laughed Sienna.

Rick winked.

Mel playfully smacked his arm. 'Well at least Jilly has good taste,' she smiled.

'Have you stayed in a lot of share houses and tried lots of different food?' asked Rick.

'Yeah, a few,' I smiled. 'I love it, you always eat something you mightn't have ever tried and better still, you learn how to cook it. That stir-fry I made last night was a recipe I got from a housemate called Tanh, years ago. He said it was an old family recipe.'

'It was pretty good that's for sure. MD raved about it,' he said.

'MD?' asked Sienna sourly.

'It was fine, Sienna,' Rick mumbled, filling his mouth with food.

'Hmph,' she grumbled, scraping her bowl clean despite her earlier protests.

'Where did you learn to cook like this?' I asked Mel, changing the subject, not wanting to discuss MD any further until I'd sorted out my head and stopped blushing like a schoolgirl every time I thought of him or heard his name.

'My mum, she was, is, a hippy, from way back,' she smiled as she thought of her mum.

'Mel grew up in a commune,' Sienna added quietly.

'Really?' I asked.

Mel shrugged. 'Yeah. It was nice. I left, clearly, but some of it stuck. I liked a lot about the way we lived. Someday I'd love a place in the hills where I can grow my own veggies and stuff,' she said.

'That sounds nice,' I smiled, thinking it sounded beautiful, peaceful, quiet. Safe. 'Wait, didn't you say you knew each other through your mums?' I asked.

'Yeah, my mum lived there before she met Dad but unlike Mel over there, my mum ditched the whole hippy lifestyle once she left, mostly anyway. She happily embraced the new world but she stayed friends with Ella, that's Mel's mum. It wasn't one of those psycho cults, they're allowed friends on the outside and people come and go whenever they want,' she added defensively, even though no one had needed her to.

'So, anyway,' continued Mel. 'When I left, I came here and I got a job at the retreat, which was right up my alley and now I live the best of both worlds,' she said, squeezing Rick's hand.

'Well, you certainly sound like my kind of people,' I added, finishing my food. 'Now, can I do the washing up?'

'No arguments here,' Sienna said. 'I have rehearsal if no one minds.'

'Of course not,' said Mel. 'Go, we'll see you tomorrow. This was nice, though, right?'

'It was,' Sienna agreed. 'Thanks for insisting on it and cooking and everything, you're a gem.'

I gathered all the plates and took them to the kitchen where I really only had to load the dishwasher and rinse the very fancy Scanpan that Mel had used. Best of all worlds indeed, I smiled to myself.

Sienna went to rehearsal and Rick and Mel went downstairs to chill out and I curled up on the couch and flicked through the television channels until I found something worth watching for a couple of hours.

CHAPTER 4

———

'What are your plans for today?' asked Mel as we ate cereal together on the balcony enjoying the perfect, sunny morning.

'I wouldn't mind taking some pictures, but I'm not really sure where to start. Everywhere looks beautiful. There might be too many choices. It's hard to know where to photograph first,' I said.

'I know, it's so beautiful here. I couldn't imagine living anywhere else. If you need a starting point, though, why don't you come up to the retreat? I could show you around, there's some beautiful spots for photographing,' she offered.

'Really? That'd be great, thanks.'

'No worries. I'll leave you the directions. Head up whenever you're ready,' she offered. 'Throw some yoga gear in, too, in case you feel like taking a class,' she suggested.

'Sure,' I smiled, thinking, *as if I have yoga gear*. But I did wonder what all the fuss was about. She must have been doing something right, she was always so calm and relaxed, zen. I could use some zen.

I left Mel to get on with her day and went to shower. I needed some new clothes, I decided when I went to get dressed. All I had were jeans and t-shirts. It was too hot for jeans, especially when you worked outside. I had to put them on anyway but then I headed over to the shopping centre and wandered the shops, picking up cute cotton shorts, a few new t-shirts that were a bit floatier and cooler than the ones I had. I added in a pair of Havianas and bought some yoga pants and a tank top from the sports store in case I did decide to indulge in some zen.

I took my loot home, changed into a pair of black and white striped shorts with a loose navy tank top. I packed my camera gear, shoved the yoga pants and top into my tote bag, slid my feet into my new thongs, grabbed a protein bar from my stash and headed back out with Mel's directions in hand.

I wound my way up into the hills of the retreat and drove down a long road surrounded by beautiful, lush green trees. If this was any indication of what was to come, it was no wonder Mel was always bursting with happiness. Finally, the driveway wound through the bush to a beautiful old house surrounded by more lush, green trees and tropical flowers and shrubs.

To the side of the house were a number of cars resting in the shade. I parked the Jeep at the end of the line and walked across the pebble path to the front of the building. I walked in through the front door to find Mel sitting behind a shiny, timber reception desk laughing with a thin, wiry man with long, almost dirty hair pulled back into a pony tail, wearing baggy black cotton pants and a sleeveless tunic.

Mel looked up at the sound of the door and a grin spread across her face. 'Hey, you came,' she beamed.

'I did,' I smiled, not sure what else to say.

'Excellent. Oh, Eric, this is my new housemate, Jilly. Jilly, Eric,' she introduced.

'Hey,' he smiled.

'Hey,' I nodded.

'Why don't I show you around? Eric here has a class in about an hour if you want to take it. Did you bring some gear you want to leave behind my desk?' she asked.

I rescued the pants and tank top I'd shoved into my tote bag, pulling out the crinkled mess as proof that I had indeed brought some gear. 'I have to warn you though, I've never done yoga,' I admitted.

'Ever?' they both asked in unified surprise.

I giggled. 'Never. Ever.'

'That would explain why there are still tags on your yoga pants,' Mel laughed, taking my gear, folding it carefully and placing it on her desk. 'Eric won't mind, will you, Eric?'

'Nope, not a bit,' he smiled brightly. 'I have a beginner's class at two, which might be better if you can hang around that long?' he said.

'Great idea,' Mel chimed in. 'That'll give you a good chance to look around and take some photos and come and have lunch with me,' she smiled.

'Excellent, I'll see you then,' Eric smiled, leaving us and walking down the corridor to somewhere else.

'I didn't bring anything for lunch, just a protein bar,' I confessed.

'Well, isn't it lucky I packed an extra salad, just in case,' she winked.

'You're quite the girl scout, aren't you?' I smiled.

'I always try to be prepared,' she admitted.

'No, you're thoughtful and kind. I haven't met one of you before,' I said.

'One of me? Like I'm an entire species all of my own,' she giggled.

'You might well be,' I suggested.

'Well, there's plenty more like me here. Come on, let me show you around. I bet there are some great spots for you to shoot,' she said.

'And you're sure no one will mind? Your boss? The owners?'

'Nope, I mentioned it to them this morning just in case but of course not. They're happy for you to wander and shoot as you please. Maybe they'll even buy something to use on their website, it needs a freshen up,' she smiled.

'Well, I'd be happy to give them a couple of shots to say thank you,' I offered.

The grounds of the retreat were enormous. We wandered along quiet, tree-lined paths that led to private huts and hiking trails, a tennis court, a sparkling swimming pool.

'We do water yoga in there. It's quite incredible what some people can do. You might need to wear in your gear a bit first, though,' Mel smiled as she led me into secret, secluded gardens where light filtered through palm fronds and if you looked between the trunks of the trees, you could see the ocean in the distance sparkling under the bright golden sun.

'This is incredible, no wonder you're always happy,' I smiled.

She laughed, 'Come on, there's still more. You could wander all day here and not encounter a single other person and we're fully booked this week,' she said, proudly.

'Wow. Bet it costs people a month's rent to stay here for a couple of days?'

'Not that much. Well, maybe,' she grinned. 'But all their food's included. We run a lot of classes, yoga, Pilates, all different levels of experience. We do guided hikes or you can go on your own. We'll teach you to cook the food you eat, all vegan, gluten free, dairy free and highly nutritious. We have a life coach who can fix the most broken person and send them back into the world as good as new, it's a pretty good deal, really,' she smiled.

'Really?' I asked suspiciously.

'Really,' she smiled, nudging me as we walked along the path. 'Well, I'll leave you to it. Make yourself at home. No where's off limits. Have fun. I'll see you for lunch when you're ready,' Mel said, farewelling me once we'd done a loop and returned to the front door.

I dug my camera out of my bag and walked over to the green lawn on the opposite side of the pebbled driveway. I stood still, closed my eyes, breathing in the clean, cool air, because it was much cooler up here. It was so quiet, too, serene. I hoped I could capture the peacefulness in the shots because I knew that's what would make them sell, not the flower or the tree or the way the sun danced between the bright green leaves, but the impact all that had, the peace it created, the tranquillity.

Opening my eyes, I slowly began to shoot, capturing little pockets of calm and beauty, like nothing I'd ever seen or felt. It wouldn't be until I got the shots on a screen or in print that I'd know for sure if I'd really achieved what I'd hoped for but I could feel it, I was capturing something special.

Slowly wandering through the grounds, I felt all the tension of my life, the loneliness of the preceding days, evaporating, leaving in its place light and hope like I hadn't felt since I was a small child. I hadn't realised how much I'd needed this, how worn down and worn out I'd become until I felt it easing, the strain leaving my body being replaced with light and something that felt like actual happiness.

Time evaporated as I lost myself in my work, lens changes, decisions, watching how the birds moved around the moss-covered birdbath or flittered on the branch of a tree as I decided the perfect angle, composition for each of the shots. I followed the trail of busy ants amongst the crunchy leaves off the hiking trails and watched the way a lizard stretched on a sun-drenched patch of quiet path, lost in this other world, capturing it all on the digital film.

My tummy rumbled, frightening away a colourful little bird I couldn't name and I looked to my wrist for the time and realised I'd left my watch at home. I fished my phone out of the tote bag I had slung across my shoulders and couldn't believe how late it was. I'd have to hurry back to have some lunch with Mel if I wanted to eat before the yoga class began and I was too hungry to do another thing without eating.

'You didn't have to hurry,' Mel scolded when I told her. 'This isn't that kind of world. But I'm glad you're here because I waited for you,' she smiled and I was glad I'd hurried.

We ate the quinoa salads with roasted pumpkin and beetroot she'd made and drizzled with leftover cashini butter, out in the pretty garden on a stone bench where the sun crept through the leaves of the frangipanis.

'This place is so peaceful, it must remind you of where you grew up,' I asked.

'A little. We never had it this grand. Lots of vegetable gardens and orchards to tend to as opposed to the beautiful gardens here, although they do have all of that as well, way down the back if you fancy the trek. But yes, a little. It's quiet and the people are kind and the philosophies are the same.'

'What sort of philosophies?' I asked, curious of this alternate lifestyle that had created such a beautiful, kind person.

'Being kind and living simply, in tune with your surroundings, that sort of thing. Taking care of yourself, making time and space for peace and thought,' she smiled.

'It sounds nice,' I said.

'It was. It is. How about you? How did you grow up?'

I stilled, as I always did when someone asked me such a question, which is why I usually avoided initiating the conversations but I'd been so intrigued by Mel's commune upbringing, I couldn't help myself. In reply, I just stuck with the good bits, the easy bits. 'Mum and Dad were good people, they were happy, we were happy, just living our ordinary lives,' I said.

'What happened?'

'That easy to read, huh? They died. When I was about eleven. Car accident.'

'That's harsh,' she said kindly.

'Yeah, but I like to think they're not too far away, you know, up there somewhere keeping an eye on things,' I lied. In fact, I hoped there was no such thing as being able to watch over your loved ones. I didn't want them seeing what had happened to us, what I'd done. They'd have been heartbroken. I didn't want them seeing any of it.

'What happened to you then?'

'We, my brother and I, went to live with my aunt, my mum's sister and her husband. It was different there but you know, nothing is the same as home, right?' I asked, trying to be honest but vague.

'Yeah, I can't imagine not having had my mum around, no matter how flaky she is. There are always plenty of mothers around when you grow up in a commune, but still, if I needed her specifically, I could always go and find her,' she said sympathetically. 'You must be very brave to have survived that loss and to live as you do,' she said.

I smiled. 'Sometimes you just have to walk the path laid out for you, right?'

'Sometimes,' she agreed. 'Or sometimes you can pick up a shovel or a rake and start making a new one,' she suggested.

I nodded. 'Maybe,' I smiled, wishing it could be that easy. Hoping.

'You coming in for the class, Jilly?' asked Eric, walking casually across the grass.

'Absolutely,' I smiled, suddenly terrified.

'Come on, I'll show you where you can change,' Mel offered, packing up our salad bowls.

Eric led the small class of five through some breathing exercises that eradicated years of pent up stress and anxiety before beginning the stretches, positions with funny names that stretched muscles I never knew I had. He was a hands-on instructor, regularly coming over to correct my positioning, to tilt my pelvis just right, tip my chin up, hold my warrior arms at the right height. Whatever it was, this yoga business left me feeling thoroughly invigorated. To end, we lay down on our mats as he took us through more breathing exercises and a few moments of meditation.

When we were done, it was like coming out of the most beautiful fog. Like opening my eyes onto a brand new, bright, shiny world I hadn't seen before, at least not in such beautiful colour. I now noticed the sun streaming through the small windows high up, how the dust bunnies danced in the rays. I felt the gentle caress of the breeze from the open window and heard the softness of Eric's voice, noticed how handsome he was in his hippy way, how his face was beautifully sculpted, that body I'd initially thought of as thin and wiry, now looked strong and defined under his tunic and I surprised myself by wondering how his hands would feel on my naked body.

'You feel alright, Jilly?' Eric asked, helping me up.

'I do. I feel amazing,' I smiled back, looking into his bright green eyes.

He smiled knowingly in return. 'Well, hopefully we'll see you again,' he said, holding my gaze just a moment longer than one normally would and I felt a little twinge in my tummy.

What was wrong with me? I thought, mentally shaking my head. Fancying two men in as many days and I couldn't have either. I smiled as brightly as I could manage and farewelled Eric to go in search of Mel.

I found Mel in a big commercial kitchen at the back of the old house, which served as the hub of the retreat.

'How did you go?' she asked.

'Great, it was amazing,' I said.

'Isn't it? We're going to get along just fine, I can tell. You're welcome to join a class any time you want,' she offered.

'Thanks. What's cooking?' I asked, finally smelling the amazing smells wafting around the kitchen.

'Chef Carmichael's making soup. Sweet potato and beans. Smells amazing, doesn't it? I'm pestering him for the recipe,' she grinned, batting her eyes at the chef who looked like he could be her grandfather.

'Fine, fine, just get out of my kitchen,' he laughed, trying to shoo her away.

'Well, I should head back home, see what I got,' I said as I gathered the things I'd left at reception.

'Did you get some good shots do you think?' she asked.

'Oh yeah, loads. This place is beautiful,' I said. 'Thanks for inviting me and the tour and the yoga and everything,' I said.

'No worries, anytime.'

At home I changed out of my new yoga gear and back into my shorts and tank top, poured a big glass of iced tea and took it with my camera to the shade of a frangipani tree by the pool. I started going through the shots I'd taken, some of my best, I thought. I already couldn't wait to go back and take some more photos, do some more yoga. There was something special about the retreat. It filled me with a goodness I hadn't felt in so long and it was coming through in my shots. I was sure I'd captured all the serenity and peace of the place, too. I couldn't wait until I got them up on a screen, printed and sized and mounted. They were going to be incredible, I thought, quite chuffed with myself.

'Hello?' called MD, startling me as he came into the backyard, fracturing the silence I'd sunken into.

'Oh, hey,' I called back, surprised to see him.

'You look relaxed,' he said, sitting on the opposite recliner.

'I've been up to Mel's retreat today taking some photos and a yoga class,' I told him.

'Yoga hey? You don't strike me as a yoga type,' he said, eyeing me as though wondering if he'd missed something in his calculations. He'd missed a lot, I was sure.

'I've never tried it before but I might well be a convert,' I smiled.

'Well, how about that,' he smiled back.

'How about you, have you ever tried it?' I asked.

'Oh, I have indeed. It's a bit quiet for me, though. I prefer pounding the pavement to work out my stress,' he said.

'Hmmm...' I mumbled, thinking how beautiful he'd look in shorts and a tank top running, sweat dripping off him. Very different to Eric.

'Who gave the class?' he asked, curiously.

'Eric,' I said, wondering if he knew him and somehow thinking MD knew everyone.

'Eric, huh,' he mumbled.

'Yeah, he was great, incredibly flexible and kind and surprisingly fit,' I offered for no reason, wondering why any of it had popped out of my mouth at all.

'Yeah, he's something,' MD mumbled. 'Rick around?' he asked, changing the subject.

'Nope, just me I'm afraid. You want a cold drink or something?' I offered.

'Sure, just a little of whatever you're having. I'm working, I gotta get back,' he said.

'No worries, come on up,' I said, leading him back into the house. 'What is it you actually do?' I asked. I'd thought he worked with Rick the way they talked, but the way he was dressed, I wasn't so sure.

'I'm a cop, slow day,' he mumbled.

'You're a cop?' I asked stopping on the stairs.

'Yeah. I thought you knew? Everyone knows.'

'Nope, I'd have remembered someone saying that,' I said, regaining my composure and continuing up the stairs, trying not to panic. Of all the jobs my new housemate's brother could have had...

I still had some brewed tea and added the necessary ingredients and lots of ice. 'It's pretty warm out there this afternoon, this should fix you up,' I offered, putting the revelation out of my mind to worry about at a later time.

He watched me with that grin of his, 'I'm already feeling better,' he said, before downing the cold drink. 'That was pretty nice,' he said.

'It's all in the brewing of your own tea,' I said.

'Right,' he smiled. 'You're quite the surprise packet, aren't you?' I shrugged.

'Well, I gotta go,' he said.

'Did you want me to give Rick a message or something?' I asked.

'Nah, that's okay, I'll catch him around somewhere,' he said and I watched him walk down the stairs in his snug jeans and black t-shirt and he was gone.

I shook my head. What was wrong with me? I was losing the plot and coming unstuck. Men were never a focus for me, I didn't seek them out and purposely complicate my life with them and here I was running around like a teenager full of hormones and nothing else to do. I distracted myself by putting away my things and doing some cleaning to take my mind off this strange influx of beautiful men. And a cop, a bloody cop.

Mel sent me a message saying she was going to try and make the soup Chef Carmichael had made and to not start anything for dinner. I was glad I'd done some cleaning because I didn't want to feel like I wasn't pulling my weight with Mel cooking two nights in a row.

Sienna was working late and going straight to rehearsal and Rick was apparently playing pool at the pub, Mel told me when she arrived home. She went about cooking the soup and telling me about the rest of her day.

'Eric was quite taken with you,' she said, with a big, cheeky smile.

'Is that so?' I asked.

'So indeed,' she said, pouring some stock into the pot of freshly chopped vegetables.

'He's single, you know,' she added. 'And they say those yogis can do things no other man can do,' she said, raising her eyebrows.

'Really?' I asked, intrigued.

'Really,' she smirked.

'Right. I'll keep that in mind then,' I said, shaking my head and getting some ciders out of the fridge for us.

It was a nice night. The soup was amazing and something I was sure to be adding to my recipe collection when I moved on. Mel and I had formed a bond since my visit to the retreat and we were comfortable with each other. I liked the feeling. Mel told me some more stories about growing up in a commune and just as she was about to ask me more about my life, a very tipsy Rick came bounding up the stairs and gathered her in his arms.

'You don't mind if I steal her for a while, do you, Jilly?' he asked, giggling like a schoolboy.

'Of course not, go!' I said, waving them off with a laugh.

Then it was quiet again. But definitely not lonely or empty. Just peaceful. I smiled and watched a bit of telly while I finished my cider and then I went to bed.

CHAPTER 5

I woke to a soft knock on my bedroom door. I rolled over and opened my reluctant eyes to see Sienna standing in my doorway with scruffy hair, wearing a short, black, cotton dressing gown covered with little pink bows.

'Good morning,' she said cheerily. 'Did you still want to go check out the markets today?' she asked.

'Oh yeah, that'd be great,' I said. I'd lost track of days and was chuffed she'd remembered. That conversation felt like weeks ago instead of days.

'No worries, you have me till lunch time. I have an afternoon shift again today, so we should probably get a wriggle on,' she smiled.

'Sure, no worries, thanks. You want first shower?' I offered.

'Nah, you go, I need coffee. It was a late night,' she smiled, leaving me to get myself ready.

Sienna was reading the paper when I came into the dining room. She had her hand curled around a big steaming mug of coffee. She'd brushed her blue hair into a shiny bob. She looked up and smiled, 'coffee machine's all warmed up, help yourself.'

I did and sat down just as she finished her coffee.

'Alright, I'm going to shower then we can get this show on the road, hey?'

Sienna was beautiful, she glowed beneath her bright blue bob but it was in a natural, no fuss kind of way. She didn't need layers of make up or designer clothing, she just glowed as she was, even though she was still in her pyjamas.

It made me wonder if I should be spending any time with her or Mel at all. They were nice and sweet and kind. I didn't spend a lot of time with people like that in my life. I purposely avoided them because it was easier, for them and me. It was harder hurting nice people. It would cut out a little bit of my soul if I hurt Sienna or Mel, I could already tell. I liked them.

Come on, Jilly, I chastised myself. I was making more out of it than I needed to. They were just good, kind people being welcoming, helping me find my feet in a new place. They had their own lives, their own friends. I was being silly, my imagination running away from my head. It was a downside of the life I lived.

This was just one more outing to help me get started. We'll have a nice time at the markets and that will be that. There's no point making any more of it. I was just adjusting, unsettled after upheaving my life, again. It was making me a little irrational which was understandable. I was just a little raw. Everything would be fine and at the end of the day, it didn't matter how nice a person was, how hard it was, if I had to leave, I had to leave.

The sundrenched balcony beckoned. I took my steaming coffee and a bowl of sugar coated Weet-Bix drowned in cold milk onto the balcony and enjoyed the sunshine. I didn't care much for the news and left the paper Sienna had been reading where she'd put it, listening to the morning sounds instead; the birds, the chatter of the trees and the distant ocean. It was much better than reading about the propaganda they called news. I had experienced first-hand how much of it was bull, made up, half assed or just totally incorrect. They were lucky if they got people's names right half the time.

I finished getting ready, brushing my hair, swiping mascara over my eyelashes and some barely-there gloss over my lips. I topped my purse up with money from the bag in my duffle and came back into the kitchen where Sienna was also ready to go.

'You're not just feeling obliged, are you?' I asked, not wanting to be a charity case. 'You don't have to go if you're feeling under the weather after last night. You could just give me directions,' I suggested, suddenly wondering if that's the only reason she was up and about with a hangover.

'What? Oh no, I'm fine now I've had some coffee. I didn't drink that much. I had my car last night, anyway. I was very well behaved. I'm actually looking forward to it. I haven't been to Eumundi in ages and it's fabulous there. Just you wait, you'll see,' she smiled.

Sienna drove us in her ageing, blue Toyota hatchback and chattered happily about nothing in particular as she navigated the way from memory and I tried to pay attention.

'So what sort of stuff do you photograph?' she asked.

'Landscapes mostly. Animals, the ocean. Occasionally people but not very often, you need permissions and things. People get tricky,' I told her.

'How did you go at the retreat?' she asked.

'Oh, it was beautiful. I think I got some really great photos.

I won't know for sure until I see them up on a screen, but I'm excited, really excited and that's always a good sign.'

'I can't wait to see some of your work,' she said.

'You will soon enough. I'll have to get some pictures printed and mounted before Saturday if I can get a spot at the markets. I'll try not to take up too much space while I put it all together,' I said.

'Oh, don't worry about that, none of us will mind a bit of mess,' she said, which was nice, quite a relief too, because sometimes it all got a bit messy as I pieced everything together. 'You didn't bring any prints with you?' she asked.

'No, I sold it all off on my last day at Paddington. I've learnt they don't travel very well, something always happens to them.'

'Do you have a website or anything?'

'Nope, nothing that fancy. I don't have a computer,' I told her.

'Really? Well, we'll have to fix that, won't we?'

'The computer or the website?' I asked, a little concerned about either.

'The website,' she giggled. 'You can use my computer,' she said.

'Won't it be expensive to set up?' I asked, suddenly alarmed at the idea of having to give out personal information I didn't have.

'Oh no, there's loads of free websites, we can have you loaded in five minutes,' she smiled.

'Wow, that's great,' I said, still unsure anything would be that easy. I avoided the internet at all costs and I just hoped Sienna wasn't pushing me to a place that forced me to leave. Not yet. I wasn't ready.

'Here we are,' she eventually announced as we drove onto a grassed car park. An oval of some sort perhaps? She passed some money through the window and followed the yellow vested attendant's directions as he waved us into a park under the shade of a tree.

We got out of the car and I drank from the bottle of water I'd thrown in my bag, watching all the people, like ants, all heading towards the same place. The sun was high and warm, the atmosphere almost electric. Markets were a special place, the eclectic sounds and smells, the great finds, the energy of the people selling things they'd made with their heart and soul, and the customers all looking for that something special they'd never find in a commercial shop. I loved the easy, carefree banter shared between stall holders the most. It didn't seem to matter where you were, they all had that in common. It was a special community.

We wandered through the stalls of beautiful handcrafted jewellery, hand-painted canvasses, sculptures, soaps, crystals, miracle cures, beach clothing, anything you could imagine, chatting about nothing, what we could see, what we'd seen before, where we'd been, what made us smile, dumplings and the funny man with the duck whistles. We ordered green smoothies and a couple of vegan chocolate balls from a pair of dreadlocked hippies wearing hemp pants. We ate the balls while waiting for our smoothies.

'Good, aren't they?' Sienna asked. 'Bet you didn't expect them to be.'

'Not a bit,' I smiled. 'But they're delicious,' I admitted.

The man with the blonde dreadlocks called our names and we collected our smoothies, taking long, cooling sips full of nourishing goodness. We wandered along and I picked up an array of vegan snacks as we encountered more. Sienna insisted I buy a crystal for luck and protection when she found out I didn't have one, as though she couldn't believe a person could exist without such a thing without the sky falling down on them. I figured I could use all the protection I could get. I bought two, black onyx to protect from negativity and amber for general protection and promised her I'd buy more next time.

'Come on, there's some people you need to meet,' she said grabbing my elbow.

'Where are we going?' I asked as she hurried me through people laden walkways.

'Just wait, you'll see,' she grinned.

Finally, we entered a quiet corner with just a few stragglers, where the air flowed better and it was just a little bit cooler. 'Pick your destiny,' Sienna announced. 'Tarot, palmistry or clairvoyant?' she asked. Clearly, despite all her pretences to the contrary, she was as much a hippy as Mel.

'What? Are you kidding?' I stumbled.

'Come on, you sound like you could use some guidance,' she said.

'What makes you say that?' I asked, concerned I'd somehow, inadvertently given away too many secrets in our mindless chatting.

'I dunno. A drifter like you drifts for a reason. You should find out if it's time to stop or where your journey will take you next. Personally, I hope it's time to stop, at least for a while,' she smiled.

It was nice of her to say. We'd only just met and I always worried people wouldn't get me, my nomadic lifestyle, my vague past. People found it either intriguing and adventurous or just plain weird. But we'd had a lovely morning and it was nice to know she was enjoying it too. It had been a while since I'd had a friend. A proper girlfriend that I just hung out with.

Considering I didn't believe in any of the mystical arts, I figured one was as good as the other, so I chose Tarot, probably because she was sitting there with nothing to do and all the others had a customer.

'Excellent choice,' gushed Sienna.

I handed over my money and shuffled the cards like the fuzzy red-haired lady insisted and selected seventeen cards. She looked like someone's kooky aunt, not some all-seeing, all knowing mystical being. I glanced over at Sienna sceptically but she just raised an eyebrow at me and nodded to the table in front of me where the woman was laying out the cards.

The kooky lady laid the cards face down in lines, which I'm sure had a significant purpose but she had a look on her face that suggested I shouldn't interrupt with silly questions while she concentrated. One by one she turned them over, explaining what they were. They were upside down for me and so well worn I couldn't make out what the intricate pictures were but she spoke of Fools and Wheels of Fortune, Justice, Lovers, Cups and Swords. I nodded politely, not believing a word of it. I couldn't afford to believe in anything or anyone other than myself but all the while Sienna sat beside me gripping my arm in anticipation of what secrets my future held.

'What does it all mean? What do you see?' Sienna asked the tarot reader before she'd barely finished turning the last card over.

'Well, together,' she started as she looked at the cards again, 'your life is about to take a huge turn. The burden that you carry will soon be relieved and you can finally rest. Your heart will get a shock too. You're not expecting to fall in love but you will and you won't even see it coming. Don't run from it. This one will be The One. You tend to handle everything on your own, but you don't have to. Not anymore.'

'What, this man is going to fix everything, be some knight in shining armour?' I asked, knowing better, knowing no one could fix anything, not in my life anyway.

'Ah, a sceptic, huh,' she smiled. 'Well, believer or not, the cards don't lie. And no, this man isn't all that will help you. There are others now. They care about you. They want to help you. Let them,' she said, as Sienna squeezed my arm giddily.

I was terrified. There was no way I'd let them help. There was no way I'd put Sienna or Mel in harm's way. This woman didn't know what she was talking about. There was no way I was falling in love and no way this life was ever going to end.

The woman gave me a kind smile, put her warm hand on mine, 'You've been alone for so long, I know it's hard to let people in but you don't have to do it on your own anymore. You're home now. You're safe,' she told me.

'Thanks,' I mumbled, as I got up to leave, uncomfortable that she could see so much truth without knowing me.

'Safe from what?' asked Sienna, curiously as we made our way back through the people.

'Who knows,' I laughed. I saw the concern in Sienna's eyes. 'You don't believe all that do you?' I asked.

'Don't mock. Di is never wrong.'

'Di?' I asked. 'That's not very mystical,' I said.

Sienna laughed and shook her head. 'You wait, you'll be eating your words. Have you seen enough though? I've gotta get to work.'

'Oh yeah, thanks. This place is great, isn't it? It'll be perfect.'

'Well make sure you phone them when you get home and see if you can book a spot for the weekend,' she said. 'Wish we had time to go to the marina for lunch, that would be a nice way to end such a lovely morning,' she added wistfully. 'Never mind, next time. Hey, they have a market there on Sundays. Maybe we should go there for brunch this week and check it out. It's only a small market, nothing like this, but it's really lovely.'

'That'd be great,' I said, as we got into the car.

Sienna pointed out lots of great spots I could photograph on the way home but I wasn't concentrating. I couldn't ignore what Di had said. How had she known all she'd said, anyway? How had she seen the life I'd been living? Known my fears?

'Do you have time to eat? There's still some stir-fry in the fridge,' I offered when we got home, trying to put Di's words out of my head.

'Absolutely,' Sienna said, getting two bowls out of the cupboard.

'Who do you think you'll fall in love with?' Sienna asked wistfully as we ate.

'What? No one,' I said, shaking my head.

'I bet he's really handsome and kind,' she smiled wistfully as though I hadn't spoken at all.

'I'm not looking for a man at all. I just ended a relationship, remember? I'm still recovering and all that,' I admonished.

'But that doesn't mean it won't happen. Since when does love run on a schedule?' she smirked. 'Di said you won't see it coming,' she reminded me.

I rolled my eyes, 'Not going to happen, so I think you and Di are going to be very disappointed,' I told her, taking our empty bowls to the dishwasher.

Sienna waggled her finger, 'You'll be eating your words,' she laughed, going to change for her shift.

'Oh, and Rick's cooking one of his blokie barbies tonight before he goes back on shift tomorrow, so don't make any plans for dinner, but fair warning, it's more often than not a torturous testosterone infused thing that takes on a life of its own,' Sienna said as she got her things ready. 'Alright, I'm outta here,' she said.

'Have a great arvo and hey, thanks for this morning.'

'Sure, no worries, it was fun,' she smiled brightly before leaving.

I had a cup of tea on the balcony and phoned the number of the market to book a stall for Saturday, Wednesday and as many subsequent weeks as they'd allow. I got lucky and had a choice of a few available stalls. I let the lady choose what would suit me best and hung up happy.

I raised my cup to my mouth, sipped my tea. I still couldn't help thinking about what Di had said. Surely it was just a random guess and it didn't really mean anything. If anything she said were true, it meant I should pack my stuff now and drive far, far away before these lovely people got caught up in my life. But I didn't have it in me.

Di was right about one thing, it was time I stood still for a minute. I needed to breathe. I liked it here. I liked my new housemates. I liked the sunshine and the sound of the ocean I was yet to properly see.

CHAPTER 6

I finished my tea, put on shorts, a t-shirt and thongs from my new collection of summer clothes and headed towards the beach and this famous Hastings Street. After unsuccessfully circling the carpark at the end, I eventually squeezed into a spot on the street and put my camera in my linen tote. I didn't want it hanging around my neck like a tourist, and headed for the golden sand hidden behind the beachfront monstrosities.

The sand stretched for miles in either direction. Cocktail bars, hotel and apartment pools, scattered the beachfront. A hub of activity filled the beach, children laughing, people talking. A lot of families sat between the flags, but many more scattered along the golden sands on towels and blankets, beneath sun umbrellas and fancy designer sun tents. Even with all the people, it was still easy enough to find a quiet spot on the sand just for myself, away from the masses of jovial tourists.

I sipped some water as I looked out over the ocean sparkling before me and watched the waves rise and fall. The whole world connected to this body of water, somewhere, somehow. Duchesses and princesses, lovers and tourists, brown and wrinkled old ladies, ordinary people, impoverished and broken people, people like me, they all looked out at the same ocean, bodies of water that all connected to become one somewhere.

It was humbling and beautiful. Di was right, again. I was home now. I felt it. The water, the sand, it connected to me, all those other people that shared it, connected to me. If my prized camera wasn't in my tote I'd have gone for a swim, become one with that beautiful ocean that glistened under the sun as though it were laden with diamonds but instead I pulled out my camera, played with the lenses until they were just right to capture the light, the sun, the sparkling ocean, the distant sailboats.

Squeals of laughter caught my attention. I looked up and two people were riding a wave to shore. It wasn't a large wave, not as big as the waves further down where the surfers gathered soaking up the sunshine but it was big enough to catch the attention of the tourists in the other direction.

As the wave riders reached the shore the young girl's voice carried on the breeze.

'That was amazing!' she cried. And why wouldn't she? She'd looked magnificent.

She hugged her companion, gathered her board under her arm and raced down the beach. I smiled and looked back down to my camera, playing with the settings until someone shouted my name. For just a second, my heart jumped up into my throat before I reminded myself no one could find me here. So I took a deep breath, looked up, shaded my eyes from the sun and saw a shirtless MD, water from the ocean still dripping from his nearly naked body, running towards me.

My camera began shooting almost without my realising. It was instinctual. How could I not capture something that beautiful?

'Oh, stop that,' he laughed, falling onto the sand beside me.

'Sorry, I hope you don't mind,' I said, shyly.

He waved it away. 'As long as you're not planning to blow them up and sell them at the markets,' he challenged, his dark eyebrow raised.

I laughed. 'Absolutely not.' I didn't add those were for my eyes only. I'd need something to remind me of how beautiful he was when it was time to move on because I suspected in a few years' time I'd doubt it was even possible to have known him.

'Beautiful day, isn't it?' he asked, looking up at the sun.

'Oh, it's gorgeous,' I agreed. 'Not working today?' I asked.

He shook his head. 'Flexible work hours mean I can spend some time on the beach without the tourists hogging the waves,' he grinned.

'That's some lifestyle you have.'

'You get much?' MD asked, nodding towards the camera and changing the subject.

'Yeah, loads,' I grinned. 'Hey was that you riding in on that wave with that girl?' I asked, suddenly realising where he'd come from.

'Yeah. You saw that?'

'You were both magnificent.'

'Magnificent, hey? I'm not sure I've been called that before.'

'Really? The girl seemed pretty thrilled.'

He smiled. 'Yeah, she's a local kid. She's been trying to get up for ages and just falls back down. So I brought her down to the smaller waves, showed her some stuff and she finally got it. Nothing better than when it all finally clicks and you get up on that wave for the first time. Nothing like it,' he grinned. 'You surf?' he asked, nodding towards the water.

'Me? Noooooo...'

'I'd be happy to teach you. Not sure you can even live in these parts without becoming one with the ocean,' he joked.

'Not sure I'm coordinated enough for that kind of thing. I'll stick to photographing it,' I told him.

'Ah, the coordination is in here,' he said, pressing his hand to my stomach, causing my breath to catch in my chest. 'And here,' he added, his hand skimming the top of my thigh.

I dared to look into his eyes and I was caught for a second, as though I rode a wave. I felt like I was flying, felt something I couldn't name. Then he smiled and my whole world tilted, just a little.

A squeal on the air shattered the moment as the girl caught another wave. MD turned to the water, sat up and cheered his young friend on and my heart swelled a little for this sweet man. Once she reached the sand she ran up to him.

'MD, did you see that? With no help,' she cried with excitement.

'You've got it now, Georgie, you don't need me, anymore,' he grinned. 'Go, grab another before the waves die for the day.'

Then she was gone and she'd taken our moment with her. Which was probably just as well.

'I've got a little time before I have to get back to work, you want to go for a walk with me?' he asked.

I should've said no. It was right to say no but my stomach still rode the wave of whatever it was that had happened in our moment and I couldn't say the word.

He stood, held out his hand to me and I took it.

We walked down to the water's edge. I took off my thongs and dropped them in my tote as we walked along the beach with the water kissing our feet. He told me about the waves, how the whole surfing thing worked, how it cleared his head. I took some more photos, for posterity more than commercial value. I wanted to remember his stories, remember this moment. I turned the camera on him as he laughed and captured a perfect moment of MD unguarded.

He laughed and waved me off again.

'You're always so serious, but then, in that moment, you weren't. It was the same the other day when you'd been surfing with Rick, for just a moment, you'd almost looked euphoric. Those moments are quick and I wanted to capture it because it was beautiful,' I explained.

He looked at me in wonder. I thought for a moment he was going to kiss me and I was terrified. I hadn't meant for that. I'd just meant to explain what I'd seen, why I'd taken his picture. But he didn't kiss me. He smiled, sweetly, honestly. 'I like the way you see things,' he said.

We'd walked to the part of the beach with the most surfers and were no longer alone. Someone called his name from over by the rocks where boards stood in a line like sentinels in the sand.

'MD, phone,' the man called.

I followed MD to where his board stood, his clothes in a messy pile beside it. He checked his messages while I took in the people around us. It was as though they existed in their own world, in their own solar system far removed from the tourists. They appeared unaware of the squealing children down the beach, the hustle and bustle of Hastings Street not far away. This was a world of its own. I wanted to capture it too but thought photographing strangers might be pushing things a bit far, instead, I watched the ocean and the beautiful men who rode its waves.

'I gotta go, duty calls,' MD said.

'No worries, I should get out of the sun, anyway,' I said as he threw on a shirt.

'This was nice, though,' he said with a smile.

I smiled back. 'It really was,' I agreed as I turned to leave and walk back down the beach with our moments haunting my heart.

I hadn't lied though, I'd forgotten a hat and I could feel the sun's tentacles burning into my shoulders. I'd taken loads of amazing photos. I was sure I already had plenty to work with, so I thought I'd try somewhere with more shade. I considered the national park rising up at the other end of the beach but it was too late in the day and I only had thongs to walk in. I bet there were just as many great shots in the woods I'd seen at the other end of Hastings Street earlier as I'd been looking for a carpark. The trails of the national park would wait another day, until I had appropriate footwear at least.

I strolled down Hastings Street, admiring the array of cute beachside shops, the incredible collection of restaurants and the casual, relaxed atmosphere. It was a healing place and I could feel it seeping into me and I let it come, welcomed it as though it were a salve or a balm.

I saw the big open windows of The Beach House, the cocktail bar where Sienna worked. I considered going in for a drink but I wasn't really dressed for it, I thought, as I saw all the men and the ladies in their resort wear huddled over tables sipping cocktails and drinking beer from tall glasses. I stopped for a moment at one of the big picture windows to see if I could see Sienna at work. I couldn't really imagine a serious side to her cheerful nature and bright blue hair. Then suddenly she popped up from behind a couch by the window with a fork in her hand. She pressed her on her back and arched as if to ease out a crick.

'Oh, hey,' she said, cheerily.

'What were you doing down there?' I asked, curiously.

She held up the fork. 'We find these things in the strangest of places, I tell you,' she laughed. 'What are you doing here?'

'I was just taking some pictures on the beach. I thought I might head down to the woods and see what I can find in there,' I told her.

'You weren't coming in for a drink?' she asked, mock pouting.

'I didn't realise you were this close to the beach or I'd have dressed more appropriately and come in for sure,' I told her.

'What do you mean?' she asked standing on her tiptoes to see the rest of my outfit over the ledge. 'You look fine, come in,' she said.

'Really? In shorts and thongs?' I asked, unconvinced.

She waved me away as though the query was silly. 'Of course, this is Noosa in the middle of the afternoon, no one cares,' she insisted.

I went inside and followed Sienna to the bar.

'What can I get you?' she asked.

'I don't know,' I said, picking up the cocktail menu and starting to read through the incredibly long list of cocktails and the elaborate details of their ingredients.

'The day's special is Margaritas,' Sienna said helpfully.

'Done,' I smiled.

'Excellent, I make a mean margarita,' she smiled. 'Go, sit. I'll bring it over,' she insisted.

I sat on the couch by the big open window and watched all the people passing by as I waited for Sienna to bring me my margarita. The people were all coming or going somewhere, all smiling and happy, towels slung over their shoulders, children with ice cream of all colours running down their hands. I wondered about the lives they led and the secrets they held.

I used to sit for hours at beaches back home after I'd first run. No one ever saw me sitting there eating ice cream, staring at the ocean, tanning on the sand like everyone else. What would they have done if they had? My face had been all over the newspapers but still, no one ever noticed me there. Considering how little people wore at the beach, it was amazing how invisible you could be.

Sienna joined me for a minute when she brought my drink, talking like a runaway train that left me smiling but having little idea what she'd said but it was too busy for her to take a proper break. I enjoyed watching the passers-by, alone with my thoughts and my memories as the lemon spritzed on my tongue and tequila surged through my veins, dulling my usually hyper aware senses, making it easier to breathe and sink into the couch upon which I had camped.

Miraculously a bowl of chips appeared and Sienna grinned at me from behind the bar as she shook another cocktail. I suspected she'd put too much weight in Di's words and was being more motherly than she should be. She'd crossed that line of friendship without me even noticing. Getting close was never a good idea with people like Sienna and Mel. They were too nice, too kind, too inquisitive. But it seemed it had already happened, without my even realising it. Bugger, I thought as Sienna brought me another margarita and sat long enough to eat a few chips before hurrying back behind the bar.

I'd have to limit our time together. Sink into my work, take lots of pictures and go to as many markets and see as many sights as possible. Surely with their schedules we'd then only see each other in passing? I didn't want it to be that way. They radiated a light and energy that made me want to be a part of their orbit, but it was safer this way, for everyone. For them and for me. It was the right thing to do whether I liked it or not.

'Hey, I'm going to go get some shots in before I lose the light,' I called to Sienna across the bar as I returned my glass.

'Well, don't hang around down there for too long, alright? It gets dark pretty fast up here and probably earlier than you're used to,' Sienna warned as I farewelled her even though she'd tried to encourage a third drink. It was only because I had my car that she finally conceded defeat and let me leave at all.

When I finally left the bar, I was dangerously close to losing light. I walked down the street towards the woods anyway with the taste of that last margarita still zinging on my tongue. Everyone seemed to be heading in the other direction, their day's done, looking for a shower and fresh clothes before dinner.

My chest felt heavy at the thought of having to distance myself from my new friends. I knew I'd feel better once I'd taken some pictures, but my heart was no longer in it. I just wanted to find a quiet corner to hide in and mope. I was sad at having to distance myself from them this soon. I would have liked some more time. They were good people. I liked them. It had been a while since I'd had a girlfriend. A real one. Not the girlfriend of a housemate who stopped by now and again or chatted about inane stuff at a barbeque. Or one of those acquaintances you bumped into regularly at parties and charity events where you pretended you were a good, honourable person. But a real friend who shared secrets and watched chic flicks and drank margaritas just because it was fun to do, because hanging out together made the day better.

In fact, I think the last time I had such a friend I was eleven and my parents were still alive. I'd long since lost track of everyone from that life. I tried not to wonder about them, what they'd grown up to do, who they'd grown up to be. Were they married? Did they have children? Did they go on holidays to the beach and shop for school supplies in January? Did they argue over breakfast tables and make love late into the night, without a care in the world? I didn't think about it because it made me envious, so much so it turned my stomach and it would do me no good to wish for things I could never have. That's just the way my life had turned out. Who I grew up to be. None of it was my fault but it was the truth just the same.

The woods were full of remnants from the day. Families packing up their picnics and collecting their scattered children. A small wedding party packing away plastic champagne flutes as their photographer zipped his equipment into bags. I walked along the winding dirt path and disappeared into the trees. The late afternoon light was filtering through the leaves turning them gold and scattering the grass and dirt underneath with crystals.

I got creative, fiddled with the lenses and took an array of shots, losing myself in the camera and seeing only what was on the other side of the viewfinder, patiently waiting for the leaves to blow just the right way or a trail of ants racing up a tree trunk to form just so. I clicked happily, sometimes quickly, knowing what sold, what made people smile, what made me smile. Beetles amongst the stones, the star flower with the purple stamen illuminated amongst the dark green foliage protecting it. The beauty of a lone jetty jutting out into the river with the fading colours of the day playing across the sky.

Sienna was right though, the sun sank fast, as though in a race with the moon. I exited the woods with the last of the picnickers before I got lost amongst the trees in the dark. It wouldn't have been the first time, but I was new to the area, I didn't know what trouble lurked here. It was best to become at least a little acquainted with the area before finding yourself stuck unaware.

I joined the people on Hastings Street as the streetlights came on. Some were still in their swimmers, or wearing sarongs and brightly pattered bikini covers heading back to their hotels after a day at the beach, a late afternoon cocktail or a spot of shopping. There was plenty to see and do. Lots of shops to get lost in. Shops filled to the brim with cute homewares or souvenirs, beachwear and personal products. You could window shop for hours or part with a lot of cash if that was your thing. I liked the feeling of blending with the tourists, the transient community who'd all come from somewhere, like me. No one belonged, yet everyone belonged for that reason.

Sienna was collecting glasses from a recently vacated table as I passed the bar. I waved as she looked up.

'All done?' she asked. 'Get anything good?'

'Yeah, I think so,' I said. 'What time do you finish?'

'Another hour. Wanna come in and wait, have another drink?' she asked.

'Nah, but thanks. Two of those are enough for me. You do make a mean margarita,' I laughed.

She laughed too. 'So I'm told. Alrighty, I gotta serve. I'll see you at home in a bit. Make sure there's some food left for me, won't you?'

I drove home thinking it'd turned out to be a pretty great day but Di's words still stuck in my head. It'd been a long time since I'd stopped, since I'd felt safe. I wasn't even sure I could, that it was in my DNA to trust. And what was that garbage about falling in love? That was enough to prove she was full of hocus pocus, that I should ignore every single word she'd uttered. I don't fall in love, it's far too dangerous, no matter how good looking the men on offer are.

Boy cars lined the street in front of our house when I arrived. Sienna wasn't kidding when she'd said it was a testosterone fuelled soiree. I was thinking it was just going to be a couple of people. Utes, black SUVs, Commodores, a couple of motorbikes lined the kerb. I squeezed into the driveway behind Mel's Prius before walking up the driveway and into the backyard to see Rick's barbeque well underway. Half a dozen blokes gathered around the barbeque like it was a God while they drank beer and laughed.

Mel spotted me as soon as I walked in. 'Oh, thank goodness you're here, the testosterone was making me gag,' she laughed.

I smiled. It was nice to have a home where people were pleased to see me. 'I'll just run my gear upstairs then and I'll come back and even out that testosterone, hey?'

I'd decided to distance myself but the barbeque smelt good and it would have been too rude to stay upstairs and cook my own food. I'd begin distancing myself in the morning. They weren't going to find out all my secrets in one barbeque.

I went upstairs and put my camera away. I liked to tuck it in the back of the wardrobe for safe keeping. I'm sure everyone downstairs was honest and reputable but, in my experience, it never paid to be careless and too trusting. I knew exactly how deceitful people could be without anyone noticing until it was too late, my aunt and uncle had trained me well, well enough to never forget no one was ever exactly as they seemed.

My hair felt a little salt caked from the sea winds. It was probably full of sand, too, I thought as I picked up a brush. Then I wondered who on earth I was trying to impress and laughed at myself. I put the brush down and went to the kitchen to dig out one of my ciders from the fridge.

'Hello,' a man called from behind.

'Shit, you scared the crap out me,' I said, gripping my pounding chest as I turned to see MD's grinning face.

'Sorry,' he grinned. 'How was the rest of your afternoon?' he asked.

'Fine. Good actually. Had a couple of margaritas at Sienna's bar, got some great shots in the woods, it was good,' I shrugged.

'Glad to hear it,' he said, reaching past me for a beer. 'Rick's serving shite down there, stashed some of the good stuff up here,' he smiled. 'You going down?' he asked after pulling the cap off his beer.

'Yep,' I said, walking out of the kitchen with MD following me down the stairs.

I felt his eyes watching me and a tingle raced up my spine. He wasn't creepy like the guy from the other share house, feeling MD's gaze moving over my body made me come alive. I mentally shook my brain clear, it didn't matter if it was creepy or not, it was a bad idea. He was a cop on top of everything else. I had to be smarter, do better. I was glad when we reached the bottom of the stairs and stepped outside into the cool evening air and Mel whisked me away to a chair.

'Was MD just scoping you out?' she asked, excitedly.

I shrugged.

She watched me closely for a minute. 'Do you fancy him?' she asked, curiously.

'What? No. Definitely not. I am not looking for a man, at all, I just left one, I sure as hell don't need another right now,' I stressed, even though I knew, that under different circumstances I would have fancied the pants off him.

'Ahuh,' she mumbled as though not believing my protest at all.

'What does that mean?' I asked.

'Nothing,' she grinned.

'What?' I asked again.

'Well, it's just... it's MD.'

'So?'

'Look at him,' she said and we both instinctively looked over to where he stood amongst the group of guys. He was watching us and raised his beer in toast. Shit. 'You might not be looking, but it seems like he is and trust me, that never happens,' she said.

'What do you mean? I bet he has girls going weak all over town,' I said, sure a guy that good looking would have no trouble with the ladies.

'Oh he does. One smile from MD and they turn to bloody jelly, it's hilarious. But he's never interested. Rarely anyway, he's only human, after all, but he's never actually interested, if you get what I mean,' she said.

'He has the occasional shag and moves on. Purely medicinal?'

'Something like that,' she said blushing.

'So why's he looking at me?' I asked, wondering what his game was.

'Probably because you're beautiful and haven't gone weak in the knees yet,' she smirked.

'Hmph,' I mumbled, knowing I wasn't nearly that beautiful and I never went weak, I knew better. But as I looked over at MD, he looked up and our eyes caught and something twinged deep inside. It felt good, really good which meant it was bad, really bad.

'Do you need me to make a salad or something?' I offered, looking for a reason to go upstairs and put some space between myself and MD.

'I wish,' she said. 'But we're not allowed to help. This is a bloke's barbeque and we have to comply or leave, no girly salads and stuff allowed. We're stuck with sausages in bread or steak sandwiches, I'm afraid.

I smirked, resisting the urge to laugh. Typical twenty something blokes trying to hold onto their traditions despite the call of adulthood and needs of the women coming into their lives, God forbid we cramp their style. But looking around, it appeared Rick was the only one to have succumbed to a serious relationship considering we were the only women in attendance and I wondered how long they could really hold on to their traditions.

Sienna came in just as Rick finished cooking, causing all the guys to stop and say hello. I suspected she was popular with Rick's friends. MD said something I couldn't hear, everyone laughed and Sienna playfully punched his arm and walked away.

'Hello, ladies,' Sienna said, greeting us as she popped the top off her beer and flopped into a chair. 'Isn't this nice, balancing out the testosterone?' she said, smiling at me and tapping her bottle to mine. 'I hope the boys are being nice,' she said.

'That they are,' smiled Mel.

'What does that mean?' asked Sienna with a gossipy grin.

'I think she's attracted an admirer,' Mel said.

'Really? Already? Wow, that was fast,' she said. 'Who might the lucky fellow be?'

'You'll never guess,' giggled Mel.

'Really?' asked Sienna, turning to look at the group of guys. 'Who?' she asked as though the suspense was too much.

'Only the unattainable MD himself,' smirked Mel.

'MD? My brother, MD?' she asked, shocked. 'Well, good luck with that,' she huffed. 'I'd warn you off, but it never works,' she said, surprising me with unexpected snarkiness. 'Sorry,' she added with a smile. 'He has issues with women. No one can figure out why. He was raised perfectly fine. Ordinarily he's a great guy. But he just can't manage anything past meaningless sex.'

'Nothing wrong with tangle free, we're all human, we all have needs, but the tangles,' I added, shaking my head.

'Now I know MD doesn't have anything to hide, he's just a fool. What about you, Jilly?'

I smiled. 'I just left a relationship, remember? I'm allowed to be snarky about men.'

'True, true,' Mel agreed.

'Yeah well, I don't care what MD does with the rest of the women in town, but you don't need him messing with your head and I don't need to be looking for a new housemate,' she smiled.

'Grubs up, ladies,' called Rick.

I put my empty cider bottle in the box of other empties and followed the girls over to the barbeque. I picked up a piece of bread and nodded to a sausage. Rick topped it with some onion and I went back to my seat to eat.

MD pulled up a chair and sat next to me. 'So, how did your shots come out today, anything good?' he asked.

'I haven't looked yet but I'm sure I got some shots I can use,' I said, remembering the shots I'd taken of him, sure they were going to be the highlight of the day.

He smiled. 'It was nice to see you on the beach today. Sorry I had to rush off.'

I shrugged. 'We all have to work. You did well to squeeze in a surf.'

'I meant what I said, I'd be happy to teach you to surf sometime,' he offered.

I laughed. 'I think I'm better off photographing the waves rather than attempting to ride them. I'd like to see you surf some of those bigger waves sometime though.'

'I wouldn't mind that. Maybe we could hang out afterwards, have a drink or something?' he suggested as Sienna sat down. 'When do we get to see some of your pictures?' he asked changing the subject but appearing to ignore the scowl Sienna threw him.

'I'm printing some up tomorrow. I'll be selling them at the Eumundi market on Saturday.'

'Hmmm, I might have to come by the market and have a look,' he said.

'You hate the markets,' Sienna interrupted.

'Maybe there's just never been anything worth seeing before,' he smirked.

Sienna rolled her eyes.

'Well, I guess I'll leave you ladies to it,' MD grumbled, taking his empty plate to the rubbish bag and re-joining his mates.

'I'm not encouraging him, you know,' I told Sienna. 'The last thing I need is messing up what we have and like I said, I'm sworn off men.'

'She isn't encouraging him,' insisted Mel. 'She's not the least bit weak kneed or giddy.'

Sienna giggled. 'It's not you. It's him. He's not nice to women and that's the last thing you need. Besides, Di said you were about to fall in love. It won't be with Mitch that's for sure,' she said.

'Mitch?' I asked smirking. I don't know what I thought the M stood for but it wasn't Mitch. I liked Mitch.

'You went to see Di without me?' groaned Mel. 'What did she say, tell me everything,' she insisted.

'She said Jilly was going to sit still for a while and fall in love,' she smiled.

'With who?' Mel asked, looking from Sienna to me and back again.

I shrugged.

'Oooh, maybe it's Eric, he was asking after you, you know. Wants to know when you're coming back. Offered to show you some of his favourite spots on the property,' she said, eyebrows raised.

'What's this about Eric?' asked MD dropping one of his empty bottles in the box nearby.

'I think he fancies our Jilly,' Mel threw out, almost as a challenge.

'What?' he asked, clearly annoyed. 'Stay away from him, Jilly,' he demanded.

'What business is it of yours? What's your problem with him, anyway?' asked Sienna.

'He's bad news. Just stay away from him, all of you,' he insisted.

'Yeah, yeah, you always say that but you never have anything to back it up. I think you're just jealous. I hear he's pretty flexible. All that yoga. Can do things no other man can do,' grinned Sienna.

MD mumbled something while scowling, huffed and walked away.

I shook my head. 'I'm not on the market, anyway,' I said, not sure what else to say.

'Well, Di's never wrong, you'll see,' Mel added. 'Tell me, what else,' she asked.

I went upstairs to get another cider while Sienna filled her in. I came into the kitchen to find MD bent over, digging one of his premium beers out from the back of the fridge.

'Hey,' I mumbled, trying to be polite but a little shaken from the earlier exchange and whatever it is that kept happening to my insides whenever MD looked at me.

'Oh, hey,' he grinned, lazily. 'Another drink?' he asked.

I nodded and he passed me a cider. 'Thanks.'

He nodded. 'So, has my sister told you I'm off limits? How much I'll ruin your life?' he asked.

I shrugged. It wouldn't have mattered what Sienna did or didn't say, I was off limits. I was worse news than MD. I wondered what he'd say to that.

'You can't believe everything my sister says. She means well but she doesn't know me as well as she thinks she does.'

'So you're not a ladies man making women weak kneed all over the coast and not following through?'

He smiled. 'Nothing is ever that black and white, Jilly.'

'No. True. I'm not looking for anything, anyway, so you best look somewhere else to alleviate your manly needs. This shop's shut for the winter,' I told him.

He laughed and again, I got the impression he didn't do it often but it suited him. 'You sure are something, Jilly.'

'Something for you to forget and ignore,' I insisted.

'See, right there, those other girls, they're not like that. They seem nice then I buy them a drink and they go all stupid and giddy. Is that the word? I can't think of any other word and I can barely get a conversation out of them. Who wants to date that? Or they're planning the wedding over breakfast or reinventing my life before the Uber eats guy has even shown up with our hash browns. They think my job's too dangerous, I surf too much. They don't see me for who I am. You on the other hand...'

'Me on the other hand am off limits, no go, don't even think about it,' I said, turning to leave.

MD grabbed my arm, turning me back into him and catching my mouth with his, stealing my breath, my sanity, the beats from my heart as his mouth greedily, hungrily moved over mine, liquefying my insides, making my heart beg for things it could never have.

He pulled away, sucking the air from my lungs. His face stayed millimetres from mine as he panted, breathless, a surprised look on his face.

'Mitch? Really?' demanded Sienna from behind us. 'Of all the women in town that you could have, you have to choose my new housemate?'

He smiled lazily at me, making my stupid heart pity pat before he turned to his sister and said, 'The heart wants what the heart wants, Sienna,' he smirked, patting her arm as he left, going down the stairs, leaving me watching him, stunned.

'Argh,' she stomped. 'He's such a shit. Now he's going to ruin everything.'

'Ruin what, Sienna? It's going to take a bit more than a killer kiss, that I didn't invite, by the way, from some hot guy to turn my life upside down.'

'Really?' she asked with her sweet puppy dog eyes.

'Besides, he just says that stuff to piss you off. It's all a lie. He's a great big fake,' I laughed. 'He's no ladies' man, it's just the women he meets don't bother to look beyond that face of his.'

She stared at me for a second, thinking.

'Don't look at me like that. I've moved a lot, I've gotten really good at reading people, listening to what they're actually saying, seeing past their bullshit. It expedites things. I don't have the time or the brain power for anything else.' I didn't tell her seeing people was how I was raised after my parents died. That seeing people, who they really were was how I survived, how my Aunt and Uncle had trained me, how I'd survived since. I had to know people quickly if I wanted to stay alive, stay free. 'I promise, still no weakness in the knees, no desire to pick out a wedding dress or any of the usual MD after affects, we're good.'

'Yeah, yeah, that's what they all say in the beginning. Come on,' laughed Sienna, rolling her eyes and leading me back down the stairs. 'Just promise me you'll be careful and won't let that bloody smile of his lead you astray.'

'I'm not twelve, Sienna. But I promise,' I added when she gave me a rare serious look.

CHAPTER 7

———

I woke up with MD's breath on my lips, as though he was there, as though he'd just left but instead it had been hours, a lifetime, since he'd kissed me in the kitchen before being admonished by Sienna. Yet still, it was all I could think about, all I could feel, as though his breath carried on the breeze, whispers of him filling my bedroom.

He'd kept his distance for the rest of the night but I'd felt him watching me. Felt him linger as though torn during his farewell. A general wave from afar wasn't enough. I'd wanted more, needed more but all there was, was a wink and he was gone.

There'd been no mess left behind, well-trained guests disposed of their own empty paper plates and empty bottles. I bid the others goodnight as they sat down to a nightcap and went to bed to sort out my head. It hadn't helped. My head was swimming this morning just as much as it had the night before.

I shouldn't even be worrying about MD. A guy like that, so accustomed to living inside his walls, so used to being treated like a thing, he didn't know how to do relationships any other way, he wasn't going to be beating down my door to whisk me away to a life of matrimonial bliss. I wasn't the kind of woman who changed a man like MD. I could never be the woman for a man like him and he'd see it soon enough and move on to one of the pretty doe-eyed types that obediently walked away and politely licked their wounds in private when he moved on, so I had nothing to worry about, really. His interest was piqued at someone not going weak at the knees, that's all. I was worried about my reaction to him, though. I was usually much better at protecting myself, distancing myself, being aware but somehow I'd been blindsided, caught off guard, knocked for six and I didn't like it. I didn't like the way my breath caught in my chest when he looked at me, or the way my heart beat strangely. I didn't like that something that happened in the pit of my stomach every time I thought of the kiss.

I waited until I heard everyone leave. One by one, their cars started up and they drove away. Sienna's was the last to leave about nine. I guess they didn't serve cocktails before ten, even somewhere like Noosa, but who knew, all I knew was she was on day shift and wouldn't be back until nearly five. Mel was working all day, Rick had gone to his shift and finally, I was alone. I needed some space, some distance. Not just because of what happened with MD but from all of it, them. I was liking them too much. I'd only been here a few days, not even a week and I'd already let down too many guards. Let them into my heart.

I tried putting it all out of my head and sat on the balcony with a cup of coffee and my camera, flicking through the shots I'd taken at the beach and in the woods, making copious notes of which ones I thought I could do something with, alterations to consider, sizing and colouring, cropping required and potential pricing. Someday I'd be somewhere long enough to invest in my own computer, maybe some fancy software on which to review my pictures. That would be nice. Sienna had already offered the use of her computer in the living room but that would just be one more level of comfort I didn't need to get used to right now, one more thing I'd have to leave behind when I had to leave. I needed to distance myself, not get any more comfortable than I already was. So I got ready and headed to the shops.

It was a standard local shopping centre, a few independent stores, a few national stores, an eatery and plenty of coffee choices, Big W, Woolworths, the usual, all with that beachside feel you'd expect, lots of tourists and families milling around, picking up supplies and what not. I bought a large latte from one of the coffee places and went into Big W and got comfortable at one of the self-serve photo kiosks.

I was right, there were plenty of great shots to choose from. From the retreat, from the beach and the woods, a few from my last weekend in Sydney and the rest stops on my way up, even though I'd taken most of those for posterity, not necessarily commercial value. That was just an added bonus. I sucked in a sharp breath as the pictures of MD came up on the screen, of him walking towards me, of him laughing, unguarded for just a moment. My loss of breath was from more than his beautiful face. In those brief moments when he'd dropped his wall, I'd seen more, seen into his soul, seen the light and the good buried in there and something inside me came to life as though it recognised his light, needed it as my lungs needed air. I realised where I was, regained my composure and moved on.

There were loads of pictures to choose from, which was great because I wanted a big selection to sell at the markets so I didn't look like a beginner. I was glad for my coffee as I settled in and carefully considered, composed and set each shot.

I went through each photo, using my notes and the fresh perspective of seeing them on the screen to decide on just the right print size and focus of each shot before sending them to the printer. With the quantity and array of sizing I'd requested it would be another day before I could collect them. I dropped my empty coffee cup in the bin by the counter after I'd paid and went to the craft section, filling a trolley with glue and white board, brown paper and assorted necessary supplies. I loaded it all in the car and went back in to pick up some groceries from the supermarket and more cider.

I felt better as I headed home. This was who I was, what made me happy, what made me whole; creating something beautiful, seeing the world, finding something new in the same things everyone saw. It was also the only record of my life, the people I met, what I saw, where I'd been, sometimes how I'd lived. I had a stack of memory cards filled with shots I'd one day load onto that computer I'd someday buy, when I stopped long enough. Until then, they'd remain in the small metal box I carried in my handbag.

It was late in the afternoon when I got home. I put all my supplies away and began making some pasta for dinner. I wasn't sure who was going to be where but it didn't matter, it was a dish that kept well in the fridge and made great leftovers.

Mel walked in just as I'd finished, grateful for the food and we ate on the balcony with the soft, gentle breeze caressing our arms.

'I hope pasta is alright for you?' I asked, not sure if I should be catering to her vegan needs.

'Oh of course, I only cook the vegan stuff because that's all I know how to cook and I love it. But I like regular food, too. The best of both worlds, remember,' she smiled.

I smiled too. I liked the way she thought. 'How was your day?' I asked.

'Great,' she grinned. 'We had a yogi visiting from overseas and she was amazing. Eric was beside himself with envy. He asked about you again,' she said, shovelling pasta into her mouth.

I shrugged. 'Still not on the market,' I told her.

'Ahuh,' she smiled. 'And how was your day?' she asked, kindly changing the subject.

'Productive. I'm all set to put together some pieces for Saturday.'

'Excellent. I can't wait to see them.'

After dinner, Mel went to read a book by some guru and not long after Sienna burst in like a tornado to change and head to rehearsal. She scoffed a few spoons of cold pasta and was gone.

I was afraid to go to bed. I was afraid to close my eyes, to sleep. I worried MD would occupy too many of my thoughts and turned on the television to block him out. It worked and I learnt how to upcycle a chest of drawers but as soon as I went to bed, when I couldn't keep my eyes open any longer, MD's face filled all the space behind my eyes and again, I slept wishing for things I could never have.

The next morning, exhausted from thinking, I headed back to the shops to collect my photos. When I got home I needed multiple trips up and down the stairs to load everything onto the big wooden table on the balcony that was soaked in sunshine.

I had a ham and tomato sandwich and made a coffee before laying the rest of my supplies on the table. I worried for a minute I was taking up too much space but Sienna had assured me it would be okay and no one was spending Friday night at home, anyway. Sienna had a gig. Mel was having dinner and drinks with her yoga mates. Rick was working. It was just me.

Sienna had invited me to her gig but she had another one Saturday night that Mel had talked me into going to after a few ciders. Perhaps I'd have to cut back my alcohol intake if I was going to make the right choices and keep my distance. Mel had invited me to join her and her work friends, even offering up Eric as a drawcard, but I'd declined with the pretence of preparing for the markets and an early start.

As was usually the case, the afternoon disappeared in the blink of an eye as I put my pieces together. When I was satisfied every piece was as good as it could be, when every piece had been boarded and I was happy with the framing, I washed as much glue off my hands as I could at the kitchen sink. Opening a cider, I sat back to assess what I'd put together as the sky turned orange with the setting of the sun.

'Knock, knock,' called MD from the doorway.

I jumped. 'You have to stop doing that,' I told him as he came out and surveyed my work with a guilty grin.

'Sorry, I knocked downstairs,' he said.

'Oh, of course, sorry. I get a bit distracted when I'm working,' I smiled.

'They're incredible,' he said, having a closer look, then looking back at me as though he couldn't quite believe I'd produced the pictures he was looking at.

I smiled. It happened now and again. I looked too ordinary to produce what people saw. Although I never could figure out what a photographer was supposed to look like.

He flipped through more of the pictures, shaking his head until he got to the end.

'Will you be alright setting everything up on your own tomorrow? I could help if you want,' he offered.

'That's kind of you, thanks, but I'll be fine. What are you doing here? Rick and Sienna are out,' I said.

'I know. Sienna has a gig, Rick's working, Mel's somewhere,' he said, lounging on one of the spare chairs.

I watched him, waiting.

He chuckled. 'I came to ask you out... on a date,' he smiled. 'Tomorrow night?' he asked.

'Sorry, can't. Going to Sienna's gig,' I told him, grateful for a valid excuse.

'Ah shit, that's right, I forgot,' he said, appearing to think.

Did that mean he was going too? Great, just what I needed, low lighting, thumping music, too much alcohol and MD.

'What about Sunday?' he suggested. But before I could answer him, he added, 'No, that won't do. No one has a date on a Sunday, do they?' he said, almost to himself. 'What about now? I know it's late notice, but what are you doing now?' he asked, starting to ramble.

'MD, it's not a good idea. Me and you. It's just not.'

'I'm going to need more of a reason than that. I like you, Jilly. I don't meet women I really like very often. It's thrown me for six for sure, but I can't get you out of my head. We should at least see what this is.'

He looked at me hopefully and something twinged inside me. Hopefully it was pity. Whatever it was, it made me give in. 'Sure, I'm free now. But it's not a date. It's just two friends hanging out. You'll probably change your mind in a couple of hours anyway and move on. But I'm already hungry and it'd take me too long to wash the rest of the glue and whatnot off to be able to cook, so how do you feel about ordering in a pizza?' I asked, thinking it would also be much less pressure and much less date like. 'Just two mates,' I reminded him.

He nodded. 'Fine. Two mates,' he smirked. 'Pizza sounds good,' he said, pulling his phone from his pocket and heading into the kitchen. 'Any preferences?' he called out.

'No anchovies,' I called back and I started packing up my collection of prints and wrapping bundles in brown paper to protect them during the short drive.

MD returned with a cider and a beer and went back to lazing in the chair opposite me.

'So, I know the M stands for Mitch, what about the D?' I asked, trying to have some sort of conversation instead of blushing.

'Ah, if I told you that I'd have to marry you or kill you,' he joked.

'Well, neither would work for me,' I smiled.

I enjoyed the look of surprise on his face. I bet most of those weak-kneed girls he met were just begging for him to marry them. He recovered well though and asked, 'What about Jilly, short for Jillian?'

'Nope, just Jilly,' I told him as the doorbell sounded downstairs.

'I got it,' he winked, jumping out of his chair before I could remind him this wasn't a date.

I took a few lungfuls of air but couldn't quite fill my lungs. It wasn't until MD returned that my heart settled and my insides seemed to exhale. What was wrong with me?

I got some plates from the kitchen and two more drinks. The pizza was good. It was hot, crunchy and really cheesy with no anchovies.

'So why'd you leave Sydney?' he asked.

I shrugged. 'Time for a change,' I told him.

'Ahuh,' he said, thinking. 'Breakup?' he asked, even though I was sure my housemates had already relayed the particulars of my life to him.

I shrugged again. 'It was inevitable really. Not much else to tell.'

He nodded and began asking questions about my work instead. What were my favourite types of places to shoot? How did I know what worked and didn't? How to get just the right light.

Once we'd finished eating, he took the empty box inside. 'I am too full to do anything. You want to watch a movie? I promise it will be completely benign,' he smiled.

'Maybe, but I don't have any,' I said.

'Sienna has a stack, come,' he insisted, heading into the living room.

'You sure she won't mind?' I asked.

'Of course not,' he said, looking at me as though I were mad. 'There'll be microwave popcorn in the pantry if you want some,' he said.

'I can't just eat her popcorn,' I said.

'Of course you can, it's from the communal house supplies, it's included in your rent,' he said.

'You're making that up,' I said.

'Nope, swear I'm not. I lived here for a few months when I was between apartments. I know her rules, I promise,' he insisted.

'Fine,' I said going into the kitchen to source and zap the popcorn while he chose and set up the movie.

I returned with the popcorn in a bowl and sat on the couch next to him. I'd been tempted to sit on the other couch but I sensed that'd have been rude, and there was popcorn to share.

MD pressed play on the remote.

'Bourne?' I asked as the movie started.

'It was either that or some romantic comedy shite,' he scoffed, draping his arm across my shoulders and it felt too nice to complain.

I smiled. I loved the Bourne movies. Somehow I identified with Jason Bourne, but I wasn't telling that to MD.

It was nice to quietly sit and watch a movie with someone with just his arm casually across my shoulders. I didn't remember the last time I did it. It was so nice that Jason was barely offering Marie money to drive him to Paris before I was asleep.

Next thing I heard was, 'Ahem,' and a series of giggles.

I gathered my senses before realising I was asleep on the couch, snuggled up beside MD, my head on his chest as I'd burrowed into the nook of his body with his arms holding me close.

'Ahem,' they called again louder and MD jumped up as though ready to save the world.

Sienna giggled, 'Settle down, Detective, it's just us,' she said, smirking beside Mel who was holding her phone as though she'd taken a photo.

'What? Detective?' I asked, my stomach sinking to my toes.

'He didn't tell you?' asked Sienna.

'I guess I didn't ask. I just assumed you were a regular cop,' I said to him. It was my own fault. I was in the habit of not asking personal questions. If I didn't ask them, they didn't ask me.

He shrugged, 'I just assumed you knew, everyone knows. Besides, there's nothing regular about me,' he winked, no doubt to infuriate his sister.

I nodded and smiled as best I could while my insides were trying desperately to run for the hills. No wonder they weren't too bothered with any other checks when they gave me the room. They had their own personal cop, a detective at that, if anything went wrong.

'Hey, did you photograph us?' MD asked Mel, noticing her phone.

'Of course,' smirked Sienna. 'It's not every day the great MD snuggles on the couch, no one would believe me without proof,' she giggled as they both walked away.

'Sorry,' he said to me. 'I guess I was tired.'

'That's okay. I daresay I fell asleep first anyway. I guess we're not good dates,' I suggested.

'Lucky we were just mates hanging out then,' he smirked.

I smiled. We both knew what this was and it had nothing to do with being mates. The second I let him drape his arm across my shoulder, it was all over. But I played along anyway. 'Lucky,' I added.

'I'm still taking you on a proper date, though' he said, tilting my chin up, his mouth meeting mine, moving against mine so deliciously I lost control of all awareness, all senses, all reason until Sienna groaned from the doorway.

MD pulled away and winked. 'Good night, ladies,' he said, grabbing his keys off the coffee table and leaving.

Sienna flopped on the couch beside me. 'Well, well, hey?' she smirked.

'Don't look at me like that,' I said. 'He just showed up. We ate pizza. I fell asleep watching a movie. That was it, until, until... just now,' I said.

'Until he kissed you,' she smirked. 'Again.'

'Yes, that,' I said.

Mel flopped into the seat on the other side of me. 'So, is MD as good a kisser as I've heard?' she asked.

I looked at her and couldn't help the smile spreading across my face.

'That good? Shit,' she giggled.

'Come on, that's my brother,' cried Sienna, pulling a face.

I laughed. 'Well, I gotta go to bed. I have to be up in a few hours to get to the market,' I said, glad for a reason to leave. I needed some space. It was happening, without my consent, fitting in, feeling something for people, for my new friends, for MD.

I needed to think about what to do. MD was a cop and not just a cop, a detective. They were like freaking blood hounds. He had access to resources that could destroy me. All he had to do was a run a fingerprint, type my name into his system and find out everything was a lie. But I couldn't leave yet. Not yet. I was tired. I needed to stay put for a while. I just had to make sure I didn't give him any reason to be suspicious. After this weekend, I'd have to do a better job of keeping them all at a distance. Which somehow I suspected wouldn't be as easy as it sounded. But I had to. For my own survival. For their protection.

CHAPTER 8

One of the permanent market stands was already busy brewing coffee, the rich aroma permeating the steamy morning air, when I arrived with my goods loaded onto a folding trolley. I bought a coffee in the biggest size they offered and wove my way through the aisles to my allocated space.

I had a small tent space with a few timber trestle tables between an old man and his son selling timber goods, quirky hooks for the hallway, chopping boards and name plaques on my left, and a middle-aged woman in a floral maxi dress on the other side selling handmade glass wind chimes that tinkled in the breeze. They each gave me a cheery hello before we all set up our wares.

I hung some of the bigger pieces from the metal rod of the tent with picture wire. The smaller pieces I put in a variety of mini easel stands I'd bought at a craft shop and some I laid out on the folding trestle table. The smallest pictures I stacked in plastic tubs for people to flip through.

Throughout the morning, there was a good flow of people. The good thing about selling at markets, it didn't matter if you were a brand name, had been around for minutes or decades, people came looking for something new and fresh and original. Word of mouth sometimes helped, particularly in places like Sydney but in places heavy with tourists, no one cared how long you'd occupied your tent.

A lot of customers asked about my work, where the shots were from, where I got my inspiration. It was always the way, people cared and they liked that they could speak with the artist, get a personal perspective. I told them no two pieces were the same, which thrilled them as it usually did. The local shots I'd taken sold the fastest.

I munched my way through the snacks I'd brought with me but what I really wanted was another coffee and some of the hippy protein balls I'd had with Sienna. I saw the lady next to me pour herself a coffee from her flask and I remembered mine, left behind in a cupboard in Sydney beside my Tupperware containers and not yet replaced.

'I remember there being a lot more than this,' smiled MD, walking into my little tent space.

He was wearing snug fitting jeans and a loose blue t-shirt that gripped his shoulders. Stubble covered his jaw and mischief twinkled in his eyes. He looked good. Too good. Disturbingly good.

'Oh, hey,' I smiled, completely forgetting I was supposed to be putting some distance between us.

'Here, thought you could use this,' he said, offering me a giant paper coffee cup.

'Oh, you're a lifesaver,' I smiled, taking a sweet, glorious sip of coffee.

'So, it's going well, then?' he asked.

'Yeah, really well,' I told him.

Another customer came in and bought a picture from the beach and walked away happy with their piece of Noosa.

MD stayed and chatted while I enjoyed my coffee. I made a couple of sales while he stood there and it was nice. He was nice, he felt nice and talking to him seemed more natural than anything had in a long time. When I finished my coffee, MD sent me off to use the ladies' room while he manned the stall. I could have hugged him, I was so grateful.

When I returned, he'd sold one more piece. It was turning out to be quite a profitable day.

'Well, I better go,' he finally announced, almost reluctantly. 'See you at the gig tonight?' he asked.

'Yep, for sure,' I answered, trying not to grin like a fool, chastising myself for breaking my own rules as easily as breathing.

'He's cute,' smiled the lady from the next stall after he'd walked away.

'Mmmmm...' I groaned. 'Isn't he just?' Too darned good looking, I thought. He kept making me forget he was a cop, a detective and I was supposed to be putting a barge pole between us.

The last of the visitors dwindled out and headed to the car park a little before the two o'clock closing time and I began packing up what was left of my stock and had a nice chat with my neighbours as we all secured our money. I had made way more than I'd expected and felt quite pleased with myself. I drove away with a satisfied smile on my face. This place had been a good choice. Having the market on twice a week was going to seriously increase my cash flow, which was great. I hated dipping into the family money. I didn't know where each note had come from and had to be careful when and where I used it and to use it sparingly, this market was definitely going to be a Godsend.

On the way home, I pulled over to the side of the road a number of times to take photos. I was in no rush and riding a high of accomplishment. Everywhere I looked there was something to see, something that needed to be immortalised, shared, remembered. As usual, I'd gotten side-tracked and before long was photographing the setting sun. The sun itself was out of my view but the rainbow of colours dancing across the sky as though the heavens had them on a puppet string photographed beautifully. Taking pictures was like a meditative release, it helped me exhale, calmed my insides, calmed my hyperactive brain.

When I finally pulled up to the kerb in front of my house, I was relaxed and ready to take on the night ahead. Lucky too, as preparations for a night of frivolity were already in full swing. My housemates and a bunch of people, some of Rick's mates from the last barbeque and a few more people I didn't know, were outside having a drink by the pool. Their spirits high as they drank beer from bottles and laughed like old friends. Rick was cooking a barbeque, his usual fare of sausages, minute steak and onions with a couple of loaves of bread and bottles of sauce ready to go. Everyone was already dressed ready for the night. After stopping for a brief hello to Mel and Sienna, I slipped upstairs to get myself ready.

Not that I really had much to wear, all I'd brought with me were jeans and t-shirts and I'd only topped up with a few extra casual tops, t-shirts, shorts and thongs. I'd have to get a bit creative. I found the most suitable t-shirt I could, black with some silver picture on it. It was the most rock and roll t-shirt I had and I paired it with my dark blue skinny jeans that were so well worn they fitted like a second skin. The only shoes I had were my one pair of black ballet flats that I'd driven up in. Not normally what I'd wear to a gig at the local pub but they'd have to do. I certainly couldn't wear my runners or my thongs. I touched up my makeup, added some smoky grey to my eyes along with eyeliner and mascara, added some lip gloss and pulled my messy hair into a pony tail, letting the natural waves trail down my back. That was the best I could manage. It would have to do.

I accepted a cider from Mel when I joined her and the others by the pool and stood as far away from MD as I possibly could, just to be safe, to see if I could get my head straight. He looked incredible too, snug blue jeans, black t-shirt that clung to his body just as I wanted to. He was still unshaven and I'd caught a whiff of him as I'd passed, soap, sun, salt and a hint of something warm and spicy that was far too enticing, that made me want to bury myself in him. It wasn't a good start.

Eating as one big group made it easy to stand to one side and be quiet, be a part of what was going on around me without actually having to do or say anything. It was easier, safer. I needed to find some equilibrium and figure out who was who in this group of people I'd be spending the evening with rather than my entire focus being about MD.

After we'd eaten, Sienna flung her guitar across her shoulders and we walked in convoy down the street. I kept to the back of the group and fell into conversation with Mel about her revitalising day of yoga, hair and nail appointments. We walked around a bunch of corners, down a few residential streets, until we eventually arrived at the pub.

It was more modern than the local pubs I was used to but still, full of character as a good pub should be, dark windows, posters advertising coming events, a queue of noisy people filled with anticipation, stretching along the wall. There was a black and purple sign out the front that said 'Tonight, The Rise of Rain, live.'

We went in through a back door leading to a room behind the stage. The room was a crazy hubbub of activity; the band, pub crew, sound people, guests, enjoying some pre-show drinks. Sienna deposited her guitar and waved as a couple of people called out greetings but we didn't stay. I followed Sienna and the others through the back-stage area, through another door and into the main room.

The room was a large, dark cube, just a few low lights on except for the well-lit bar. The room had that strange, haunted, eerie feel pubs have when they're empty, as though the ghosts of nights past still clung to the walls looking for mischief.

The long bar stretched across one end of the room, a scattering of tall round tables to stand at and put your drinks on, filled most of the space between the bar and the small dance floor in front of a raised stage. The stage had already been set and held some microphones, a couple of shiny guitars leaning against amps and a black drum kit with the band's name on the front in purple glitter, was set up at the back.

One of the bar staff greeted Sienna familiarly as we crossed the room, handed her a drink and Sienna farewelled us. We wished her luck and they both went backstage. Rick and some of the others headed to the bar, Mel went to the bathroom and suddenly I was alone with MD.

'Are you avoiding me?' he asked with a knowing smirk, angling his body too close, backing me up against the table so I couldn't escape.

'Nope, why would I do that?' I asked, trying to keep control of my suddenly frenetic insides. 'Just friends remember?' I'd decided it would be easy enough to put that barge pole between us in a filled pub. I'd just blend in with the masses, I thought. No one had told me we'd be walking into an empty bar. I hadn't planned for that. I hadn't planned for nowhere to hide.

'Hmmm...' he mumbled, eyeing me cautiously as Rick returned with our drinks.

Mel returned from the bathroom and the four of us gathered around the tall table, the others finding their own preferred vantage points. There was no way I was going to be able to keep away from MD if it was just the four of us. It would be impossible. The boys quickly fell into a conversation about sports or something and Mel was asking how my first day at the markets had gone. Brilliant, I was telling her, then, without warning, MD's hand wrapped around mine.

It took all my concentration not to audibly gasp from the surprise of it. I wasn't his girlfriend, for goodness sake. Holding hands was too intimate for my liking, too familiar. It says too much. It took me by surprise but aside from making a fuss and shaking him free, there wasn't much I could do. It certainly wasn't the time or place to make a scene and if I was being honest, it felt nice and my heart refused to agree with my head. For the first time in a while, my heart won and I gave in. Just for a minute, I told myself.

I was glad when the drinks were finished and MD went to the bar seconds before the doors opened and people began filling the room. I could finally think straight again. My brain told my heart to shut up and I excused myself to go to the toilet, thinking it was the perfect way to get lost for a while.

When I came out of the bathroom, the pub was full, the noise of jovial chatter deafening. I could see the table where my friends were. A few more people had joined them, eagerly awaiting the night to begin. My cider sat waiting for me next to MD's beer. I could easily disappear for as long as I wanted among all these people. Maybe even find someone else to hook up with to throw MD off but as he glanced around looking for me, ignoring the conversations going on around him, my heart sank. I couldn't do that to him. I didn't know why. I didn't know what it was about him, but somehow he'd gotten to me, a dangerous connection had been formed and I knew I couldn't hurt him. Not like this, anyway. Not today. My heart wouldn't let me.

He spotted me, his dark eyes serious, his features appearing even more chiselled and dangerous as our eyes connected across the room sending a bolt of electricity through me. I smiled, though I suspected it was lopsided as I was trying not to grin like a fool. I didn't even have the sense to chastise myself.

I returned to my friends and MD passed me my drink.

'You alright?' he asked, whispering it close to my ear with his arm casually draped around my waist.

'Ahuh,' I said, turning towards the stage as the band began to take their places.

MD's hand stayed on my hip, pulled me to him, against his beautiful body. I gave up the fight and relaxed into him as Sienna strummed the first notes on her guitar.

I glanced around to see people's reaction to her, to the band. They must have been popular to draw such a crowd. I noticed a number of girls looking my way, giving me the evil eye. They looked me up and down, whispering to each other, scowling right at me, making no effort to hide their contempt. I turned away, surprised. I'd been the new girl in town more times than I could count but no one had ever looked at me like that.

'Ignore them,' Mel said, leaning across the table. 'You have the ungettable man draped all over you. They'll be wondering who the hell you are and how the hell you got MD to do what he's doing.'

'What do you mean? I didn't ask him to do anything,' I said. 'And he's not doing anything Rick's not,' I said defensively.

'That's the point,' she smirked. 'MD doesn't choose his women until the night is ending and look at him, he's making his declarations pretty clear.'

'Mel, what are you telling her?' MD demanded.

'Nothing,' she smirked.

'Am I going to need an escort to go to the toilet?' I asked.

Mel giggled.

MD scowled.

Sienna began singing and she was incredible, captivating and beautiful.

The band, The Rise of Rain, was a folky rock sound. They sang all originals and everyone in the bar shut up to listen. They were mesmerising, their sound intoxicating. Every one of them fell into their own spell as they played, taking us with them as they lulled us into submission.

The set was over too soon. But it was a good chance to get some air. It was my turn to buy a round for the four of us, so I told MD I was going to the bar.

'Hell no,' he declared. 'You'll be eaten alive. I'll go,' he insisted in a do not mess with me voice that sent something fluttering deep in my belly. I think it was my belly anyway. I hoped it was, any lower and I was in more trouble than I wanted to consider.

Mel giggled, shuffling over next to me. 'I've never seen him be this protective. He's kind of hot like that,' she said.

'Mel, really? Are you telling me you've never seen MD with a girl?' I asked.

'Of course I have. But usually it's one in the morning and they're drunk as skunks, snogging while deciding whose place they'll go to. Usually hers by the way. He likes the option of leaving when he feels like it.'

'Seriously?' I asked, trying not to laugh. 'He's such a cliché.'

'You're not upset?' she asked.

I shook my head. I couldn't allow myself to be swept up into anything else. No strings attached fun, I could do, it was my only option. It was what I knew, it was safe and familiar.

MD returned. 'I hope you're not filling her head with stupid stories, Mel?' MD scowled.

'Never,' she smirked, going back to stand beside Rick whose arm instinctively wound across her shoulders.

'Don't listen to a word she says,' he said, tilting my face to his. 'A man's only a cad until he meets someone he fancies the hell out of,' he winked.

Oh shit, there goes the idea that he's just having fun.

With nothing but his finger under my chin he drew my mouth to his in a long, sensual kiss that made my toes curl, that I never, ever wanted to end. As he pulled away, our eyes seemed lost in each other for a second before he winked.

I could feel every pair of eyes on us. He ignored them all as though he didn't even notice and nodded to the stage as Sienna and her band returned for another set and I turned to watch. He draped his arm around my waist, pulling me protectively against his strong body, kissing me sweetly on my head and suddenly I didn't mind a bit. It felt natural and perfect and why shouldn't I get a little piece of what everyone else had?

As Sienna and her band finished their next set and I'd finished the two ciders that had appeared in front of me. I needed the bathroom.

'I'll come with you,' insisted MD as Mel had disappeared to dance with some friends and hadn't returned yet.

'Don't be ridiculous, you are not escorting me to the bloody toilet,' I laughed, walking away before he could do anything about it.

There was a small line for the toilets and I stood at the back and shuffled forward with everyone else. See, I wanted to tell MD, no problem.

I went into a cubicle when it was my turn and came out to wash my hands. There was a row of girls, faces full of flawlessly applied makeup and hair that flowed perfectly, standing at the basins, talking and fixing their makeup. I squished in at the end and washed my hands in the spare basin, looked up to check my own makeup in the mirror and I saw they were watching me.

I took a deep breath, ignoring them and I turned to dry my hands. As the dryer stopped, one of them asked, 'So, who the fuck are you?'

I looked at her surprised. I didn't know what to say. I wasn't anybody.

All of a sudden it seemed all three of them had herded me into the corner and were gathering the interest of every other woman in the room.

'Well?' asked the girl again. She had long, straight brown hair, big brown eyes and a fabulous tan. 'Who are you and why is MD fawning all over you like a love-sick puppy?' she demanded.

'What? He is not,' I said, hoping she was being dramatic. MD didn't look like he'd do lovesick puppy.

'Yeah, who are you exactly?' asked another girl joining the throng. She had blonde curly hair, was pretty, slim, petite.

I didn't do well trapped and I didn't like spectacles. Just as I was trying to subdue the panic building inside so I could figure out how I was going to push past them all, Sienna reached in, grabbed my hand and told them all to 'Bugger off and stop gossiping like old hags,' As she pulled me to safety.

Sienna put her arm around my shoulder and steered me out with Mel leading the way.

'Has he slept with all of those women?'

Mel laughed. 'God no. A couple, yeah, but most of those women wouldn't have a hope in hell with MD. But they'd like to and that's the problem. He doesn't give any of them a second look and in walks you and he's dripping all over you like a love-sick teenager,' she chuckled.

'Don't worry about them,' insisted Sienna as we met MD waiting just outside the door.

'They had her bloody corralled into the corner for crying out loud,' scoffed Sienna. 'Look after her, would you? I've got another set to play,' she grumbled at MD before walking away.

'You alright?' asked Mel, kindly.

'Yeah, I'm alright. Hey, thanks for rescuing me,' I said.

'No worries. You coming back to the table?' she asked.

'In a minute,' MD said.

She nodded and returned to the table, her job done.

'You sure you're alright?' MD asked, examining my face, for what I wasn't sure, a sign of damage, a lie, something.

'Of course I am. But bloody hell you've whipped everyone into quite a frenzy,' I told him, realising how funny it actually was.

He grumbled his displeasure as a couple of girls cooed, 'Hey, MD,' as they walked past, as though I wasn't there at all.

'You wanna go?' he asked, ignoring them.

'No, no, I want to see Sienna's last set,' I told him.

'You sure?' he asked, concerned.

'Absolutely,' I smiled. Those girls were not going to ruin my night.

He nodded, pulled me to him and kissed me, his hands either side of my face, holding me there, my blood pumping hard as the kiss deepened, heated, and I thought I might rip his shirt off right there. That'd give those bitches something to talk about.

He pulled away, resting his forehead on mine as he caught his breath. 'You sure you don't want to get out of here?' he smiled, mischief filling his eyes as they turned molten.

Something inside me came alive and all I wanted to do was crawl into bed with this man and never come out. I also wanted to believe that the sooner we got the whole business of sex over with, the sooner my brain could go back to proper functioning and he'd be ready to move on and things could get back to normal. It was too much. All these feelings. They had to stop. But somehow, I doubted sex was going to be the answer and I suspected if he moved on once we got the anticipation of sex out of the way, I wouldn't cope as well I thought. I suspected I was doing the unthinkable. I was falling for MD.

We returned to the table to watch the rest of Sienna's set. I tried limiting my alcohol intake. I'd been more shaken than I'd let on and I was worried about whatever this thing with MD was and wanted a clear head. But drinks appeared and I drank them anyway.

When the set was over, we waited for Sienna to have a rest and talk to her adoring fans as she walked through the pub to us. Someone passed her a drink and everyone began telling her how brilliant she was.

'Did you like it?' she asked me.

'Are you kidding? You were incredible,' I told her. 'I can't believe you haven't been signed yet.'

'Oh from your mouth to the powers that be,' she smiled.

People were leaving in droves, heading off to dance clubs or heading home. Most of our entourage had dispersed and moved on. It was just the five of us left and a guy Rick worked with who was too drunk to make sense but insisted on babbling on to Rick. But finally, we could hear each other speak and no one had to shout.

'Where did the name of the band come from? It's very cool,' I said.

'Rain is my middle name,' she said. 'So we just played around with that. Would be a shame to waste something that quirky,' she said.

'Your middle name is Rain?' I asked, suppressing a grin.

'Yeah, it's mum's hippy influence but thankfully Dad had the sense to insist we had respectable first names,' she said.

'We? What then does the D in MD actually stand for?' I asked, barely able to hide my glee at the prospect of MD having a quirky middle name.

I could feel MD scowling behind me, the scowl radiated off him, it must be good, I thought.

'Yeah, Mitch, what does the D stand for?' Sienna giggled.

'Nothing,' he said, scowling and taking a long drink of his beer.

'You're such a killjoy,' Sienna smirked.

Rick's friend finally stumbled away after a pretty girl. 'What are you talking about?' Rick asked.

'What the D in MD stands for,' said Mel. 'He won't tell us,' she said.

'You don't even know?' I asked her.

'No way,' she said. 'That's like the best kept secret in the whole Sunshine Coast,' she giggled.

'Secret?' scoffed Rick, way over the line of drunk. 'I thought everyone knew he was the great D'Artagnan,' he said dramatically, laughing.

'D'Artagnan?' I smiled. 'As in the musketeer?'

'Come on,' MD begged. 'It's not like I got to choose it,' he defended.

'Well, I think it suits you,' I told him as a brewing scuffle by the bar distracted everyone else.

'How's that?' he asked.

'D'Artagnan was strong, sexy, brave; I could go on,' I smiled.

He smiled. 'I like the way you see me,' he whispered. 'Can we go now?' he begged, his voice hot on my ear. 'Please?' he said pulling me against him as he kissed me so dangerously I thought sparks would fly off us.

He pulled away and I stared at him stunned, breathless.

'Come on, let's go to my place,' he mumbled, reaching for my hand as the scuffle ended.

It hit me like a brick wall. His place. He never goes back to his place. I couldn't do it. It was out of control. Everything was out of control. Everyone was watching us, perhaps sensing something was about to happen. 'Sorry, I can't,' I whispered, before walking out.

It was one thing to pretend I could live like this, have a man like him when I thought it was just a fling, that I could just enjoy him before he got bored and moved on. But this? No. Not if he was playing for keeps. Not if he was serious. Even with my brain fogged with alcohol, I knew I couldn't go down that path with him. That at some point, I'd have to do something awful, that I'd have to leave him and I wouldn't hurt him. I couldn't. I had to stop it now. He'd invited me to his place, which meant he didn't want an escape route. He was serious about whatever was going on here. I wasn't the girl for him. He had to know that. Some detective.

MD followed me out, I could sense him, then I could hear his feet on the footpath as he chased me. 'Jilly! Jilly! Wait,' he called out to me.

I turned. Our friends had followed us out but kept their distance.

'Jilly, what's going on? What was that?' MD asked, reaching for my hand.

I looked up, into his beautiful eyes. They were hurt. They were afraid and confused. A little piece of my heart broke off, floated away, knowing that I'd done that to him. I hated myself for it. He was a good man, but we were already in too deep. It was a place we shouldn't be. He shouldn't be. I could never be. It was better to walk away now. If I let it go any further, it would just be worse for both of us.

'I'm so sorry,' I said, tears filling my eyes. 'I know everyone keeps warning me about you, saying things, but MD it's not me who should be watching out for you, it's the other way around. Trust me, you don't want to do this, not with me,' I told him, a few stray tears rolling down my face. I reached up, touching his beautiful face, his strong jaw that I'd desperately wanted to kiss into the wee hours of the morning. 'I'm so sorry. If I'd seen this coming, I'd never have let it happen,' I said, before walking away, leaving poor stunned MD on the street to watch me.

As I navigated the dark streets, I debated not going home at all. Perhaps I should just get the hell out of town now? Or get a room somewhere and come back for my stuff in a couple of days when everyone was at work? But all my money was in my room. My camera was at home even though I'd considered bringing it to take some pictures of Sienna playing. So I went home.

I'd beaten them home. They hadn't caught up to me along the way or caught a taxi. They probably didn't want to see me, anyway, not after what I'd done to MD. It was better this way, I thought as I climbed the stairs to my room but it didn't make it any easier.

I washed the night off, snuggled into my jammies. Still feeling the buzz of alcohol, I drank some water before climbing into bed and tried to figure out how to fix this mess without having to leave.

I heard everyone come home not long after I'd gone to bed but I just lay there listening to them moving around the house, filling it. I heard the fridge door open, the jingling of bottles and someone going back down the stairs, a few voices then steps coming towards my room. The door opened but I pretended to be asleep and then not long later, my cheeks wet with fallen tears, I was.

CHAPTER 9

It was early when I woke, my eyes crusty from tears, my body dehydrated, my heart just a little bit broken from denying it something it so desperately wanted, for the look on MD's face. It wasn't about the sex, he'd put himself out there, done something he'd never done before, he'd followed his heart and I'd rejected him. I'd said too much, thrown him for six after the amazing kisses and he'd been crushed.

I quickly showered as quietly as I could so I didn't wake Sienna. We were supposed to go to the marina markets together, have brunch, but I thought it would be best if I went on my own. They'd all kept drinking into the wee hours, I'd heard them as I'd drifted off to sleep, so Sienna should sleep for a while yet, I thought.

I dressed in shorts, t-shirt, thongs, put my camera and some water into my tote bag and headed to the kitchen for a piece of toast. I'd get coffee and something more substantial later.

When I passed through the lounge room, I saw MD stretched

out on the sofa, sound asleep, a blanket over him. He was too big for the couch. His body stretched over the ends, fell over the sides but he slept anyway, the stubble on his jaw thicker, his face soft and relaxed. Sienna was standing at the kitchen bench when I finally tore my eyes away from MD, a steaming coffee in her hand as she read the paper, fully dressed and groomed, ready for the day. I hadn't heard her make a sound. I was losing my touch.

'Good morning,' she said cheerily.

'Morning,' I replied suspiciously. 'What are you doing up?' I asked.

'We're going to the markets,' she said as though I was mad. 'Coffee?' she asked.

I nodded and she popped a pod into the machine beside her.

'What's he doing on the couch?' I asked, indicating MD. 'Isn't there a spare room downstairs?'

'There is but he didn't want to miss you. He forgets he sleeps like the dead after a few beers, though,' she smiled. 'What happened with you two, anyway?'

I shrugged.

'You should give him a break. He's new at this. He's not going to know all the rules.'

'It's not that. It's not him, I mean. It's me. I'm not someone he should be getting close to. None of you should, but you're all too bloody nice for your own good,' I smiled, accepting the coffee.

She smiled, 'Not sure any of us have been told that before. So why? What's going on?'

'Nothing. It doesn't matter,' I said, trying to wave it away.

'Fine. For now,' she conceded. 'But give him a break, eh?' she begged.

'Why me, Sienna?'

'What?'

'Why me? Why'd MD choose me? There are plenty of women who'd kill to date him. Why me?'

She shrugged. 'Why not you? Yes, he's a shit and you shouldn't fancy him and he could've picked anyone in town to mess with other than my new housemate,' she smiled. 'But why not you?' she asked, confused.

I raised an eyebrow.

'Come on, you're beautiful and fun and you don't fall for his shit, maybe that's just what he needs. Like he said, the heart wants what the heart wants, I guess. Who knows what goes on inside that head of his? Come on, let's get outta here or you'll be having a heart to heart before breakfast and I'm way too hungover to referee,' she smiled.

I sculled the coffee, thankful she'd put too much milk in it. I couldn't help but glance over at MD as I walked out of the kitchen. He was so bloody handsome with his face soft in sleep with that little boy softness some men get when the worries of the world are at bay, despite the sexy as hell stubble covering his jaw. The sight of him tugged at my heart whether I wanted it to or not. The heart indeed. It had no business sticking its head up after all this time.

Sienna rolled her eyes and grabbed my arm, 'Trust me, he'll still be right there when we get back.'

I hoped so and it terrified me.

The marina markets had a different feel to Eumundi. They were cheery and bright, a little fancier. People wandered lazily with coffees in hand along the sun-drenched pier looking at the lovely beachy items on offer; clothing, home wares, homemade cards and glass items. With the sun already warming our skin it was hard not to feel better.

After we'd done a lap, I followed Sienna into a nice cafe overlooking the river.

'What did you think?' she asked after the waiter went off to organise our bacon and eggs for breakfast.

'I love it. It's different to Eumundi, brighter somehow. I think I'd need some different stock here but that's okay, I have an idea of what might work,' I said, already imagining the kinds of bright, cheerful beach shots I could print. They'd be a bit of a contrast to my usual work, which was a bit artier with a lot of moody black and whites but the idea of the happier shots felt right. It suited the area, the people in their blues and whites, their resort wear and the sun that drenched the whole marina.

'Excellent,' she said as the waiter brought us orange juice and coffee.

We talked while we ate our eggs about Sienna's hopes for the band, how the group of friends had come together. 'It's a small music scene up here, everyone knows everyone and somehow we just started jamming together and we fit. We were working on originals and playing them before we'd even realised we'd formed a band and by then we were in love and there was no turning back,' she smiled. 'Hopefully someday we'll get our music in front of the right people and that'll be that. We try, but it's not easy in such a small demographic like Australia, but we'll get there and we're having fun along the way,' she said, lighting up as she spoke about what she loved.

'I've got it,' I insisted when the waiter bought the bill over. 'As a thank you for helping me get set up' I added when she looked like she was going to argue.

We stopped a couple of times along the drive home so I could take some pictures and by the time we arrived home in the late morning, the sun high, I felt better.

I was making too much of this thing with MD, with everyone. My past wasn't going to be an issue for them. They would never have a reason to find out who I was and my past had no way of finding me. It's not like MD was going to be proposing for goodness sake. It was the booze mixed with the recent chaos of moving and everything that had happened with Michael, I decided. I'd blown everything out of proportion. I'd still have to keep my distance, not let any of these relationships go any further, but there was no need to be a paranoid cow about it. I could relax. I had to relax.

MD was still lying on the couch when we walked in, but he was awake and watching cartoons. My heart swelled with feeling for him. I almost laughed at myself for how quickly I was able to throw out every single one of my rules.

'Coffee?' Sienna asked.

'Please,' MD and I echoed as MD threw off his blanket and sat up.

MD was next to naked in nothing but a pair of boxers. I watched him as he sat and rubbed his face, stretched his perfectly fit body, unable to turn away. He was perfect. He was clearly fit, worked out enough for his muscles to be nicely defined, more than a hint of a six pack, definition in his strong arms and thighs, a tattoo of some sort on his left shoulder, not too much hair on his chest, just enough, a perfect snail trail...

'Would you put on some clothes, Mitch, seriously,' Sienna scoffed with a smirk when she brought in our coffee. 'Now, is it safe for me to leave you two alone?' she asked.

I nodded. Although now I'd seen him practically naked, I could hardly remember what it was we'd fought about.

MD smirked.

Sienna rolled her eyes and took the paper and her coffee to her bedroom.

'Sit?' MD asked, putting on his discarded jeans and sitting back down on the couch.

Shit, how was I supposed to concentrate while he was shirtless? I sat anyway and tried to smile.

'So what happened last night?' he asked.

I shrugged.

He raised a challenging eyebrow. He had a way with facial expressions and the intensity of that challenging eyebrow made me want to confess everything. I bet he was a master interrogator. I almost laughed. What would he do if I did confess everything? That would throw him back on his butt and wipe the smirk off his face. But I liked the smirk. I liked the intensity in his eyes. I liked how he could be so many things all at once and still be sexy as hell.

'I guess I panicked,' I confessed.

'About what?' he asked.

'You. This.'

'Why?'

'Mel said you never take women home. You invited me to your place. I panicked. I thought you were getting too close.'

'What's wrong with that?'

'Why me, MD?' I asked, seeing as I didn't believe the answer I'd gotten from Sienna.

'I don't know,' he said quietly. 'You're beautiful, that's for sure,' he said.

'There were far more beautiful women in the pub last night ready to throw themselves at you,' I said.

He shook his head. 'You have no idea how beautiful you are then. But it's not just that,' he said, putting his hand up when I was about to protest. 'I don't know what it is, it's just something. There's something about you and from the minute I saw you, you were under my skin, you were in my brain and I couldn't think about anything but you.

'I go to sleep thinking about you, wondering what you're doing, wondering what it'd be like to kiss you, wondering what's going on inside that mind of yours. I just can't get you out of my head, your smile, your eyes, it's like we've known each other for a hundred years, not a week. I can't explain it. It makes no sense.'

When he looked at me, he looked afraid, vulnerable, so beautiful I couldn't help reaching up to touch him, to kiss him, whisper soft kisses. I stopped before it got too heated, leaning my forehead on his, not wanting to part but knowing I had to.

'Tell me,' he whispered.

I shook my head. 'You don't want to know. You're far too beautiful a man for me and sooner or later you'll realise it and the other stuff, my past, none of it will matter,' I said, picking up my handbag to leave.

He grabbed my arm, spun me around. 'No, Jilly, no. You can't do that to me. I'm going to prove to you that this isn't just a flying fancy,' he insisted.

'It had better be a flying fancy or we're all screwed,' I told him, running down the stairs.

He caught up to me outside. 'Jilly, stop, come on,' he begged. 'What is it you're so afraid of?'

'Everything. I'm afraid of everything, MD,' I said, very nearly saying more but grateful for his ringing phone.

He pulled it from his pocket and snapped, 'What?' at the caller.

After a few grunts he hung up. 'I gotta go, one of the galleries was just robbed and the owner was nearly killed. But we're not done, Jilly, not by a long shot,' he insisted, pulling my mouth to his and kissing me hard, like there was no tomorrow and all we had was this one very second. Then he was gone.

I'd lost all my fight, gave up and went back upstairs and made another coffee. I'd just taken it onto the balcony when Sienna came out.

'You guys sort everything out?' she asked.

I shrugged.

'Where is he?'

'He got a call, he had to go,' I told her.

She nodded. 'Are you alright, Jilly?' she asked.

'Of course,' I told her.

'No, I don't mean right this second, but in general.'

I shrugged. 'I'm not the good person you all assume I am, but I'm trying,' I told her.

'What does that mean?' she asked, concerned.

I shook my head. 'I'm probably making more out of it than I need to, I just panic when my walls are breached and trust me, you guys have already gotten closer than anyone has in a long time. We all have pasts though, don't we?'

'Sure, I guess.'

'Well, mine haunts me a bit more than some and I worry that good people like you would get hurt if it ever caught up with me.'

She nodded. 'How far in the past are we talking?' she asked.

'Twelve years, or there abouts.'

'You would have just been a kid, Jilly?'

'I was,' I said, trying not to see any of it behind my eyes as I blinked, as I so often did, especially when the wounds were freshly opened.

'You can't persecute yourself forever for something that happened when you were thirteen,' she scoffed. 'Geez, no one made any sense at thirteen and we all wish we could erase our entire teenage years,' she said.

I knew the sort of stuff she was referring to. I'd seen it on television shows; funny teenage angst, bad haircuts and clothes and poor choices, boys, drinking. I wished that's all it was. I smiled though because she was being kind. 'Thanks,' I said, squeezing her hand. 'I'm going to go see if I can get some photos, I'll see you later.'

'Sure, have fun,' she smiled.

I sat on the beach with an icy Frappuccino and my camera. I was conflicted. Now was when I should run, when I usually ran but I just couldn't bring myself to do it. I didn't want to. For the first time in as long as I could remember, I really wanted to stay. I wanted to live. I liked this place, the sun, the sense of community. I liked the markets. I liked my friends. I really liked MD. I didn't know what to do. It had always been so simple. How had I let that change? Because I took the nice house with the nice people instead of the dump with the wasted surfers, that's how. I needed a plan. I had to figure it out. Somehow. Instead I fell asleep in the sun, amongst the squeals of happy children and the crashing waves.

I woke hungry, thirsty, my face feeling raw from the sun. I walked up to Hastings Street, careful to avoid the bar where Sienna was working an afternoon shift and headed for one of the Parisian styled cafes for a light lunch. I watched the people passing and wondered about them while I waited for my food. It was something I'd always liked to do, imagine their lives, wonder how they, regular people, lived, and imagine for just a moment what it would be like to be them instead of me.

The hiking trails leading into the national park at the end of the street tempted me some more. I could see the rise in the hill better from here and it looked beautiful and I could only imagine the views from up there, the shots I'd find inside the hidden nooks of rocks and trees. The waiter assured me, if I wanted to make a good go of it and get lots of great photos, I'd be better off with a whole day to spare and the appropriate footwear. I made a mental note to throw my runners in the car.

Sienna called as the sun was setting and I was enjoying a cold iced tea on the balcony. 'We're all heading to the surf club for dinner. Will you come?'

'After last night, I don't know,' I said, reluctantly.

'Come on, what's a night at the pub without a little drama,' she laughed. 'Come, it'll be fun, I promise. And, they make the best schnitzels in town. Come, please,' she begged.

I knew I should stay home, put some distance between us all, it made sense, at least until I got my head straight but I was hungry and with all that was going on, I didn't feel like being alone.

I knew it was selfish. But I had to believe everything would be alright. How would they ever find out the truth, anyway? No one else had ever come close to figuring it out before. It was only when official documentation was required, signing of leases, marriage proposals, too many questions about my past, that I had to run. It was just food. I'd be careful.

CHAPTER 10

I found my friends amongst an extended group of people who had taken over the balcony where the breeze coming up off the ocean turned the heat from the day into a perfect balmy evening. I recognised some of the faces from the night before but there were many I didn't. I got a few scowls from a group of pretty girls who had gone to far too much effort for such a venue but I ignored them as my friends welcomed me into their fold of camaraderie.

'I'm glad you came. I saved you a seat,' said Sienna, taking a collection of handbags off the seat beside her and redistributing them back to their owners.

She introduced me to a few people in our immediate vicinity, those she'd been chatting to but there were too many to bother introducing me to everyone.

'So you're the one who's got Paige and the other hangers on up in arms,' Justine, a girl across the table giggled as her man handed her a drink before going to chat to his mates against the railing.

'Shush, you'll scare her off,' laughed Sienna. 'She's like a cat, you can't go spooking her or you'll have to deal with MD,' she joked.

'Ah, someone to finally give MD a run for his money, hey?' Justine joked in return.

I shook my head at them. Where was he, anyway, I wondered, looking around for him but I couldn't see him in amongst the unfamiliar faces. I needed to see him even though I knew I had a lot of explaining to do, a lot of apologising and I'd rather not do it here in front of this audience but still, seeing him made my insides stop spinning. He made everything make sense, made it better and I needed to see him.

'He's not here,' Sienna whispered.

'Who?' I asked stupidly.

Sienna giggled. 'He's working. That case has everyone worked up. He told me I had to keep an eye on you, though.'

'Really? Doesn't he think I can look after myself?' I asked, a little offended he'd think of me as such a damsel, even though it was nice that someone might care.

'I think he's more concerned you'll pack up and go,' she said, raising her eyebrows in challenge.

'I thought about it,' I told her.

'Well don't,' she smiled as Rick appeared with a round of drinks for me, Sienna and Mel.

They were right, the schnitzels were sensational and I did need the laughs and the friendship for perspective. My worries felt less amongst the people. I liked hearing their stories, about their lives. It was good to get out of my own head for a while.

After we'd eaten and the evening began to wear on, people went home, moved into smaller groups, Sienna, Mel, Rick and I went inside to play a game of pool. A lot of the tourists had left and mostly locals remained having quiet beers, catching up with friends.

We were playing in teams. The first game was Mel and Rick against Sienna and me.

'You've played this before?' Rick quizzed with a curiously raised eyebrow as I hit the winning shot for us, beating Rick and Mel easily.

'Indeed I have,' I admitted with a smirk.

We switched it up for the second game. Rick took Sienna and gave me Mel. I knew they were ganging up on me. I'd seen Mel play, terribly, and they both had evil smirks on their faces.

Mel and I were giving them a good run for their money, though and having a great laugh. She bent down, showing too much cleavage in an effort to put Rick off or talked in Sienna's ear, anytime they looked to be gaining too much advantage. Not that she needed to. If I wanted to I could have won in just a couple of shots. I'd lived in a house once with a pool table and spent far too much time practicing.

'Oh, this will go down well,' Rick muttered.

'What?' Mel and I asked as Sienna took her shot.

He indicated with his head.

'Eric! Hey!' cried Mel, letting Eric wrap his arms around her in a hug.

He nodded to Rick with apprehension and to Sienna who greeted him a little more warmly. Then he turned to me. 'Hey, Jilly, how are you?' he asked, smoothly. 'I've been waiting for you to come back. Did Mellie tell you I offered to show you some of my favourite spots at the retreat?' he asked.

'Ahuh. Yeah, she did,' I answered nervously while Rick stood close beside me, leaning against the table with his arms crossed.

'I've just been a little busy working. I kind of go where inspiration takes me.'

'Well, this is my formal invitation, then. Perhaps some time this week? We get great afternoon light up there and then perhaps we could have dinner or something afterwards?' he asked, his body inching too close, despite Rick's imposing presence.

I nearly spluttered my drink. 'Um, I'm sorry, I don't think I can,' I said. Even though I didn't know what was going on with MD and me, I was pretty sure accepting dinner invitations from other men would not impress MD.

'Why not?' he asked, moving closer and trailing a finger along my jaw. 'I think we could learn a lot from each other,' he drawled.

I took his hand and moved it away from my face but he took it as an invitation to hold hands and gripped mine like a vice. I tried to pull my hand free but he wasn't letting it go and I didn't want to make a scene. I had to fess up even if it might have been an over exaggeration, especially as I didn't really know where things stood after our confrontation that morning. 'I'm sorry Eric, but I'm kind of seeing someone,' I said, still trying to pull my hand free.

'Kind of isn't actually, though, is it?' he asked, challenging me with a salacious grin.

'It's MD, Eric. She's seeing MD,' Rick said, stepping in and wrenching my hand free of Eric's.

'MD? You're kidding, right?' he asked Rick, me, anyone. Then to me he asked. 'You really think that arsehole is a better choice than me? He doesn't date women, Jilly, he fucks them and walks away. You deserve so much better.'

'I'm sorry Eric, I really like MD,' I said, taking a step sideways.

'Then you're a fool,' he spat, shaking his head and walking over to the bar.

He stood at the bar, threw back a couple of shots with a beer chaser, scowling at us before he walked out.

'Are you okay?' Sienna asked.

I shrugged, took my shot and potted the black, making Mel and I winners. 'I think I'm done, I'm going to go,' I said.

'You sure?' asked Mel, concerned.

'Yeah, yeah. I'm not worried about him. It's fine. I'm just tired,' I told them. It was true, too, guys like Eric I could handle. They were a dime a dozen in my world and usually that was the guy I'd choose, slightly narcissistic, too self-obsessed to dig, to notice, easy to keep at an arm's length. Guys like MD on the other hand…

We'd had a great night. For the first time I could remember I belonged somewhere. I hadn't forced myself to fit, it had just happened and I suddenly had a lot to lose, a lot of damage that could be left behind.

What would they do if they knew truth about me? I knew what they would do, what would happen if they found out and they wouldn't be inviting me to stay. Rick wouldn't protect me from the likes of Eric. They would be horrified, betrayed. They would never forgive me. Despite what Sienna said about my age at the time. I did it all the same. I'd killed a man. They would hate me. MD would hate me.

All it would take is for MD to put two and two together if something didn't add up. They'd be stuck in the middle, tainted by my past. That kind of thing never leaves you, it follows you forever. They didn't deserve that. What would happen to MD's career if his colleagues found out about us? Half of the Noosa locals had seen him draped over me at Sienna's gig. What would happen if his superiors found out who I was? How would that look for him? It could ruin his career. What I was doing was entirely selfish. For my own self-preservation. It had to stop. My past could taint everyone's future. It was for their own protection, and mine. As of tomorrow, I was going to have to do better if I wanted to stay.

I stared at the ceiling thinking about all the places I'd been and all the people I'd known on this ridiculous journey. There'd been the old lady in the big house. She was old, hard of hearing and the house was big enough that she'd never even known I was there, camped out in an unused room. That was my favourite place even though I'd never spoken to her. We'd made good roomies, she and I. It was surprisingly easy to stay out of her way. I'd get up and walk the forty-five-minute journey to the bus stop in the dark every morning. It was far too early for any of the people I'd once known to be there, not that they'd recognise me after I'd cut off all my hair, dyed it black and dressed like a Goth.

Once I got to the bus stop, I blended in with the uni students, even though I was far too young for university. Disguises were a key element of my upbringing, changing the way I looked, making myself unrecognisable, it became as natural to me as brushing my hair. I'd been too bland before to stand out anyway but after everything that had happened, I was sure people knew who that bland version of me was, what I'd done.

Anyway, I'd catch the express bus into the city and disembark with the masses. Then I'd get on another to whichever far away location I'd chosen for the day, the beach usually or Marion Shopping Centre where it was easy to go unnoticed. I'd buy groceries from a variety of faraway supermarkets, never becoming a regular at any. Then I'd return with the masses when the sun went down and sneak back in through the window I'd left unlocked on the other side of the old lady's house.

Everything was easier when the old lady went on her jaunts. I could stay home, watch television, bake, use the swimming pool, read lots of the stories from the big bookshelves crammed with every type of book. I just had to keep an eye out for the cleaning lady. But she tended to shirk her duties when the old lady was out of town. Which was good for me and I soon figured out her pattern.

They were good years. I learnt things from the old textbooks and from the stories I read in the pages of the novels crammed onto the shelves. It was there I first learnt about photography from an old textbook and then I saw how beautiful a photograph could be when the old lady received a coffee table book of photography in the post for Christmas one year. I'd never seen anything as beautiful as those pictures. So, for my fifteenth birthday, I took some of the family money and bought myself a fancy camera.

One shot was all it took for me to fall in love. As soon as I looked through that lens, saw something only I could see, captured a small moment in time, something extraordinary amongst the ordinary, something changed in me, clicked into place, like magic.

They were good times. I was safe and happy there. I could breathe. I hadn't felt like that since. Not until now.

When the old lady died, I was heartbroken and couldn't settle anywhere for a long time, maybe not ever, until now, even Michael was just a means to an end that I'd never expected to go where it did. When I left her house, I snuck into the back of a road train when the man loading it was distracted by a mate offering him a smoke and got off when it stopped, which was up north where my skin burned, feeling as dry as beef jerky and dripped with beads of sweat at the same time. I watched some sensational sunsets and made friends with a few beach bums heading west with a spare seat in an old, dust-red station wagon.

The point is, I reminded myself, before getting carried away, is that I knew how to be invisible. I knew how to avoid people and still co-exist. I lived with that old lady for years and we never once crossed paths. I could do that again. I'd have to if I wanted to stay and I really did want to stay. I wanted to stay in this place where the sun never burned too hot, where it was never cold, where people welcomed you like an old friend, where trees offered shelter from the bustle of the world and the markets overflowed with kindness and life. But the only way I could stay was if I knew they'd never find out who I was, if I never put their lives in danger because of what I'd done.

I got back up and showered, so I wouldn't have to in the morning, set the alarm on my phone with a sound that wouldn't wake Sienna and went to sleep, confident this was the only option, but far from pleased about it.

CHAPTER 11

It was still dark outside when my alarm tinkled on the cupboard beside me. I dressed quietly in the silent house, stocked my tote bag with snacks; muesli bars, rice crackers, nuts, lots of water and my camera. I held my thongs in my hand to avoid any accidental slapping sounds they'd make on the floor as I crept down the hallway, the stairs, then I quietly closed the front door and hurried for the Jeep parked on the street as though it were a getaway car.

There were cute beachside towns all the way up and down the coast. It wouldn't be hard to whittle away days exploring them and taking copious photos. It'd just be like those early days when I lived with the old lady, and it would be good to spend time just me and my camera, seeing what I could find on the other side of the viewfinder. Then I could waste days at the shops getting them printed.

I decided to totally immerse myself in my work. Build up my

stock. It was win, win every way and a plausible excuse when the girls quizzed me, because I suspected they would.

I'd miss the company of my new friends, of MD, but I could make more or just go it alone. I've never minded my own company. It's good for the soul and I could use some time with myself, think about how I was going to handle this situation, maybe where I might go next, what's in store, that sort of thing.

The sun rose as I drove, pinks and purples streaking across the sky before the sun finally made its grand appearance. I stopped a couple of times where it was safe to capture the colours and light and shadows through the trees and over the ocean. Already I felt calmer, purposeful. Yes, this was a good idea.

When I'd had enough of driving, I followed the next exit sign into a town. I parked in a mostly empty carpark surrounded by big white buildings, scattered with tall willowy palms. I put on my oversized sunglasses and walked to the esplanade, trying to get a feel for the place and the people.

It was a different feel to Noosa. Even the buildings were different, older, whiter. As I made my way to the esplanade, I could see even the people were different. There were more retirees, fewer families, fewer young people and no surfers wandering the damp sand with their boards tucked under their arms. Noosa began the day slowly, lazily, unless you surfed the early waves and gathered your zen for the day. Here had an early bird buzz about it.

People filled the cafes drinking cappuccinos and freshly squeezed juice as they tucked into big breakfasts of eggs, bacon, mushrooms, tomatoes, little sausages and toast. They struck me as tourists and I guessed this was their big meal before a day of sightseeing and light snacks. A travel reporter had mentioned it on the telly once and it had been a useful survival tool in those early days. Or maybe these were just hungry retirees keen to start their day with an outing and sick of resisting the good things in life like big breakfasts. A big hot breakfast certainly beat cereal, toast or muesli, especially if someone else was cooking it for you.

I'd resisted too many good things in my life, too. I was here giving up my friends and MD. That alone deserved a big breakfast. I found a table recently vacated by a white-haired couple wearing matching pastel pink polo shirts and white linen pants, sun visors and runners. I sat in a chair overlooking the ocean, which was perfect and calm, clear blue, matching the perfect blue sky.

'Heeeey, what can I get ya? Coffee? Juice to start?' asked a perky middle-aged man with a thick bushy moustache, blue Hawaiian shirt and tan, long shorts, as he handed me a menu.

'Sure, double shot latte and a pineapple juice, thanks. Oh and just give me one of those big breakfasts doing the rounds,' I asked, already knowing there'd be nothing more satisfying on the menu.

He smiled knowingly, 'Sure thing, love,' he said, taking back the menu and clearing away all the spare cutlery.

I looked up and down the coastline while I ate, trying to see where I should take my camera. Everywhere had potential. The beach, its surrounds, all practically glowed under the golden sun.

The sky was a perfect periwinkle blue. It was a good day for shooting high-end colourful prints for the Marina. I could trial the brighter, more colourful shots at Eumundi too, see how they fared against my regular work, which was already selling well there.

A sense of calm filled me while I quietly ate, as though I'd left my troubles behind in the sleeping house in Noosa. I'd needed this change of scenery, I thought, for clarity, for peace, to remember who I was and my purpose and why I couldn't have lovely friends and a beautiful man like MD.

Leaving the sunny café with a full tummy, a takeaway coffee and tips for some great spots to shoot from the waiter, I felt better, stronger, purposeful. As I walked along the esplanade, I could feel the sun already beating down on my shoulders. It was going to be a hot day. I needed something else to wear or I was going burn to a crisp and a hat. I'd need a hat. I stepped into a beachwear shop I would never normally shop in but it was convenient. It wasn't the sort of town that held a great deal of other options, especially not on the esplanade.

I bought a long, light blue, cotton maxi dress that would protect my legs but still keep me nice and cool. I topped it off with a big floppy hat to keep the sun from scorching my head and shoulders and bought a tube of sunscreen, which I instantly lathered on my arms, feet and chest. I popped on my sunglasses and I was a new person. It was as easy as that to change how one looked, how one felt.

The waiter had given me directions to a little secluded inlet behind the sand dunes. I followed his directions and found a small lake hidden far away from the prying eyes and destructive nature of people. There were birds and flowers, flowing water, sand crabs and little tiny fish. It was just what I needed, some space to be me. To be reminded the world was full of beauty. That my troubles were insignificant in the grand scheme of the universe.

I took out my camera, moving around carefully so I didn't disturb the little eco system and let myself feel what I saw. I connected with that part of me that took over whenever my eye met the viewfinder and let the magic happen.

Losing all track of time, I let the lens guide me. I lost myself in shooting the water birds with their long, arched beaks, the pools of water glistening like jewels in the sun, the schools of tiny iridescent fish, the hills shadowed in the distance, even the sun itself, bright white against the bright blue of the sky.

It wasn't until the sun began to set that I realised how late it was, that I'd skipped lunch and lost track of an entire day but I already knew I'd gotten a lot of great shots and couldn't wait to see them in print. My tummy rumbled as I put my sunglasses into my tote and held my hat in my hand as I headed back along the esplanade.

Streetlights now lit the footpaths. The already full cafes appeared to glow in the evening light, the chatter of customers filling the street. My rumbling stomach told me I needed more to eat than one of the muesli bars in my bag.

I stopped at the café where I'd had my delicious big breakfast and the waiter with the bushy moustache and the Hawaiian shirt gave me a friendly wave.

'How'd you go?' he asked after giving a table their menus.

'Great, thanks. Lost the whole day though and now I'm starving. I was going to see what you had going here for dinner but it looks pretty busy,' I said, looking around and not seeing a single available table.

'They'll probably start freeing up in about an hour if you can wait that long. We have some fresh salmon on the specials board tonight that is amazing,' he declared animatedly.

My tummy grumbled at the thought. 'Maybe some other time. I don't think I can wait an hour,' I laughed.

'Excuse me,' interrupted an old lady with short, curly brown hair and makeup caked into her wrinkles. 'We have a spare seat at our table if you'd like to join us,' she offered.

'What? No, really, I couldn't impose,' I told her.

'Impose? Goodness no, we'd love to talk to someone other than ourselves for a while,' she chuckled.

In the seconds it took me to decide, another waiter delivered a serve of the salmon to a nearby table. It looked so good my mouth watered.

'Thank you, that's very kind. I'd love to join you,' I told them.

My friendly waiter pulled out the chair for me and I sat.

'Well, go on Robert, get the girl a menu and a glass. Oh and don't forget the cutlery,' she ordered. To me she said, 'I don't know why they do that, take away the spare cutlery. Surely it can't be that much of a bother to wash,' she laughed. 'Anyway, dear, I'm Doris and this is my husband John and that's May next to you. Her husband, Arty, wasn't feeling well tonight, got too much sun today, that's how come there's a spare seat,' she told me. 'Now, how come you're out here eating dinner all by yourself?' she asked.

'I've just moved to Noosa. I came up here today to take some photos and lost track of time. I'm a photographer. I have a stall at Eumundi,' I told them.

'Ooh, a photographer,' May cooed as though it was something glamorous. 'We were going to go to those markets one day Dorrie, weren't we?' she questioned.

'Oh we were. We could stop by and see you. Would we like your photos?' asked Doris.

'I hope so. I like them,' I smiled.

'And what about your boyfriend, doesn't he mind you wandering all over the place all day and night?' asked May.

'Oh, no boyfriend,' I smiled as they poured me a glass of wine from the bottle in the middle of the table after Robert brought my glass, cutlery and a menu.

'A pretty thing like you must have the fellas queuing up,' said John.

I laughed, thinking of MD and Eric, and Michael recently left behind in Sydney. Perhaps I did, I thought with a smile. 'No. I just left one of those in Sydney. There is a man in Noosa, a really beautiful man but well, it's complicated,' I told them.

'Dear, love is never as complicated as your generation makes it out to be,' smiled Doris.

'Perhaps,' I smiled. 'But in my case it's actually true. I have a past that I sense is catching up to me, and it's better if I just keep my distance from him and everyone,' I told them, feeling unusually chatty.

I blamed the wine and the anonymity, the combination always loosened the tongue, especially around kind older people who treated everyone like their grandchildren. But it was true, that was the biggest problem. Somehow I could feel my past closing in. I sensed it pushing at my walls, forcing its way through and I was worried that this time, I wasn't going to be able to escape it or protect the people I had begun to care about. Not this time.

'Well, that doesn't make any sense at all,' added John. 'I was in Korea, you know and I tell you, nothing got more complicated than that and I also tell you, the only way any of us got through it was by leaning on each other, looking out for each other, that sort of thing. You can't go through life handling all your problems on your own, love. There's nothing wrong with leaning on someone once in a while,' he said.

'But what if by leaning on them, they might get hurt? Like really hurt. At the very least, it could ruin their lives.'

'Do they know that's the risk?' he asked.

'No. No way.'

'Well, shouldn't it be their decision to make? The world is full of danger, you can't protect everyone all of the time.'

'I don't want to protect everyone. Just these people. Or more so, I don't want to be the cause of their pain. But I see your point,' I said, wondering again what my friends, what MD would decide if they knew the truth and wondering if I could survive their choice, if they walked away, if they turned me in. 'Certainly wise words though, John. Something to think about. Now, tell me, what are you all doing sunning yourselves in these lovely parts?' I asked as Robert delivered my salmon and another bottle of wine.

'We're from Melbourne, but we chipped in and bought a place up here to share,' Doris told me. 'It's getting bloody cold down there this time of year and our old bones aren't what they used to be. They don't take too kindly to the cold these days. It's never winter up here though. The sun keeps our bones nice and warm,' she smiled.

'We'd live up here year-round if it wasn't for our array of grandchildren,' added May.

'How do you all know each other?' I asked.

'Dorrie and I have been best friends for as long as either of us can remember,' May smiled. 'Luckily our blokes have always got on or they'd be freezing their bony butts off back in Melbourne,' she giggled.

After that we talked about their enormous array of grandchildren, who was who, what they did, too many funny anecdotes to count and I felt a longing to be them someday, to be telling strangers funny stories about my kooky grandchildren while I sunned myself in faraway lands with the love of my life. Perhaps MD? It was sad to know that would never be me.

I was grateful when the subject turned to my photography, what inspired me, how did I know the right compositions and light and things, then somehow we got onto the subject of my nomadic lifestyle and some of the places I'd lived.

'Don't you get tired with all that moving around?' asked Doris.

'Sometimes, but it's pretty great too. I get to meet incredible people like all of you and I feel like I've lived a hundred lives.'

'One is exhausting enough for me,' chuckled John, pouring us more wine.

I left them to it once I'd finished eating and we'd emptied the second bottle of wine. They ordered a third and dessert while insisting I stay but I had to drive back to Noosa and it was getting late and I'd had my wine allowance for the evening. I dropped enough notes onto the table to cover my meal and one of the bottles of wine, despite their protests, and walked back to the Jeep with a smile on my face. People like that were one of the great treats of the life I led. I imagine people who lived ordinary lives didn't meet extraordinary people like John and Doris and May, or not as often as I did anyway and they always had great words of wisdom and stories to share.

As I drove back to Noosa enveloped in night, I wondered if I should at least consider John's advice and let my friends decide the risks they were willing to take to have me in their lives. I knew MD would have to turn me in though, he was a cop, he must have some obligation but would they stand by me? As I pulled up outside our dark house, I knew I wasn't nearly brave enough to test John's theory. I didn't think I'd do very well if they wanted nothing more to do with me.

Only Mel's car was in the driveway and all the lights were off. Mel must have been asleep. I guessed Sienna was either working, gigging or rehearsing and congratulated myself as I quietly climbed the stairs, quickly showered and climbed into bed, ready to do it all again in the morning. It was just like old times with the old lady and I went to sleep smiling as I thought of those easier days when I hadn't had to lie every day.

CHAPTER 12

I hadn't heard Sienna come home. It must have been late seeing as I'd tossed and turned for a while and still hadn't heard her come in. I thanked my good fortune as I snuck out again in the morning under the cover of darkness.

I drove to the top end of the beach after stopping by the McDonald's drive-through for pancakes and a coffee. I needed a plan for the day but I was tired and wasn't sure I fancied another long day. But where else was there to hide where I wouldn't run into my housemates? I didn't know the area well enough to know where was safe, where they went, where their friends went.

Thankfully, I felt a little revived after I'd refuelled and the caffeine hit my system. As I wondered about safe places to hide for the day, I had a sudden urge to get as far away from Noosa as possible. I couldn't explain it, but it consumed me, this desperate need to get into the Jeep and drive and not look back. I filled the Jeep with petrol and headed down to the Gold Coast. It was a couple of hours of freeway and the further I got, the more this need to drive that was crushing on my chest eased and I could breathe again. I followed the signs to the hinterland, winding my way through the lush green hills until I found a cute town filled with tourists and beautiful clean air to lose myself in.

I wandered through the little shops with another coffee, finally feeling relaxed as I looked at all the knickknacks and things that other people liked to clutter their homes. When you moved as much as I did and so often at short notice, there was no space in your life for knickknacks. None the less, I found myself buying a pair of hand carved bluebirds. They'd be my reminder of Mel and Sienna who were as beautiful and sweet and innocent as the bluebirds and they'd remind me why I had to do what I was doing to protect them, regardless of what John said about people making their own choices. I couldn't stand the thought of ruining their beautiful outlook on the world, on people, and I couldn't bare the thought of seeing fear and disappointment in their eyes when they found out who I was, the things Peter and Aunt Joanne had made me do. What I had done.

I had a pasty and a cream bun from a busy bakery and was sitting outside on a wooden bench in the shade eating when my phone beeped to signal a message.

'Where are you?' asked Sienna.

'Shooting down the coast,' I replied.

'K,' was all she said, but I knew my absence two mornings in a row had raised her suspicion. People didn't usually notice when I was gone but Sienna and Mel weren't the type of people I usually spent time with. It was strange for people to notice. Perhaps even a good strange. Even Michael who was about to propose never really checked up on me and when he did, it was only to see if he had time to squeeze in a session with one of his hookers. He'd say things like, 'Will you be home for dinner?' 'Shall I wait up?' 'Will we make the seven o'clock movie?' all innocent enough if you weren't aware of his hobbies. That guy could have gone ten times a day and still been as randy as a rabbit.

I was used to coming and going whenever I fancied for as long as I fancied. It made life for someone like me a whole lot easier. The dirty surfers wouldn't have noticed but I should have known it wouldn't be that easy with Sienna and Mel as housemates. But this was my life. I had to let it go. Sienna and Mel would adjust.

After I'd eaten, I found a few quiet spots to shoot, to regain my equilibrium. There were some great forest-like shots that looked both eerie and magnificent depending on the angle, the exposure and how I captured the light. I lost sight of the people moving around me as I immersed myself in this other world, found myself creeping into forest edges and losing track of another day.

My phone beeped as I was trying to shoot what looked like a mamma and a baby marsupial of some sort, scaring them both back into the bushes. It was Sienna again. 'Rick's having a BBQ tonight, see you then?' she asked.

'Unlikely I'll make it back in time,' I told her, feeling awful doing so, knowing I could have if I'd wanted to.

It hurt to lie to her, to distance myself but I had to do it. I couldn't let them find out who I was or what I'd done or worse, have them caught in the crossfire if it all came to light and dragged us all down.

I tried finding more shots to take, but I'd lost my enthusiasm. Imagining my friends all gathering for the testosterone-filled barbeque without me killed my enthusiasm. It was hot today. They'd all probably jump in the pool to cool off at some point. I wondered if MD would be there. If he'd solved his case. I wondered if he'd be there in his boardies ready to rip off his shirt and jump in the pool with the others.

The image of him, his beautiful body covered in glistening water droplets made me smile before I caught myself. It wouldn't do anyone any good, particularly me, to go thinking that way about things I could never have. I had no right to fantasise about MD. If he knew the truth he'd want nothing to do with me. I was sure of it. If he knew the truth, it'd be over for me. It'd have all been for nothing and not only could I not put him in real danger, my secrets could ruin his career and I wouldn't do that to him. He was a good man. He didn't deserve that. We weren't even a couple, nothing had really happened, but he could lose everything anyway. Harbouring a criminal. I'd seen that on the telly. They said it was as bad as being the criminal. Did it matter if he didn't know? I didn't want to risk finding out.

I left the hinterland and headed to the beach, sat on the sand and watched the water, killing time. There was a happy family on the sand, parents, a couple of small children, maybe five and six years old, their hair wet from swimming as they built sandcastles. I smiled. That had been my family once. I'd built sandcastles with my brother under the watchful, admiring eyes of my parents who'd praised every mound I created. I'd forgotten about those long-ago summers. Summers where we ate cold salad dinners while watching the cricket, barbeques outside and running under the sprinkler to cool off with Beau our Border Collie chasing us, barking and trying to lap at the water spurting into the air.

Beau had died with my parents. I'd lost everything that day. I wondered who I'd have become if that day hadn't happened. If we'd decided to go to somewhere else that day. I wondered if I could have been sitting on a Gold Coast beach building sandcastles with my own family, a husband, children of my own?

Instead, I was running, always running, from my past, from myself, never able to have any of those things. Never able to buy a plane ticket or have a job or even go to the doctor. No one deserved a life like this, a life where I had to constantly push people away or live with boyfriends I barely liked just to be safe and have a roof over my head. But I was free and I was safe and I guess for me, that was a lot to be grateful for.

The barbeque was going to go late into the night. I was too afraid to go home. Instead, I ate fast food for dinner and then drove past all the beautiful beach-front hotels, again, wishing for things I couldn't have. Ensuite bathrooms, free toiletries, room service and a comfortable bed were for other people. I passed them all longingly, heading to an out of the way truck stop to sleep in the Jeep instead.

The sun woke me in the morning. My mouth was dry, I needed a shower and my back ached.

I drove to a nearby shopping centre, grateful for consumerism and early starts and headed straight for Kmart. I bought a change of clothes; another maxi dress, a pair of undies and a clean bra, a brush and some deodorant as well as a toothbrush and toothpaste, thankful for self-serve check outs and not having to deal with inquisitive, chatty, checkout chicks.

After freshening up and changing in a toilet cubicle, I felt a million times better. I was sure I no longer smelt of sweat and sleep, so I headed to the food court for a coffee and a muffin; raspberry and white chocolate, still warm from the oven.

Refuelled, I figured it was finally safe to go home. I had a market stall to man and had to make a detour home for my stock. I figured by the time I drove back up the coast, everyone should be getting on with their day.

It took a couple of hours to get back up the coast and as I'd hoped, everyone had gone for the day once I got home. Home? I hadn't considered anywhere home in such a long time. It was nice. I didn't want to lose it and it reminded me I was doing the right thing.

I grabbed some snacks out of the cupboard and filled up my new coffee thermos, loaded the car with my stock and headed to Eumundi.

People were already filling the aisles when I arrived at the markets under the cover of thick black clouds. No one else paid them any attention, continuing to make their way into the markets, shop and laugh as usual, so I ignored them too and hurried to my stall. I took my place between June, the lady with her glass wind chimes and Frank, the wood guy. It was just the older guy today and not the son, turned out he had a day job. I quickly set up my stock and flopped into my fold up chair.

'Big night?' laughed June as her wind chimes tinkled in the breeze.

I smiled. 'Something like that,' I said.

'You're brave to be out and about,' Frank added.

'What do you mean?'

'There was another one of those nasty robberies yesterday. That really fancy jewellery store in the village. Bold as bloody brass if you ask me. You never know who they're going to target. You should take care out and about on your own.'

'I heard,' added June. 'A lovely young girl pretended to be sick, so while the jeweller helped her, her parents robbed them blind and they didn't even realise until after they were gone.'

My blood went cold. Suddenly I understood my desperate need to get out of Noosa the day before. My past was here. It was on my doorstep, creeping up behind me.

The customers started coming before I had a chance to come up with a plan or pack up and run like I should have so I put it out of my mind. They weren't here for me. They were here because here was as good a place as any and before long they'd be somewhere else. Those were the rules. Never stay too long anywhere or you get sloppy. People start remembering you, looking for you, waiting for you.

So I lost myself in the conversations of tourists. I smiled. I listened to their stories and let the time pass unnoticed.

But in the break between customers, and even though I'd been avoiding him along with everyone else, I thought of MD. I'd secretly hoped for a visit from him but I knew he was working, that he'd be working even harder now his case load had been added to, and there was no time for a detective like him to be swanning about the Eumundi markets when he had a case to solve and people to protect. I was surprised at how empty and sad I felt without him. No one had made me feel that way. Ever. Not even Nick Perry. But I'd still been a teenager then. All I'd cared about then was he'd had great hair and a car. He'd smelt good and was a great kisser. He'd everything a teenage girl could wish for. I smiled at the memory. MD had all those things plus intelligence, wit, charm and he was sexy as hell. And as for the kissing, it just about did me in every time. I was just glad he wasn't trying to get a confession out of me because I'd have no hope if he were. I'd almost confessed everything as it was.

The day had a steady enough flow that I was able to put MD and everything else out of my mind for a while. But the customers died off after lunch and the aisles were looking like a dusty ghost town.

'Where'd everyone go?' I asked my neighbour.

'Weather must be coming in,' June said as she poured herself some coffee.

I remembered then, the heavy black clouds I'd seen on the way in, they'd been fat to bursting. No one else had paid them any attention so I was sure they'd blow over. But what if they didn't? I looked up at the top of my tent and noticed the poor coverage we had from a torrential downpour.

'Should I be worried?' I asked

She shrugged, 'Maybe. I don't have anything that could be damaged by a little rain, but you might,' she said.

I waited a while, went to the toilet, got a couple of protein balls and still there were no customers. Rain or no rain, I wasn't in the mood to sit around selling to no one. Despite still having an hour left, I packed and headed back to Noosa.

The clouds had gone and the sky appeared to be laughing at me once I returned home. I checked the time. I didn't know what shift Sienna was working, which meant she could be home any minute. I had to find somewhere else to go. I showered and changed into shorts and a t-shirt and headed back out.

I drove towards the beach as though it were a magnet pulling me along. As I went through the roundabout near the surf club, I saw the trails leading up into the national park. It was a perfect place to escape and hide and it was past time I took my camera for a walk up the headland.

CHAPTER 13

I was only mid-afternoon, still plenty of light left in the day and there were a lot of people heading up and down the trail, many decked out in their running gear, some tourists in dresses and sandals, so I figured I still had plenty of time to get up and down again before the sun disappeared. I put on my runners, grabbed my water and tucked my phone into my pocket and my camera around my neck.

I worked my way up the hill, enjoying the burn in my thighs and using my camera and the incredible view over the ocean as an excuse to take a lot of rests and great shots I looked forward to developing. People were passing, going up and going down, some laboured like me, some ran with barely a panted breath but I ignored them all and focussed on me, on the view, on clearing my head and appreciating a little piece of paradise.

I stopped at each of the lookouts and when I finally reached Hell's Gates, I felt a surreal sense of accomplishment. It had been steeper than I'd anticipated and I was more unfit than I'd expected. But it was worth it. The view from the lookout at the top was breathtaking. I took so many shots I lost count. Everything was beautiful, every sailboat and swimmer, every bird swooping for its dinner and every wave cresting in the distance. It all needed to be immortalised. People needed to be able to hang what I saw on their walls, to look at it every day. This is what made life better. This is what connected you to the world, perhaps to something greater than just our meagre existence.

When I had finally photographed every element of the view, of the horizon and all the scenes in between, I took a step back, let others take their shots and guzzled some water. I sat on the rocks with the other tourists and breathed in the clean air and revelled at the perfect blue sky. How insignificant me and my woes felt in the most glorious of ways.

That perfect blue sky wouldn't last much longer though, so I knew I had to head back. I went inland, took the Tanglewood trek, through the trees, which was a whole other beautiful, ethereal and mystical experience. My finger hurt from all the shots I was taking, felt compelled to take.

Runners began zooming past me, a few giving me quizzical looks as I stopped to take some more shots and I realised I'd done it again, gotten lost in my own bubble, lost track of the time. It was getting darker which meant it would soon be night and I wouldn't be able to see my way down.

I wasn't dressed for running but I had worn my runners, so I ran, trying desperately to outrun the night. Bend after bend I ran and I shouted at myself, why couldn't you have just gone back the way you came with all the other bloody tourists? But no, I had to take the bloody scenic route. I had to stop and photograph everything, every little nook and shadow.

I puffed and puffed, my legs and lungs burning as though a fire tore through them but I had to keep going. I could collapse at the bottom, I thought, anything but being stuck up a mountain in the dark. It was becoming more and more difficult to see as it was with all the tall, lush trees blocking out what was left of the sun.

The wind picked up and the dark clouds from earlier blew over what was left of the sky. I saw a billion more potential photographs stream past almost in a blur but I couldn't stop to capture them. I had to keep going. Surely I was almost at the bottom. I kept thinking, I must be about to come out into the grassed picnic area that met with the carpark and the safety of my Jeep but the path just kept going and going, never seeming to end.

As I came out of a turn, sure that this must be the final one, my foot caught a rock I couldn't see in the haze of light. My ankle twisted and I hit the ground. Having protected only my prized camera, pain shot through my hip and elbow, which had taken the full brunt of the fall.

After I caught my breath, I tried standing but it hurt too much to put any pressure on my injured foot. Panic began to bubble in the pit of my stomach as I imagined all the things that could happen to a person stuck up here in the dark, all the creatures that would come out during the night, hungry animals looking for an easy meal.

Out of fear I pulled out my phone. I'd have to call for help, Sienna, Mel, maybe MD. I had no choice. But as I looked at my glowing screen, I saw I had no reception. Tears filled my eyes. I'd been alone for most of my life but I had never felt as alone as I did in that moment.

Would anyone even come looking for me? Would they know where to look? How could they? For all anyone knew I was still down on the Gold Coast. I'd done a great job of avoiding them these last days. They probably wouldn't think anything of me not replying to their text messages if they sent any. I was really wondering if there was something in what John had said about leaning on people and trusting them. Trusting might be better than being alone, I thought as it dawned on me no one would be coming to save me. Not this time. I was on my own. Again. Just as I'd insisted I needed to be. I didn't like it so much anymore, not now I was back here in the darkness.

I hadn't seen any of the joggers in a while either, all smart enough to get out before night descended. Sienna had warned me that first day I'd photographed the woods how quickly and early night came in these parts. But still I came up way too late in the day to be dallying about taking photos along the scenic route.

When I heard the distant sound of voices, I thought my brain was playing tricks on me. Maybe it was just sound drifting on the breeze from somewhere else? Who else would be up here in the dark? But then the sound was getting closer. The voices were male and they sounded laboured as they spoke to each other as though they were running. I had to let them know I was here in case there was some other route they could take that I couldn't see and so they didn't run right over me.

'Hello?' I called, turning on the assistive light on my phone as the first droplets from the morning's threatening black clouds fell. The light was bright enough for them to see me, for me to see my immediate surroundings but not enough to see my way down and around the bends, even if I could find a stick to support my busted ankle. But the men would definitely see me as they came down the hill. I'd never felt so relieved in all my life. Now I just had to hope they weren't sleazy Eric types.

Three men rounded the corner, blinding me with the headlamps attached to their foreheads. I blinked a few times before I could see them smiling at me, confused and surprised. They wore drill pants and long sleeve tees that hugged their fit bodies. They stopped when they saw me.

'Hey, what are you doing there?' the guy in the middle asked.

'I fell. I've hurt my ankle. Can you send up help when you get to the bottom?' I asked.

'Ah, we can do better than that,' said the guy to his left, scooping me into his arms.

'What? Don't be silly, you can't carry me all the way down,' I told him.

'Of course I can,' he said as though the idea of anything else was just plain silly. 'It's your lucky day. Someone always gets stuck up here when it rains so the boss always sends a few of us out for a training run, just in case,' he smiled.

'Hey aren't you one of the girls from Rick's place?' asked the third guy, having a proper look at me as he came over to inspect my ankle.

'I am. The new roommate,' I said.

'Ah, MD's girl,' said the first guy, recognition dawning.

'What? No, I'm no-one's girl,' I said defensively.

'Don't let MD hear you say that,' said the guy cradling me in his arms.

The first guy pulled out a phone and dialled.

'How do you have reception?' I asked, annoyed that he did and I didn't and now I had to rely on their help.

'Have a delivery for you mate, meet us in the carpark at the bottom of the headlands,' he said into the phone. Then to me he said, 'I'm search and rescue, I carry a Sat Phone,' he smirked.

'Come on, let's get you out of here before those clouds really open up and you get hyperthermia and MD carves us up.'

It didn't take long to get to the bottom, not just because they were fit and hustled, but because it actually wasn't far. If I'd been able to see, I probably could have limped down with the aid of a big stick before anyone even missed me.

MD was waiting at the base for us, his arms crossed over his chest with a scowl on his face. It had been days since I'd seen him, I'd almost forgotten how beautiful he was, forgotten that thing that happened in the pit of my stomach when his eyes met mine and all I wanted to do was fall into him and feel safe. Instead I just stared at him, watched him. He looked angry as a caged animal.

Cameron sat me on a picnic table protected from the rain by the branches of a tree. Steve went to get a first aid kit from the car and Drew went to try and diffuse MD.

MD was having none of it and stormed over to where I was sitting. 'Do you have any idea how worried everyone's been about you?'

'What? Why?'

'Why? Are you kidding me? You've basically disappeared off the planet for three days. No one's seen you and the last anyone heard from you was yesterday afternoon when you were on the bloody Gold Coast and never came home and now I get a bloody call from Cam to come and get you,' he fumed.

'MD, come on...' I tried.

'No Jilly. I'm mad. In fact, I'm bloody pissed as hell. I've been working my arse off on this bloody case, worried sick about you because my sister keeps calling to see if I've heard from you. What the hell's going on?' he demanded as Steve returned with his first aid kit. 'We're not done,' MD snapped, walking a few steps away to give Steve space, running his hand through his hair.

Steve twisted my ankle gently to see how bad the damage was. 'Not too bad, just a sprain,' he declared, as he went about strapping it. 'Take some Panadol and keep off it for a few days and you'll be fine,' he insisted, packing up his things. 'Well, we're done here if it's safe to leave you two alone?' he smirked.

'Yeah, yeah, course. Thanks guys,' MD said, shaking their hands. 'Owe you all a beer, eh,' he smiled as they left.

'Thanks,' I called and they waved in reply.

'Come on, we can finish this at home,' he said, helping me off the table and providing enough support for me to hobble to his black SUV.

'What about my car?' I asked.

'Give me the keys and I'll sort it out,' he said, holding his hand out.

We drove in silence but the tension was thick. I looked over at him. He had a couple of day's growth on his jaw and shadows under his eyes but God, he was really handsome. I had no right to be thinking lustful thoughts, but I couldn't help myself. Even the way his bicep jutting out from the sleeve of his navy t-shirt flexed as he gripped the wheel sent bolts of lust through my body. He would haunt me this one, I knew it.

'Stop it,' he demanded.

'What?' I asked innocently, blushing.

'Stop looking at me like that. I'm mad at you. I'm allowed to be mad. It's not just my sister you disappeared from. I haven't heard from you or seen you since Sunday morning, Jilly. Why? What did I do?' he begged.

'You? It's not you, MD. I keep telling you, it's me. You're all better off having nothing to do with me.'

'Why don't you let us decide what we are and are not better off being a part of,' he grumbled.

'Yeah, someone else said the same thing to me a couple of days ago,' I mumbled.

'What someone?'

'Just a guy I met. John.' I saw MD's face change and my heart sank. 'It wasn't like that. He was old and married. I had dinner with him and his wife and their friend,' I clarified.

'So you'll tell strangers what's going on but not me?'

'I didn't tell anyone what's going on, just that I didn't want any of you getting caught in the middle.'

'The middle of what?'

'Nothing. It doesn't even matter. It's not going to be a problem anyway,' I said, despite the feeling it was closing in on me, my past was too close and I didn't know how to stop it. My insides felt like a balloon in those moments before that last breath of air was forced in, that one breath too many that would burst pieces everywhere.

As I looked at his beautiful face, all the muscles in his body taut like an animal, I decided I'd just finish the week. It was safer for everyone. I needed the money boost from the markets and to offload all the stock I'd just created and then I had to leave. Find a big city to blend into. Maybe Melbourne. I hadn't been there in a while and my hair was longer now, a different colour and if I made a few other subtle changes, some glasses, new style of clothes, no one would ever recognise me.

'I can hear you thinking. Stop it,' he insisted.

'Really? And what is it I'm thinking?' I asked smugly.

'You're thinking about leaving. You're making plans,' he said, catching me off guard.

'Whatever,' I huffed.

'Jilly, you can't leave. You can't insert yourself into our lives and then leave,' he said.

'I didn't insert myself into your lives. It's you lot that have forced your way into mine. I don't need friends. I do just fine on my own,' I defended.

'I bet you do. But it doesn't have to be that way,' he said, turning into our driveway.

He opened the door, but before he got out, he said, 'We're not done talking about this, I promise you. I'm not giving in that easily,' he insisted before coming around to my side and helping me out.

I leant against his strong body as he helped me hobble to the door. What I would be losing when I left was not lost on me in the least and for the first time in a long time, I was sad. Really sad. He was probably the loveliest man I'd ever know. Strong, reliable, principled and so ridiculously handsome my breath caught in my chest every time he looked at me. It was not going to be easy to walk away from him but it was for his own good.

Looking at the stairs, I wondered how I was going to get up them. Even leaning on MD would be tough. The staircase just wasn't wide enough for us both. Before I could give it too much more thought, MD scooped me up, looked at me with a smirk on his face and carried me up the stairs as though I weighed nothing.

He dropped me on the couch as Sienna and Mel who'd been buzzing about in the kitchen came out.

'What happened?' demanded Sienna.

'She got herself stuck on the Tanglewood trail after dark with a sprained ankle,' he told them. 'She was just lucky Steve and the boys were training or she'd have been up there freezing her arse off all night.'

'Shit, Jilly, anything could have happened to you if you'd been stuck up there all night and we'd have had no way to find you,' Sienna scolded.

'I didn't mean to and I actually wasn't even that far up,' I told her.

'But when you didn't come home we wouldn't have even known where to look for you. Especially as the last any of us heard, you were down on the Goldie,' she challenged.

'That's my queue,' MD said. 'I have to check in,' he added before going out onto the back balcony while I prepared for a lecture from Sienna.

'What's going on with you, Jilly?' she asked once MD had left the room and Mel sat down as eager for the answers as Sienna.

'What do you mean?' I asked, trying to buy time, feeling unprepared for this confrontation.

Sienna scowled. 'Why have you been avoiding us?' she demanded.

'Don't be ridiculous,' I scoffed, unconvincingly, even to my own ears.

'We're not stupid Jilly. What's going on?'

'Nothing. It's just stuff. It doesn't even matter,' I said, trying to fob them off.

'No way, that's not fair,' Sienna said. 'You're not that person.'

'What person is that?' I asked. 'Because I might be,' I challenged.

'No, you're not. You're a good person. I can tell,' she insisted.

'What if I'm not?' I asked.

'You're not a bad person, Jilly. We'd be able to tell. We have a sixth sense,' Mel added. 'I don't know what happened to you in the past, but it's not who you are now,' she said.

'No, it's not,' I told them. 'But that doesn't mean my past can't still do some damage or that people I care about won't get caught up in the cross fire,' I told them.

'We can look after ourselves. We can make our own choices. We don't need you to make them for us,' she said.

'Hmmmm...' I thought remembering John and MD had both said the same thing.

'And don't get me started on what you're doing to MD,' Sienna said. 'I know he can be a shit but he really likes you, he's really put himself out there and what you're doing, disappearing for days on end without a word, you have no idea what that will do to him and for what? No good reason that I can see. We're all grownups, Jilly, we can make our own choices about our friends and the risks we're willing to take. You don't have to protect everyone like some kind of martyr. You have to let people in. You can't live your life this way, it's crazy.'

'You people make it very hard for someone to walk away, you know,' I smiled, comforted by how much they cared and how prepared they were to fight for my friendship when they hardly knew me and didn't know the truth.

'Do you want to walk away?' she asked.

'For the first time in a long time, maybe even ever, no. Not at all,' I admitted.

'Then don't,' she said, as though anything was that easy.

'Fine,' I conceded.

'Fine,' she smirked victoriously. 'And go easy on him, would you? Give him a chance,' she said as MD finished his call and came back in through the sliding door in the dining room.

I nodded. I couldn't fight anymore. I wanted to, knew I should, but I couldn't. And really, how could anyone even find me here? I don't exist. Last I heard my brother and Aunt Joanne were locked up so these robberies couldn't be them, had to be someone else and unless MD needed official documents, why would he even think to question who I was? He had no reason to question anything, as long as I kept my mouth shut and didn't give myself away. It was time to just give in and Sienna was right, I had to give people a chance. I couldn't keep living like this. It was killing me.

'Everything okay?' MD asked, sitting on the coffee table in front of me.

'Yeah, all's good,' I smiled.

'Glad to hear it. I gotta go,' he said, standing up. 'You have to keep your foot up and stay off it,' he insisted, lifting my foot to put it on a pillow he'd put on the coffee table and sending sparks of electricity through my leg and suddenly I was very glad I might get a chance to see what comes next with this beautiful man. I just hoped we both got out of whatever this was intact. He kissed me quickly and left.

'Well, good, now that that's all sorted, I'm ordering pizza,' Sienna decided, walking into the kitchen.

Sienna returned with a tub of ice cream. 'Appetisers,' she smiled. 'Now, tell us just how lovely the boys from rescue were,' she said with a naughty smile.

CHAPTER 14

I gave my friends a break and made sure I was still in the house when they left for work in the morning. I was in my pyjamas eating Coco Pops and drinking coffee at the dining table while Sienna and Mel rushed around getting themselves ready for their work day.

'You going to be alright here, Jilly?' asked Mel. 'You could come hang out at the retreat if you want, so I'm close by if you need something. There's a TV room no one really uses,' she offered.

'No, no, don't be silly. It's just a sprained ankle, I'll be fine. I'll just rest it for a couple of hours and I bet it will be good as new by this afternoon,' I insisted.

'Well don't you go doing too much too soon,' Sienna warned.

'Yes, doctor,' I laughed.

She playfully punched my arm with a smile and hurried down the stairs with Mel right behind her.

After they'd gone, despite Sienna's warning, I carefully tested my ankle, tried putting pressure on it or rolling it but it was too stiff and sore to do anything. I put some ice in a tea towel and rested it on my ankle while I sat on the couch and looked through the photos on my camera. I really needed to get some shots printed if I was going to have enough stock for the markets on Saturday now that I was staying but until the swelling in my ankle went down I couldn't drive.

Sitting on the couch wasn't doing me any good, though. I couldn't stop my brain from thinking. I was a creature of habit. I had programmed myself for survival. But it seemed my human need for connection was also strong. I'd always been able to override it but now, now it was hard. Now it was begging me to give these people a chance, to let them in.

I'd met a lot of nice people in my life, a lot of people I could have made real connections with, I supposed, under different circumstances. I'd had some fun over the years but nothing, none of those people had made me feel this way, as though leaving would break me in two. None of the men I'd shared my body with had made me feel the way MD made me feel without even touching me. MD made me feel things I'd only ever read about in the books in the old lady's library. MD made me want to confess everything just so we could start fresh and be whole. MD made me want things, things I'd long ago given up wanting and it terrified me.

I hobbled into the kitchen to dispose of the melting ice pack and made some toast before hobbling back to the couch. All this hobbling and thinking and feeling was bloody exhausting. I turned on the telly to watch morning TV but fell asleep during one of those live commercials about vacuum cleaners.

After watching Ellen and eating some two-minute noodles for lunch, I tested my ankle again. The swelling had gone down, enough anyway. I tested it and it still hurt to roll but I didn't have to hobble quite as much when I walked to my bedroom so I decided to strap it and brave an outing before I died of boredom.

As my car had appeared out the front while I slept, I took it to Big W to put in my order for photos. I needed the help of a trolley to lean on like a crutch as I walked to the back of the shop but then I got to sit for a while and that was nice. I ordered more photos than I think I ever had and was quite pleased with myself. They were going to look great. Getting stuck on the hiking trail was going to be worth it after all from the photos I'd seen.

As I drove home, I was mentally going through the supplies in the fridge trying to come up with something for dinner when I saw MD's black SUV parked on the road in front of our house. My heart skipped a beat and I shook my head. I'd lost it. I was in big trouble, I smirked as I got out.

MD was in the downstairs living room playing a video game with Rick. My heart sank a little.

'Hey,' I called half-heartedly before heading for the stairs, not wanting to interrupt them.

'Hey,' called MD as he dropped his controller in Rick's lap and jumped off the couch. 'I was waiting for you,' he said when he reached me.

'Really?' I smiled.

He smiled back and led me back outside.

'What are you doing out and about, you're supposed to be resting your ankle,' he reprimanded.

'I just went to order some photos for the weekend,' I defended. 'What's up?' I asked, changing the subject.

He shrugged then tilted my mouth up to his and kissed me. I suddenly thought if he was that good at kissing, how good would he be at everything else? I felt myself blush as the image of him naked flashed through my mind.

'What?' MD asked, curiously.

'Nothing,' I said, embarrassed.

He smirked as though he knew exactly what I'd been thinking.

He led me to the bench seat under the frangipani tree. 'Sorry I had to leave yesterday, this case is bigger than I expected and I still don't seem to have your number,' he said.

'Oh, of course,' I said, taking his phone and typing in my number for him.

'That wasn't all. Although I really wanted to see you,' he said, tapping my nose playfully. 'I wondered if you would go on a date with me?'

'A date?'

'Yep, a date. A proper one this time, with proper cutlery and drinks and chivalry and things,' he said, nervously.

'Well, if there's chivalry and cutlery,' I smiled, completely incapable of fighting anymore. 'Sure.'

'Excellent. Saturday? Seven?'

When I hesitated he added, 'Come on, we need to talk, we need to see this through. Why can't you just enjoy it? God, spending time with you, kissing you, it feels so good. Doesn't it?' he begged.

I nodded because he was right. It did feel good and every minute I spent with him left me wanting more, every kiss, every smile he gifted sent my world spinning. I no longer had the heart to fight him, to push him away, my brain screamed at me but my heart danced with joy.

'Saturday then? Seven?' he asked quietly.

'Yes and yes,' I whispered, unable to stop myself as Sienna came in.

'Oh hey, you two,' she said coming over. 'How's the case? You've been suspiciously quiet the last few days,' she said to MD.

'Yeah, it's a crazy one. It seems there's been a spate of robberies all the way up the coast. We're the next stop. They use one girl as a decoy and then clean the place out before anyone realises what's going on, usually jewellery or easy to carry valuables. One was a bloody bank if you can believe people still bother with all the tech and security they have these days but I suppose they still have the most money. Pregnant lady collapsed, the manager came running and left the teller alone behind the counter and the bloke was gone with a bag full of money before anyone knew what was happening. Anyway, they're getting desperate if they're hurting people. It's not their usual MO but we can't bloody find them, they're like ghosts. You guys make sure you're extra careful when you're shopping okay? Stay away from the fancy places,' he said.

'Like that'll be tough,' laughed Sienna.

My heart seemed to stop. It wasn't just one time. It wasn't just a copycat. Ice ran through my body and my breath stuck in my throat.

'Jilly? Are you alright?' asked MD.

'Yeah, yeah, just not enough water today I think,' I lied with a smile.

'Alright, well go hydrate, I gotta go. There's no stopping 'till they're caught,' he said, kissing me quickly and walking away.

'You sure you're alright?' asked Sienna.

'Oh yeah, of course, just a long couple of days,' I told her as we headed inside.

'How did you go at the markets yesterday?'

'Fine. The weather scared everyone off around lunchtime but

until then it'd been great. I should have moved up here years ago,' I said.

'Wow, that's great,' she said cheerfully, honestly pleased. 'We'll have to sort out that website for you, if you ever have anything left to put on it,' she smiled. 'Or perhaps you're not charging enough,' she suggested, as we climbed the stairs. 'I might come by on Saturday and have a look,' she offered.

I couldn't stop thinking about what MD had said about the case he was working on. It was all too familiar. Sickeningly familiar. But how? I couldn't figure out how. It was impossible. But still, I felt sick to my stomach.

I reminded myself to breathe, that I was safe. I was invisible. I was just as much a ghost as they were. I had to believe that. No one knew I was here. I didn't exist anywhere. It wouldn't cross anyone's mind to look for me here. They'd think I was in a big city where I'd easily blend, which is where I should be, I chastised myself, instead of here, putting all my friends in danger.

But everything would be fine if I just lay low. If it really was my brother, Neil, and Aunt Joanne, they wouldn't be trolling the markets for bargains or art investments by up and comers so I'd be safe there. I was safe here, in my home. I'd surely be safe on my date with MD. I didn't look like my thirteen-year-old self anymore. I didn't use my real name. They wouldn't be expecting to see me here, living a normal, boring life. But I'd keep it simple anyway. I wouldn't risk wandering around taking new photos. I'd just get creative with what I had, reuse some of the older shots. If I could stick to that, I'd be fine, just until MD sorted it all out. I couldn't leave now anyway. It was too risky. I couldn't chance crossing paths with Neil and Aunt Joanne.

Everyone was busy coming and going from the house but I sensed they were keeping a close eye on me. I wished they wouldn't because my brain was too busy processing a lot of information, not to mention, preparing for this date with MD. How I was going to get through that, I wasn't sure. But I had to. Cancelling would cause MD to ask too many questions, get too nosey and I had to believe I was safe. That there was no reason for my past to find me. Not here. Not now.

I was afraid to leave the house in the morning but I had to. I had to go on with my life as usual, not cause my housemates to worry any more than they already were. I tried putting everything out of my mind and drove to the shops to collect my photos. In and out, I told myself.

My eyes kept darting to the rear vision mirror, my heart stuck permanently in my chest. When I got out of the car in the big bustling car park, I felt a wave of nausea, of discomfort, swim through me and looked over my shoulder. There was no one there. Even so, my skin prickled with fear, as though someone was watching me. It's just paranoia, Jilly, I tried telling myself. It had to be paranoia. I checked over my shoulder, anyway, found nothing but a young mother, mollycoddling her children, families laughing as they lugged barbeque supplies to their cars and people in their swimmers running in for a cheap feed.

I picked up my order and felt better once I was back in the safety of my car. Stop it, Jilly, stop it, I kept repeating to myself. I was overreacting. It couldn't be them, anyway, I'd read they'd been locked up for a long time. We'd done some awful things as a team, they were paying the price for all of us, I reminded myself as I drove for home.

Sitting on the balcony sorting out my photos calmed me. I was safe there, at home, in my bubble. That was all I knew. It was easy then to bury myself in my work as I prepared my prints for sale. I felt better, calmer for it too. By the time I was done, I had an enormous collection ready to go and felt quite pleased with myself. The photographs had come up better than I could have hoped. The real proof would be how well they sold but I was confident they'd sell easily enough.

My ankle was aching after all the moving around, so I took some Panadol and lay on the couch to watch afternoon sitcoms. I was still there when Sienna buzzed through at the end of the day.

'You coming to the gig?' she asked.

'Nah, I don't think my ankle will hold up,' I told her. 'Good luck though, break a leg. That's what they say, right?'

She laughed. 'Something like that. Will you be alright?'

'Yeah, I'll be fine, don't worry about me. Just go and be brilliant.'

Mel was going out to the commune to have dinner with her mum while Rick was on shift. It was just me. I scrambled some eggs for dinner, ate them with toast and tomato sauce in front of the telly watching Neighbours. I fell asleep after I'd drunk too many ciders trying to numb my brain.

'Jilly, wake up,' Sienna said, gently rocking me.

'Oh shit, again?' I scolded myself with a laugh. 'How was the gig?'

'Awesome. You alright?'

'Yeah, course,' I told her.

'You sure? You didn't sound alright.'

'What was I doing?' I asked, concerned I'd given away some secrets.

'Moaning, sweating,' she said.

I felt my forehead, it was wet with perspiration and I could then feel my whole body was wet. 'Must have just been a bad dream,' I smiled as though it was nothing but I knew it wasn't and feared they were back, the dreams, the nightmares. They'd haunted me after I'd run, sometimes it was a replay of the things we'd done, what they'd made us do, sometimes it was Uncle Peter looming over me with that look on his face that made me sick to my stomach, the look in his eyes as the bullet hit...

'Alright then, if you're sure,' Sienna said, unconvinced. 'Well, I'm off to bed,' she added reluctantly.

'Me too, that couch is far too comfy,' I told her as I followed her down the hall.

'So I'm told.' She laughed. 'Good night,' she said, going into her room.

I sat on the edge of my bed, praying it wasn't true. I couldn't survive the dreams again. I couldn't keep reliving it.

CHAPTER 15

Thankfully I'd managed a relatively peaceful sleep. I didn't wake covered in sweat, anyway, that was something. I needed to be rested and alert, just in case, if for no other reason than to maintain the walls, to not crumble, to pretend all was fine with my world. Keeping up pretences required stamina and I couldn't afford to be weary.

Sitting at my market stall felt comfortable, like home. It was what I knew. I was in my element. I was able to keep my wits about me because it was second nature. I was in control and I had a bird's eye view of everyone passing by. But THEY wouldn't pass by. Not here. Not them. It wasn't classy enough for them. Even though they didn't have an ounce of class in their bodies, there was nothing for them to take here and that's all they'd be thinking about.

I shared some laughs with my neighbours but it was busy. It made it easy to keep busy and distracted, keep focussed on what was important, what mattered.

Sienna had said she'd stop by to check on things. But I didn't really expect her to, not with her gig schedule. She'd come home late the night before from a gig and had to prepare for another, so I suspected she'd sleep half the day away.

Apparently that wasn't her way, though, I thought as I saw her and Mel walking into my stall, shining their light and brightness over everything. Even the strangers who were flipping through photographs in the plastic tubs stopped to look at them and soak up their energy.

'Here, for you,' Mel beamed, handing me a smoothie and a bag of cacao vegan balls.

'I love you guys, thanks,' I said, grateful.

'How's it going? Still selling well I see,' said Sienna as Mel started rummaging through some of the prints.

'Yeah, going great,' I said as a customer came in saying they'd seen a picture at their friend's house and had to have one as well.

I raised my eyebrows at Sienna after the customer had left, feeling like a celebrity.

'I told you,' she said. 'You're brilliant and waaaay undercharging,' she insisted as she looked at the price of the print she held in her hand.

'Well it's going to be hard to jack up the prices now, isn't it?'

'Every couple of weeks, add a dollar or two and make sure you start at a higher price point at the Marina and we'll have them even higher on the website. You're going to be a star, you know,' she gushed as they gathered their things to leave. 'I have to go get a reading and then we're outta here. Will I see you at the gig?' she asked.

'Nope, she has a date,' smirked Mel and I realised I'd hardly seen Sienna to tell her.

'Are you kidding me?' she smiled. 'My brother is taking you on a date? A real date?'

'He is,' I said.

'Are you sure because I'm not really sure he knows what one is,' she said and Mel and I laughed.

'He insists there'll be proper cutlery, drinks and chivalry and everything,' I smiled.

'Well, how about that,' she smiled. 'Do you have something to wear? You can raid my wardrobe if you need,' she offered.

'Thanks, but I picked up a dress the other day when I revamped my wardrobe, I even have shoes.'

'Don't go getting too fancy now,' she giggled as they left.

As the day ended and I packed up my stock. It seemed my new, brighter work had been just as popular as my moodier, artier black and whites. I was quite pleased with myself, with my tidy little profit. Heading for home, I was so pleased with how my day had ended that I forgot to look in the rear vision mirror a single time.

I poured a cider to drink while I was getting ready. I needed to put everything else out of my mind. I wanted to give MD my full attention. He deserved that, even if it was only for one night because I had no idea how this night would play out or what tomorrow would bring. This might be all we ever get.

Suddenly I was nervous and very glad everyone had already left for Sienna's gig. My palms were sweaty as I blow dried my hair and tried applying mascara and what not. At least I'd succeeded in pushing my other worries to the side. That was something. I smiled as I zipped up my blue linen shift dress.

When I was done I looked in the mirror. My cheeks were pink with nerves but I looked better than I had in the last few weeks.

My brown hair had become sun kissed, my blue grey eyes seemed brighter, my skin tanned and glowing. This place of light and happiness was clearly good for me. It was showing on my face.

There was a knock at the top of the stairs, 'Hello,' MD called down the hallway.

'Oh, hey,' I called back, sticking my head out of my bedroom door.

I squirted some perfume, a light fruity scent that wasn't too overpowering and went to meet him in the hallway.

'You look sensational,' he grinned.

'Well you did insist it was a proper date with cutlery and chivalry and everything,' I smiled, thinking he looked pretty darned good himself in snug black jeans, and navy collared shirt with the top few buttons undone, the shirt hanging free.

He looked at my lips and frowned.

'What's the matter?' I asked.

'I really want to kiss you, but I was trying to think how to do that without messing up your lips,' he said, confused.

I smiled and pulled his mouth to mine, revelling in the feeling that shot through my body and the lusciousness of his warm mouth. When we were done, I wiped my lip-gloss from his mouth and smiled.

'Well,' he smirked. 'Easy as that hey?'

'So, where are we going?' I asked as we drove away.

'To the marina. There's a very fancy steak place that serves great cocktails and has a sensational view of the river,' he said.

'Oooh, very nice indeed.'

He held my hand comfortably as he drove, like we'd been doing it for years. 'I hope so, I don't do this very often,' he said.

'So I'm told,' I smiled, amused by him.

'Really? What has my sister been saying about me?' he asked, concerned.

I shrugged and smiled. 'Nothing much.'

He shook his head. 'Well, don't believe a word of it. Just because I don't lead women on by taking them out to dinner and whatever, doesn't mean I'm the shit my sister thinks I am.'

'I know. I think it's good you don't lead them on. You're a good man MD. I see that. I see it in those unguarded moments. I saw it on the beach that day. I know what it's like to walk away to protect another, when they become more invested than you. It's the kind thing to do. I get it. It's lonely though, right?'

He smiled tightly, squeezed my hand. 'One day you'll tell me all those secrets you have locked away. One day you'll let me help you.'

I tried to smile. He was sweet. But I didn't see how him knowing would ever be okay. No matter how much I liked him, I needed my freedom more. And with this case he was working on and all the memories it dredged up, I remembered the stories Uncle Pete would tell me, how it would be if I got locked up. Would MD let that happen? Would he be the one to turn the locks?

MD held my hand as we walked from the car to the restaurant. It felt nice. I felt safe and cared for.

My tummy was a bundle of nerves as he ushered me forward following the waiter to our window table with his hand on the small of my back. An intimate gesture and I felt a twinge of guilt for the lies. I put it out of my mind, determined to enjoy this while I could because it was feeling pretty incredible and I'd already missed out on too much in my life. I needed this.

I couldn't walk away from it, from him, not right now, so I was going to enjoy him right up until the very last minute. I knew it was cruel, unfair. MD didn't deserve to be hurt by me. I just didn't have the strength to stop it now. Instead of walking away, I looked up and smiled at him as he ordered us drinks and played footsies with him under the table as we looked out over the river sparkling with lights.

'Where did you grow up?' he asked. 'I feel like I've known you forever but I know nothing about you.'

'Adelaide. How about you?'

'Local, born and bred. I did my first year on the force in Brisbane but then I transferred back here and worked my way up. I love it up here. It's home. Why'd you leave Adelaide?'

I shrugged, trying to make light of it. 'I wanted to see places,' I said, which was partly true.

'And your family? You must miss them?' he said.

I shook my head. 'No, there's no one left to miss anymore,' I said.

'Your parents are gone?' he asked.

'Yep, long time ago now,' I said, waving it off.

'Any siblings?'

'Not really,' I said. 'I had a brother, but we're not close.' Hard to be close when he's in gaol but then we were never actually close before that, not since we were really small, before Mum and Dad died. But I didn't talk about that, not with anyone, no matter how handsome they were or how they made my insides quiver with just a smile. 'Is Sienna your only sibling?' I asked, changing the subject.

'Yep and really, that's debatable,' he smiled.

'You can't say that. She's one of the most amazing people I've ever met,' I scolded.'

'She's alright,' he smiled, as though even he knew she was more than alright.

'And your folks travel a lot. Do you miss them?' I asked.

'They travel so much we can hardly keep track of them. They email and call and send postcards but we don't see much of them anymore. Not that we saw much of them before that. They had pubs to run, which took most of their time, so it was mostly just Sienna and me looking out for each other growing up,' he said.

Our drinks arrived and we ordered food. But I'd lost my appetite. There were too many butterflies taking flight in my tummy, I couldn't even think about food. Every time he reached for my hand or his foot moved under the table, it was like the earth's axis went out of kilter.

MD moved on to a much easier subject and asked me about photography, how I'd discovered my love for it and I happily recounted the first time I'd taken pictures in my late teens and how it had made me feel, especially when I saw the prints. I was easily addicted. I left out all the bits about how it was the only record of my existence, that without the photos there was no proof I was alive at all, no witness to where I'd been and what I'd seen and the incredible people I'd known and hurt along the way. Not just boyfriends, but friends mostly, friends who cared too much just because they were good and kind people.

'So, you always wanted to be a cop?' I asked, desperately trying to turn the subject onto him.

'More or less,' he said. 'I toyed with being a fireman with Rick, but it wasn't for me. Also thought about joining the forces but with Mum and Dad working as much as they did and talking about travelling, I didn't want to leave Sienna on her own. But really, it had always been the police force anyway. I've wanted to be a policeman since I was five,' he smiled.

'And is it everything you hoped it would be?'

'And then some,' he smiled as our food arrived with another round of drinks.

We ate, talking about not much, how the markets had gone that day, where I'd been photographing, he suggested some great spots I hadn't yet found and offered to take me to them. He told a funny surfing story about him and Rick and how they went surfing up and down the coast one summer when they lived like bums before they went into training.

'We still go for a week now and again, but it's not the same now we're responsible grownups, but that's okay,' he said as the waiter cleared our plates.

I anxiously sipped my drink. Those nerves returning. I suspected how the evening was going to end and now my palms were sweating because I knew I wouldn't fight it. I liked him too much.

The waiter returned, offering us dessert menus. I was tempted if only to prolong the evening's end but I was full, so I said no thanks.

MD eyed me cautiously over his glass. 'You wanna get outta here?' he asked.

I nodded.

He went and settled the bill at the counter while I finished my drink, sculling my martini and enjoying the burn as it went down and entered my blood stream. I needed to quell the nerves in my tummy before they rendered me incoherent. I looked around at the restaurant, the other patrons unaware of my first date nerves.

Then I wondered, is that all it was? Was it something more?

This was definitely the type of place where Neil and Joanne would eat. Suddenly I felt sick to my stomach and stared back out at the view of the river, hoping no one had seen my face. I was glad when MD returned and we left.

We walked back to the car, MD's arm draped over my shoulders. I leant in closer, needing the safety of him, breathed in the clean night air and I felt better. The anxiety dissipated and I could focus on MD. It was a beautiful night, still warm, a bright high moon lighting the way and I felt lucky, blessed even. I couldn't ever remember feeling blessed.

MD unlocked the car but before he opened the door for me, he turned me and pulled my mouth to his in a deep, passionate kiss that curled my toes and stopped my heart.

'That's better,' he smiled when he was done. Then he opened the door for me.

'So,' he said nervously once he was in his seat and he'd turned on the car. He looked at me as though unsure how to broach the subject of what happened next. It was very sweet to see him lost for words.

I reached for his hand, lacing my fingers through his and looked into his beautiful eyes, 'So,' I countered. 'What exactly did you have in mind?'

He grinned, reaching his spare hand to the side of my face, he leant over kissing me, hard, breathtakingly, making every one of his intentions very clear.

'Right, then,' I stumbled.

He placed his hand on my thigh as he drove, a little faster than he had on the way to the restaurant, I noticed. His hand crept up my thigh, inch by inch and the anticipation was killing me. I countered by putting my hand on his thigh, almost salivating over the hardness of it, remembering how beautiful he'd been when he was practically naked on Sienna's couch and it took all my strength not to slide my hand much further up.

He pulled into the garage of his building, turned off the car and leapt across the seats, kissing me, his hand riding up my thigh, taking my dress with it as he groaned. It was hot, it was sexy and I just wanted him naked.

'Come on,' he said, almost throwing his door off its hinges.

He took my hand, nearly dragging me up the three flights of stairs to his top floor apartment.

As soon as the door closed, both his hands gripped the sides of my face and pulled my mouth to his. His was hot and wet. We were panting and breathless. I couldn't wait. I pulled off his shirt and felt my way over his beautiful body. I couldn't stop there, I'd had a preview of what was underneath and I wanted it all for myself. Reaching for the button of his jeans, feeling his erection as I did, I smiled beneath his mouth. His jeans were gone, then his boxers were gone and I looked at him, softly trailing my fingertips over his body, thinking he was just perfect and I was the luckiest girl in the world.

When I looked into his eyes they'd gone soft and dark. He unzipped my dress, letting it fall to the floor. He trailed a finger between my breasts and down, over my flat stomach, stopping at the top of my panties. His finger skimmed along the skin just above the elastic. His touch was electric and my head fell back as I groaned. He kissed my neck but I could feel him smiling.

'This is going to be fun,' he whispered in a low growl close to my ear and I practically orgasmed.

He held me steady as I stepped out of my shoes then he led me to the bedroom. Once inside, he held my mouth to his in that intimate, desperate way of his as he edged me backwards to the bed, unclipping my bra as he did.

As I lay where he pushed me and he cupped one of my freed breasts with his hand, every cell in my body caught fire. My skin was alive, burning from the inside out, his kisses scorching in their wake. He slid my panties from my hips with easy, practiced manoeuvring, his mouth never leaving my body and then his hand, his fingers, found my centre and elicited deep guttural groans I thought surely had come from someone other than me.

He found my mouth again and I reached for him, desperate to touch him, feel him. He groaned, grabbed my hands, holding them above my head, kissing me, hot, hard, desperate. He kissed my neck, sorted out the necessary protection, and then came back to my mouth.

I couldn't move beneath him, I wanted him so much I could cry. As if sensing how far gone I was, he held my eyes with his as he slowly filled me.

God, he felt good, too good, sinfully good. My eyes near rolled back in my head. I closed my eyes and my head fell backwards as I groaned.

'Look at me,' he begged.

Opening my eyes, I looked at him and as he began to move and something changed between us, something clicked, a link formed I feared could never be broken. He kissed me, deep, soft, his tongue and mouth moving in rhythm with his body.

Is this what being loved felt like? If it was even an inkling of what it felt like then it was no wonder people went to the ends of the earth, moved mountains and did crazy things to find it, to keep it.

Then sweet and beautiful became hot and fast and desperate

and incredible. As he moved faster I felt the beauty of an orgasm building almost violently inside me. I wanted him to slow down, I wanted to make it last, savour every second but I couldn't speak, I couldn't have slowed him anyway, it was too perfect, too amazing and then I cried out from the surprise of it, the intensity of it, as my body shuddered from the sweet release.

After, we lay there, still joined, our bodies slick with sweat. I held him to me, never wanting him to move, feeling his heavy breaths on my neck, feeling his heart beating fast in his chest.

When we finally parted he pulled me close. I nestled against him, fitting perfectly as his fingertips stroked the length of my back, over my buttocks, my skin tingling under his touch. It was a while before either of us could speak but there really wasn't a lot to say before he kissed me and it started all over again.

We took our time exploring every inch of each other, teasing and tantalising, everything slow and sensual before we eventually fell asleep, sated and exhausted, wrapped tight in each other.

I woke with a start, taking a second to get my bearings and remember where I was. I felt MD move, his body tight against mine, spooning me as though we were one and the whole delicious night came flooding back.

MD's phone was ringing, that's why I'd woken. He groaned and reached over to the bedside for it.

'Yeah,' he answered. He grunted a few times then hung up.

He pulled me against him, kissing me slow and sweet. 'I gotta go, there's been another robbery,' he said. 'You can stay here, though. I can drop you home if you really want but you should stay here, naked in my bed until I get back,' he smiled, lazily.

I rolled my eyes but I liked the idea of him going off to work thinking about me naked in his bed. I stretched up and kissed him. 'Alright, I'll wait right here,' I said, rolling over and snuggling close to his pillow, smelling him and stretching my legs into the warmth he'd just left behind. I watched him get dressed through half-closed eyes and hoped he wouldn't be long before falling back to sleep with a smile on my face.

CHAPTER 16

The sun was up when I woke but it was early. MD was still gone. I got up, threw on his discarded shirt from the night before and went in search of coffee. I checked my phone while the coffee brewed. News of MD's callout had already spread. There was a message from Sienna offering me a lift to the markets.

'Yes, please,' I messaged her. I'd completely forgotten about the marina markets in my post coital bliss.

I had a quick shower and had thankfully thrown a few supplies in my tote bag just in case I didn't make it home, some make up, deodorant, a change of undies. Sienna arrived not long after with a change of clothes.

'They were in the washing basket, I didn't go through your stuff,' she said.

'No worries, appreciate it,' I said, quickly getting dressed.

'I put the pictures you had bundled up into the car as well, hope that's okay.'

'Seriously, you're a lifesaver. I completely forgot about the markets when he left in the middle of the night.'

'Thought you might,' she smirked.

I shook my head. 'Is it weird for you? Are you okay with it? With me and MD?' I asked.

'Yeah, of course. I'm glad he has maybe found someone he might like to keep for a while,' she said.

'What about you? Why haven't you found someone you'd like to keep for a while?' I asked.

She shrugged. 'There's Seb, we have a bit of something when we've had too much to drink,' she said, referring to the guitarist from her band. 'But I don't know, I don't want to jeopardise the music. That's all I care about right now,' she said, as we headed out.

I was excited to see what this new market would bring. Every market was different, the people were different making the vibe different but they were all the same at their foundation. People who were passionate about what they did, always found something in common. It was the passion that connected us. Sellers and buyers because the buyers came searching for us. They knew there was something special about our work, whatever it was. It didn't matter if we were photographers, painters, designers or craftsmen, passion was always the common denominator.

I'd lost my nerves too, those prickles of anxiety from the last couple of days had found someone else to annoy. Maybe some good sex was all I'd needed all along. I was safe. I knew I was safe. Paranoia was part of my life. I knew it well, we coexisted every day and that was okay but I couldn't let it take over. I'd be no good to myself or anyone else. Besides, my insides were still buzzing from what MD had done to me and I didn't think anything was going to be able to penetrate that. I felt invincible. He made me feel invincible.

'How was dinner?' Sienna asked with a smirk.

'Amazing,' I told her. 'Sensational view of the river, excellent food, was a great night,' I smiled.

'So my brother knows how to treat a lady after all, hey?' she smiled.

'I guess he does,' I smirked as I remembered just how well he'd treated me. 'How was your gig?' I asked before I gave way too many details to MD's sister.

'Excellent. We tried some new material and they loved it,' she gushed.

'Of course they did,' I told her. 'You know you're going to be a superstar someday.'

'Oh,' she said, waving that idea off but I could see she was pleased with the compliment.

'Mark my words,' I told her as she turned into the marina car park.

Sienna parked her car where MD and I had parked for our date. I would have smiled but instead I noticed all the cars, the extraordinary amount of police cars. There were cops everywhere and they were filing in and out of the restaurant MD and I had been to the night before like ants.

'What's going on?' I asked, my breath catching, my heart pounding.

'Dunno,' she said.

We walked along the boardwalk to my allocated space at the end of the row of stalls, the only vacant space. Everyone around us was too distracted by the cops and activity to notice us, both customers and stall holders were watching the activity across the marina as though it were a tantalising soap opera.

'It'll be quiet with all of them fussing about,' said a girl selling beach wear in the next stall as she reluctantly tore her eyes away and began hanging some of the clothes she was selling onto racks.

'I'm going to go see what's happening,' said Sienna as I anxiously tried to ignore the police, ignored my neighbour and set up the prints despite all that was going on. I let the colourful, cheery beach shots dominate but I'd had to boost the supply with my usual moodier work after having sold so much the day before.

I was chatting with my neighbour about her clothes when Sienna returned. 'We gotta go,' she said, shaken.

'What? We just got here?' I said.

'MD says we gotta go, that you've gotta get outta here, now,' she demanded in a tone so far from her usual sweet perkiness it caught me off guard and made me a little sick to my stomach.

We quickly bundled up my stuff, barely muttered a goodbye to my perplexed neighbour and Sienna hurried me to the car. Once we were both in, she roared off like a rally driver and headed for home.

'Sienna, what's going on?' I begged.

'I don't know but Mitch was really freaked. Said I had to get you out of there. He had his cop voice on and you don't mess with Mitch when he has his cop voice on.'

She roared up the driveway and stopped the car with a jolt. 'I'll bring everything in. Mitch said to get you inside, you're not to leave and we're not to let in anyone but him,' she said. 'Go!' she demanded when I hadn't moved.

My heart pounded with suspicion as I grabbed a parcel of prints and went inside and up the stairs. The house was quiet. Rick was still on shift and Mel's car was in the drive so I guessed she was still asleep. I dropped my stuff in my room and went into the kitchen to make coffee. I suspected I needed something stronger but it was far too early in the morning and I needed my wits.

I heard Sienna bring a few parcels inside and drop them by the door then I heard the lock click into place before she started up the stairs. I was worried. We didn't lock doors when we were home and I didn't have to run from market stalls. Not the new me, anyway. I suspected the old me had caught up and I wondered if I should just grab my stuff and go. No, give them a chance. At least find out what's going on first. Make a proper plan.

Sienna tried pretending things were normal when she came upstairs. She pottered about humming, pouring coffee, putting bread in the toaster then went to the toilet. I couldn't stand it anymore. Something had happened at the Marina and MD knew something. While Sienna was distracted, I went into my bedroom and threw everything I could into my duffle bag. The toilet flushed so I left my bag just inside my bedroom door and went to meet Sienna in the kitchen where we drank our coffee, speculating over MD's behaviour.

'All I know is there was a robbery. He says it matches the case he's working on. Brad, he's MD's boss, we've known him since we were all at school, told me there was a distraction, a girl and while the manager was tending to her, the other two emptied out the till. They think he must have realised what was going on and instinctively protected the money. People do that. They shouldn't. You're supposed to just let them take everything and pay attention so you can give the police as much information as possible,' she went on.

My heart sank. Suddenly I was sweating all over and my empty stomach began contracting as though it desperately wanted to heave.

'You alright?' Sienna asked.

'Yeah,' I said. 'It's just, that's where we had dinner, it's surreal,' I lied. But really, I was wondering how early they'd been casing the place, if they'd seen me, if they'd recognised me. 'I gotta go,' I whispered, hurrying down the hall to grab my bag.

'What are you doing?' Sienna asked, as though only just comprehending what I meant.

'I have to go Sienna, let me past,' I insisted when she blocked my way.

'Mitch said you had to stay here,' she said in a whisper.

'I don't care. It'll be better for everyone if I just go,' I said sadly. 'Here, this should cover my rent until you can replace me,' I said, shoving a handful of notes into her hand and pushing past while she was confused.

I was halfway down the driveway when I looked up and saw MD at the other end. We both stopped. Our eyes locked and I knew he knew. It didn't matter. Not anymore.

I kept walking. He held his arm out to stop me. 'Let me go, MD, you know it's the best thing for everyone,' I insisted.

'No, I don't,' he snapped. 'Get inside. Now!' he demanded and I saw what Sienna meant about his cop voice. It had my knees shaking in a whole other way to his kisses.

He grabbed me by the elbow and dragged me back inside and followed me up the stairs.

I dumped my bag at the top of the stairs so it would be handy when it was time for me to try again.

'Sit!' he demanded, pointing to the sofa.

I went to sit and Sienna followed.

'Not you,' he told her.

'What?' she asked.

'Just go Sienna, you don't want to be here for this,' I told her.

'No, I'm staying,' she insisted. 'You know I'm only going to listen in the hallway, anyway,' she pleaded.

'Fine,' he mumbled.

I shrugged. She'd regret her choice soon enough.

'Will you tell us what's going on?' Sienna asked in a quiet voice, perhaps knowing exactly what worked best with her brother when his face was full of thunder.

'We got fingerprints from the crime scene,' he said. 'They ran them through the system and we got lucky, they were in there. Bernie, the waiter had scratched the guy's neck and I suspect the DNA will match,' MD mumbled.

'And?' coaxed Sienna.

'It belongs to a Neil Adams, not long out of gaol. We suspected it was him, just the right MO.'

'So?' asked Sienna.

MD didn't take his eyes off me. He barely blinked. 'There were other fingerprints too, not at the counter or where he'd eaten dinner, but we dusted the whole place trying to piece everything together. There was a set belonging to a Sydney Adams,' he said, staring at me as my face paled. 'I saw her picture, Jilly. She looked a lot like a younger version of you,' he whispered. 'Everyone thought you were dead,' he said, tears filling his eyes as tears filled mine.

'Who the hell's Sydney Adams?' asked Sienna looking from one of us to the other, confused.

'Me,' I whispered in the smallest voice. 'Please, MD, let me go,' I begged so quietly I wasn't sure if he even heard me.

He squatted before me, held my hands in his. Mine looked tiny and fragile against his now. I looked up into his beautiful eyes, through my tears and he looked as frightened as I felt, as frail as my hands looked. I touched his handsome face, 'I'm so sorry,' I whispered, ignoring the tears falling down my face.

'Were you helping him?' he asked quietly.

'God, no,' I said, shocked he could even think it. 'No, never. I swear,' I said, my hands shaking. He closed his hands around mine tighter in an effort to stop them.

'Tell me everything,' he begged.

I shook my head, looked into his eyes, pleading, 'No. MD, no. I can't,' I whispered.

'You have to,' he begged, squishing onto the sofa beside me. 'Jilly, you have to.'

I shook my head. 'I have to go. You have to let me go,' I begged.

'I can't do that,' he said, leaning his forehead on mine.

'But he'll kill me,' I said, my voice shaking. 'MD, they'll kill me,' I cried.

CHAPTER 17

'What's going on?' asked Mel sleepily, walking into the room.

Sienna was sitting still, staring at the wall in shock. I was staring too while MD clung to me, holding me to his chest, his arms wrapped around me tightly as though he could protect me from them, from everything, as though if he held me tight enough nothing could penetrate our beautiful bubble.

'Nothing,' he told Mel, his voice cracking. 'You should go back downstairs,' he told her.

'No. I will not,' she insisted.

'Sienna?' he begged.

'Fine, fine,' she conceded. 'Let's go make some coffee and I'll fill you in,' she said, leading Mel into the kitchen.

The girls returned with steaming cups of coffee. I felt stronger after a few sips. The situation became clearer. I'd had it right all along. I couldn't put these people in danger. I loved them. I'd only been here a few weeks and already I was closer to them than I had been to anyone since my parents had died. I would never forgive myself if Neil or Aunt Joanne hurt them. If they were caught up in the fallout of it.

I pried myself out of MD's arms. 'I have to go, you know I do,' I told him.

'What? No. No,' he begged.

'MD I have to. Otherwise, everyone's in danger. Sienna. Mel. You. Your careers, you could lose it all.'

'I can look after myself,' he said.

'Can they?' I asked. 'You know he'll find me. Once word gets out you found my prints, Neil will know I'm nearby. I have their money, I did... Aunt Joanne won't just walk away if she knows I'm here. Neil's manipulative enough to get answers from people without them even knowing, no one is safe while I'm here.'

'It doesn't matter because I'm not leaving this house,' he said.

'What? You have a job to do. You have to catch them,' I pleaded.

'Which we can do much better if you're here, with your help.'

'MD, come on, you know that won't happen. You know I can't help you if I'm locked up. Please, let me go,' I begged.

'No one is locking you up, Jilly, you were just a kid,' MD insisted.

'Why would you be locked up?' asked Mel.

I looked from her to Sienna. They had no idea. I couldn't shatter their world, their image of me. I couldn't turn them into people who don't trust anymore. I looked at MD and even he didn't seem to comprehend. 'You don't know,' I whispered.

'Know what?' he asked.

'About Peter?' I said, waiting for his face to show a sign of recognition, of understanding, of hate.

'I know about Peter,' he said.

'You know? Then why am I still sitting here?'

He shook his head, scowling. 'We all know it was self-defence Jilly.'

'That doesn't matter. That's not for you to decide. That's what a jury decides.'

'Well, I decided,' he shouted.

I held his hands, made him look at me. 'MD, do not ruin your career for me. Don't,' I begged.

'You were just a kid,' he pleaded.

There was a knock on the door to the living room. We didn't use our upstairs entrance so Sienna had to hunt for the key then MD made us wait in the kitchen while he answered the door with his gun in his hand.

'Shit Jilly, this is bad, isn't it?' asked Sienna pointlessly.

'Really bad,' I said, looking to see if I could sneak out.

'No,' Sienna said, grabbing my arm. 'Stop running. Let Mitch help you,' she begged.

'You can come out, ladies,' MD called from the living room.

We went back in and there was another man standing with MD. A tall, handsome man, just a few years older than MD. His dark blonde hair was short, his dark blue eyes were wary. He had a scar above his eye and another on his chin that just made him look sexy and dangerous.

'Hey, Brad,' Sienna said, greeting the man familiarly.

'Hey, Sienna,' he smiled.

I was at the end of the three and as I stepped out and instinctively towards MD, the man, Brad, said, 'Well, hello there, Sydney. Aren't you a sight for sore eyes?'

I froze. I didn't move, I didn't speak.

'It's alright,' MD said, reaching for me. 'He just wants to hear what happened.'

'Which bit, twelve years ago or last night?' I asked, sensing this Brad was more suspicious of me than my friends.

'Both,' said Brad.

'Last night I had nothing to do with, I promise you,' I said. Brad nodded so I continued. 'I don't really know where to start, what exactly you want to hear,' I said.

'How about you start at the very beginning,' he offered, kinder, as Mel placed a coffee on the table for him and we all sat down.

'Well, I guess the beginning was when Mum and Dad died,' I said as MD passed me my coffee and slid an arm around me. Brad watched him carefully, his face giving nothing away.

'We had to go and live with Aunty Jo and Uncle Peter. No one knew about their life. Mum always thought Peter had a really good job and that's why they led their glamorous life, lived in a nice house, wore fancy clothes and jewellery and drove a fancy car. But it wasn't. They said no one lived with them without paying their dues. So they trained us. Aunt Joanne showed me how to use make up and clothes to change the way I looked, to make me look older. They'd put me in all sorts of get ups and made me create dramatic diversions while they did what they did.

'I tried not to think about it, what we were doing, what I was doing. If I did a good job, they treated me fine, if I didn't, well, I'm sure you've seen the hospital records. Anyway, Neil jumped right in, loved every second. Although I always suspected he and Aunt Joanne had some sort of relationship going on but I didn't want to know. She was my mother's sister. It just didn't make sense but they'd disappear together all the time, watch movies in her bedroom with the door locked when Peter was out scouting for places to rob.'

'What about that last day?' Brad asked.

I shrugged. 'I'm not really sure what happened. Maybe we stayed in the one place too long, got lazy, I don't know. But I did what I was supposed to do. The husband was out the back and I faked a diabetic attack. I went out the back with the wife, she gave me some orange juice and I left through the back door seeing we'd gone out the back for some air. I gave the others plenty of time. I got into Peter's car and then we heard the sirens. He took off, leaving Neil and Jo there.'

'What happened next?'

'When we got home, Peter was furious. He was throwing things and punching walls. He was out of his mind. Then he said to me,' I sobbed and took a sip of my coffee as I remembered.

I closed my eyes, trying to move away from MD but he wouldn't let me go. 'Then Peter says, "if Jo's locked up then I had to take her place. In every way." He dragged me to the couch and pushed me down. I was only thirteen, he was a big guy and I felt like a rag doll being thrown down. I hit my head on the arm,' I said, rubbing my head as though it had just happened.

'Then he started ripping at my dress. He pulled my pants down and pulled down his own. He grabbed my hand and made me hold him, and, you know, while he did things with his hand. It hurt. I screamed. He slapped me. I was out for a few seconds and when I came to my pants were gone, he'd spread my legs as far as he could and was hovering over me. I knew what he was going to do. Then I remembered the gun Jo kept under the couch. She kept them all over the house so she could never be surprised. Either he didn't know it was there, he forgot or he didn't know I knew. Anyway, I was half off the couch by then anyway, not that he cared, he was holding onto the parts he wanted. I dug for the gun and I just pulled the trigger. I didn't even know if there were bullets in it. But there was and he fell on me. There was blood everywhere, so much blood and I didn't know what to do,' I said through my tears. 'I didn't know,' I sobbed, looking from MD to Brad.

'So, after I pushed him off me, I changed my clothes and took all the money from under the floorboards in their bedroom and I left. I couldn't go to gaol if Aunt Joanne was there. She'd kill me for what I did to Peter. Now they'll both want to kill me. Neil will want to kill me for taking the money. He liked the money.'

'Where is it? The money?' Brad asked.

'In a washing bag in my wardrobe. It's yours, I've barely used it, only when I was really desperate.'

No one spoke. The room was dead silent.

Sienna broke it, in a squeaky voice she asked, 'Where did you go?'

'I was stuck. I was thirteen. I had no family, no friends, no ID to go to a hotel if they even believed I was old enough. But there was a lady. I used to watch her sometimes at the bus stop while I was waiting for the bus to go to school. She'd get off the Greyhound some mornings with just an overnight bag in the crook of her arm. She'd walk across the bridge to the car park and get into her car. I always wondered where she went and one day I broke in and laid in the back seat of her car, just to see. She lived in this really big house. It was huge, the closest thing I'd ever seen to a mansion. After that, I sometimes skipped school and watched the house, just wondering what it would be like to live there. She lived alone. A lady came to help with the cleaning and the cooking but that was all. Then, one time when she got on the Greyhound to go wherever it was she went, I went inside the house and had a look around. There were all these beautiful rooms and she only used about three or four. You could tell the cleaning lady didn't even touch the others. So after... I left, I moved in. She didn't even know I was there. That's how big the house was. I lived there for three years. Then she died. One morning, she was just dead in her recliner, so I left. I felt bad leaving her for the cleaning lady to find but what could I do? Since then I've mostly lived with boyfriends or in share houses. I stay for as long as I can but move on if they start getting too close, too nosey, ask too many questions or require paperwork of any sort. The last boyfriend was going to propose. I couldn't apply for a marriage licence or anything, not that I loved him.'

'What about your driver's licence, your car?' asked Mel.

'How much trouble do you want me to be in?' I asked, sipping my cold coffee.

'You don't have a licence and your car is not registered?' asked Sienna.

I nodded. 'An old boyfriend said I could have it if I got it running. It was just rusting in his backyard. I fixed it up and I left not long after. I tried not to drive much for a long time, since I got here is probably the most I've ever driven. Usually I just use it to get from one place to the next.'

The room was quiet again and MD had me in a grip like a vice even though he wasn't speaking.

'It's alright,' I told Brad. 'I know what you have to do,' I said.

He shook his head. 'Your version of events fit with the crime scene. We'd always figured it was self-defence. The poor guy's pants were around his ankles,' he smirked. 'There'll be talks and I can't guarantee, but it was self-defence. You were a kid,' he said, patting my hand. 'For now, though, we have to stop them before they kill someone and we have to keep them from killing you,' he said. 'MD's right, we need to keep you safe but we also need your help.'

'How can I help?' I asked.

'Tell us how to stop them, how they think,' he said.

'I don't know much about Neil and Aunt Joanne. I'm assuming that's who he's with, that some fool let them both out?'

Brad nodded.

'But when Peter was in charge, he'd watch a place for days. That's how we did things. Peter would do the watching and the planning, give us all instructions down to the minutest detail. Then when the day came to do what we did, Peter would drive, so no one would ever know how we did it, and no one could implicate him from his previous visits. We were a four-man team. I don't know how they'd be doing it now if it was just the two of them. Or how they'd be creating the distractions without me. They used me because I was young and looked vulnerable. Aunt Joanne looked old and haggard even then.'

Brad was suspiciously quiet.

'What is it?' asked MD, finally speaking.

'Joanne had a daughter eight months after going into prison. The girl was put into a foster home and everyone forgot about her,' he said, pulling his phone out of his pocket and dialling. He asked someone to find out about Joanne's daughter and then we all just sat there in the quiet room sipping our cold coffee.

'I'm going to make more,' said Mel, needing something to do.

She cleared away our cups and the sound of the coffee machine was welcome in the silence. We all jumped when Brad's phone rang. He answered, grunted a few times and hung up.

'She's gone,' he said. 'They say she ran away and the timing is about the same as when Joanne and Neil were let out.'

I nodded, taking it in.

'There's more,' he said. 'They always wondered who the father was as she didn't have any of Peter's DNA. Going by what you've said, the child has to be Neil's.'

I shook my head. 'He was fourteen!' I shouted. 'Fucking perverted bitch,' I said, pulling away from MD and storming out of the room.

I grabbed my bag from the top of the stairs and ran down them.

'Jilly,' cried MD, chasing me.

He had longer, stronger legs than me and caught up with me before I could unlock the door. He pulled the bag out of my hands and carefully put it out of my reach. 'Don't go,' he begged. 'Let me help you. Please,' he begged.

'Why? Why would you want me now?'

'Are you kidding?' he asked.

'No, I'm not, MD. I'm a mess. My life's a mess. I'm a criminal, the things we did… I might go to prison for killing my uncle, a career criminal who almost raped me. Why would you want anything to do with me? How can you even look at me?'

'Jilly, I'm looking. I can't stop looking. All that stuff from your past, it happened twelve years ago and is nothing to do with who you are. It tells me that you're incredible, you're strong, you're a survivor. Jilly, you're amazing.'

'I don't even know who I am, MD. I'm not Jilly, I'm Sydney, but even that doesn't feel right. I'm no one. I live in nowhere land. On paper, I barely exist, I'm a ghost,' I told him.

'You exist with me,' he said, pulling my hand to his heart. 'You exist in here. You can't leave me. Not now. Please, stay. Let me help you,' he begged.

I couldn't fight anymore. I couldn't run. I couldn't even move and I let him pull me to him and I cried. I cried because it was over. Whatever happened next, the past was over. I didn't have to run anymore. I didn't have to be alone anymore. I had MD and Sienna and Mel, if they still wanted to be my friends. I was ready to fight. I was ready to take charge of my life. Aunt Joanne and Neil couldn't keep doing this to me, making me afraid, making me run. I wasn't thirteen anymore and I had a niece, or a cousin, a something, that didn't deserve the life they were inflicting. I looked into MD's heartbroken, fearful eyes. I couldn't leave him. I couldn't break him.

I reached up and softly touched his face. 'You're an incredible man, MD. A good and beautiful man,' I told him as he gathered me to him as though hanging on for dear life.

We went back up the stairs and Brad, Sienna and Mel, all looked up, the girls' faces tear-stained.

'You know you're all in danger if I stay, right? If they find out I'm alive, that I'm here, they'll want revenge for Peter. They'll want their money and they won't care who they hurt to get it. You all know that, right?'

They nodded.

'So you'll stay?' asked Sienna.

'If you'll have me?' I asked.

She jumped of the couch and smashed into me, wrapping her arms around me. 'Everything'll be alright, Jilly. It will. Wait, do I still call you Jilly?' she asked.

I shrugged.

'I don't care what your name is,' she said. 'Now,' she said, taking charge. 'Brad, you'd better stay here and have some lunch while MD goes home to collect some things. He can stay here with us until this is all over. Rick's off shift tomorrow, but even still, there's a spare room downstairs if you want a couple of guys to stay, the more the merrier, right?' she said, looking at MD for confirmation.

MD nodded. 'I'll be back in a few,' he said. 'Promise you'll stay,' he begged, his eyes pleading with me.

I nodded. 'I'll stay, I promise,' I said.

He kissed me quickly, his mouth lingering for a moment longer and he was gone. Sienna and Mel went to make sandwiches and I sat next to scary Brad all alone.

'You're one heck of a woman, Sydney,' he said, shaking his head.

'Is that a compliment, I can't quite tell?' I told him.

He smiled. 'It's a compliment.'

'You will catch them, won't you?' I begged.

He nodded solemnly. 'We'll catch them,' he promised.

'And you'll keep those two safe. If it's getting too dangerous, you move me, you use me as bait or something, anything to keep them safe. Promise me,' I begged.

He nodded. 'I promise.'

'And MD?' I asked.

'Don't you worry about him,' Brad insisted, patting my hand like my Dad used to do when I was upset. It had been a long time since I'd missed my parents. There hadn't been time for missing dead parents and lost childhoods but I missed them now. I missed them so much it ached, deep inside my belly. There was black hole that ached so bad I didn't think I could stand it.

CHAPTER 18

Everyone had something to do and got on with doing it. MD went home to collect his things. Mel went downstairs to create a workspace for MD, Brad and their team.

'Just stay here, Jilly. They don't know you're here yet. They don't even know you exist. They'll hear whispers soon enough but they won't get very far asking for Sydney Adams. Just stay out of sight and let them think you were just another tourist passing through town,' Brad insisted.

'It'll be okay, Jilly. I've known Brad a long time, he knows what he's doing,' Sienna assured me before she quickly changed and dashed out for a shift.

What was there left for me to do? Nothing. I'd created this whole mess. I'd brought this mess to the safety of their home and dumped it in their laps. They went about their business as though nothing had happened. Brad and MD were upending their lives to help and I was left sitting on the couch, alone, with nothing to do to fix any of it. I wanted to cry but it seemed I'd cried my tear ducts dry.

I went downstairs for my duffle bag. Both Mel and Brad looked up, watching me carefully as they rearranged furniture to make space for desks and chairs and computers. I ignored them, picked up my duffle bag and went back upstairs, their sighs of relief following me up the stairs.

I had nothing else to do but shower and get changed. MD was sitting on my bed flicking through a magazine when I finished. I was wearing nothing but my dressing gown, my damp hair hanging loose, my make up all washed away.

'Hey,' I said, not sure what else to say.

'Hey,' he smiled, reaching for my hand and pulling me to the bed beside him and pulling me into an all consuming hug.

'I'm sorry I lied to you,' I told him.

'You did warn me it was me who had to watch out for you, not the other way around,' he said with a smile in his voice.

'Well, you should have listened,' I told him.

'I'm glad I didn't,' he said.

'What now? How long is it going to take you lot to find them so everyone can get their lives back?' I asked.

He shrugged. 'Hopefully soon.'

'How soon is soon?' I asked.

'There's no schedule. It takes as long as it takes but the sooner the better,' he said.

'And what am I supposed to do until then?'

'You stay here,' he snapped.

'And do what?' I asked, already frustrated.

'Well, now,' he coughed, stretched out and kicked the door

shut. 'I have an idea or two,' he smirked, pulling my mouth to his and pushing me back onto the bed.

The dressing gown provided easy access and he wasn't wasting it. His hand slid up the inside of my thigh. He skipped the expected destination and ran his hand over my stomach instead, igniting tingles of anticipation and setting my skin on fire. He pushed the robe open and reached for my bare breast as I pulled his t-shirt over his head.

'Now that's what I'm talking about,' he mumbled with a grin. 'I think I'm going to enjoy staying here for a while.'

'Wait, wait,' I said, putting my hand on his beautiful chest to stop him.

'You're kidding, right?' he asked.

I shook my head. 'Do you really want to do this? Now?'

'Yes,' he said emphatically.

'Really? After everything I just said, everything you know about me, you still want to do this?'

'Yes, I do,' he said, rolling to the side and running his hand through his hair. 'Do you? Or do you want out, is that what this is?' he asked. 'Cos if I was just another convenient guy and you want out, you need to say so and you need to say so now.'

'What? No, I don't want out, MD and you weren't the least bit convenient,' I said, running my hand up his chest. 'I really like you and I don't want to lose you. But it's a lot, for everyone, for you. You don't need to feel obliged to keep this going. You officially have permission to end the chivalry,' I told him.

'That's what you think I'm doing? You think it's chivalry?'

I shrugged.

'Honey, I do not do anything I don't want to, ask anyone. You, I definitely want to do,' he smiled. 'I want to be here for you. I want to keep doing whatever this is we started. I don't care who you were or what you did when you were thirteen, which by the way, was not your fault. I care about who you are now.'

'It's all the same. I'm the same. I killed someone, MD. I shot him and I walked away and left him to die. That has to mean something to you, you're a cop, a man, a good man.'

'It means you defended yourself. If you hadn't killed him Jilly, who knows what else he would have done. A man that angry wasn't going to stop with raping you and you know it. You're a victim. None of this is your fault.'

I nodded, tears filling my eyes.

'Hey, come here,' he said, pulling me to him. 'You did what you had to do. None of us like killing a person but sometimes you have no choice. Don't let it define you. Don't let him and his actions, define you.'

He pulled the robe over my shoulder and held me so tight I almost believed everything would be alright, that he'd make it alright.

I must have fallen asleep. When I woke, MD was gone. The upstairs was dark but I could see the light downstairs, could hear people working and I could smell pizza. It smelt good. I was suddenly starving hungry and went into the kitchen to make some dinner. A plate piled with pizza was on the bench covered with cling wrap. A sticky note with a smiley face was stuck to the top inviting me to eat.

'Hey,' MD whispered from behind me, making me jump. 'Sorry,' he smiled.

'What's going on?' I asked. 'Where is everyone?'

'Out. Downstairs. You going to eat?' he asked, nodding towards the pizza.

'Yeah, thanks,' I said, unwrapping the pizza as he walked up behind me and slipped his arms around me, nuzzling into my neck.

'Sorry I left you,' he said.

'That's okay. It was good to sleep. I didn't get much last night,' I smiled, remembering the incredible night at MD's before the world fell apart.

'Mmmmm...' he groaned. 'Me neither,' he said lazily, kissing my neck.

'I'm sorry about before. I'm feeling better now, though,' I said, turning to face him.

I was wedged up against the bench, still in just my dressing gown and he looked down at me with his handsome, brooding eyes, stubble growing along his jaw creating sexy dark shadows.

He kissed me good, made my toes curl and my stomach flip but just as the fire started erupting in my belly, he pulled away and winked, 'You missed your chance.'

'What? Nah, uh,' I said, pulling him towards me by his waistband.

He chuckled, raised his eyebrows. 'Jilly,' he drawled. 'I have a whole team of guys working downstairs.'

I shrugged. 'They won't miss you for a little bit, will they?' I said, sliding my hands up under his shirt.

Someone called out to him from downstairs and I rolled my eyes at their timing.

He laughed, playfully tapping me on the nose. 'We'd be needing more than a little bit, anyway,' he drawled, kissing me so I'd remember before walking away, leaving me groaning.

I took the plate of pizza to the couch and ate it cold in front of the television watching old sitcoms. They seemed funnier than they had before and I wondered if it was because a weight had been lifted by not having to hide anymore.

I fell asleep and woke to MD, shaking my shoulder and whispering my name.

'Come to bed,' he whispered.

I suddenly remembered we were now sharing a bed and I liked the idea of sleeping next to him indefinitely and let him take my hand and lead me there. I put on a t-shirt and climbed in beside him. He pulled me to his bare chest and wrapped his arms around me tight. I could feel his legs were bare too but he'd left on his trunks. Rolling over I snuggled against him, liking the smell of him, the feel of him, the sounds of his breath above my head.

MD was still snuggled beside me when I woke. He must have sensed I was awake. 'Good morning,' he mumbled, his voice croaky from sleep.

'Morning,' I said, smiling, liking that he was still there.

'You feeling better this morning? You know, about everything?' he asked.

'A little,' I said.

'Good,' he said, running his hand up my bare thigh. 'Because I believe we have unfinished business,' he said, parting my legs and nuzzling my neck.

'Don't you have work to do?' I asked, even though I hoped he was going nowhere.

He looked over his shoulder to the clock. 'Nope, I have time,' he said.

'Even with your sister across the hallway?'

'I'll be quiet, I promise,' he smiled as he went about doing his thing.

I reached for him and indeed we did have some business to take care of, I thought with a smile.

I didn't see MD for the rest of the day. He was downstairs in amongst the hubbub of activity. They were scouring security cameras from every shop, restaurant or service provider that matched Neil and Joanne's preferred places to rob to see if they could find them doing any preliminary scouting. All the shops were on alert, but it was hard for them to report strange activity, any unusual people coming through when the whole town traded in such a transient, tourist community. Everyone was new and everything was unusual.

I assumed Rick was downstairs in amongst the activity, probably trying to sleep. Sienna had gone to work, then she had rehearsal for a big gig they had coming up and Mel was at the yoga retreat. I camped out on the couch and raided Sienna's DVD supply and watched far too many romcoms. I ate a sandwich, made a stir-fry and went to bed while they were still working downstairs.

A while later I felt MD climb into bed and his arms wrap around me but he was gone before I woke in the morning.

I couldn't spend another day on the couch. I was already feeling brain dead from boredom. After a coffee on the balcony, I decided to raid the pantry for baking supplies. I'd learnt to bake when I'd lived in the old lady's mansion. While she was away on her little jaunts, I'd scour her cookbooks and tried as many recipes as I could. Sometimes I'd leave her treats in the fridge. I'd spy on her and the cleaning lady but I never heard the old lady thank her. Did she know it was me, after all? Maybe. I'd never know.

I made a chocolate cake, cut a slice for myself and took the rest downstairs for the boys. MD eyed me cautiously from the far corner where he was working as I sliced up cake for those who wanted it.

I ate my piece of cake on the balcony with another coffee but I was still bored. I watched how the sun hit the flowers in the garden, how the pool sparkled under the sun's rays, the loneliness of the floating pool lounge and thought I might as well use my time to my benefit. I'd had to cancel my stalls at the markets. Who knew when I'd be able to return? Even after they'd caught Neil and Aunt Joanne, I still had charges to answer to for killing Peter. Brad didn't see it would be a problem, but surely it would, surely it mattered?

It was sad to think no one would see my pictures, that I wouldn't be able to sit next to June again and enjoy the tinkling of her wind chimes or listen to the wood man's stories of his grandchildren and times gone by. Would they notice I wasn't there? Would they care? Would they wonder where I'd gone? Would they see my picture in the paper, read the story of how I killed a man and walked away? Would they be glad I was gone? Would I ever be able to return there or anywhere without the world knowing who I was and what I'd done?

MD's team were all keenly watching their monitors when I came down the stairs and went out the door. I looked around the garden, wondering where to begin. I went over to a white flower with a pink centre, who knew what any of them were. I'd never learnt but they were pretty. I adjusted the camera a number of times to get a variety of shots. Then I turned to the pool and took a variety of shots of the water from different angles, some with the lone lounger floating under the sun.

I moved over to a bush in the corner with lots of little pink flowers. There were bees buzzing in and out and I got some great shots. I was really pleased. Too often we forgot to look in our own backyards for inspiration.

'What are you doing?' snapped MD from behind me.

I jumped. 'Would you stop doing that?' I demanded.

He huffed. 'Would you get back inside?' he begged.

'What? Why? I'm safe in the backyard, aren't I?'

'Jilly, you're not safe anywhere,' he said, walking over, taking my hand and dragging me inside like a child.

I huffed.

'Jilly, you have to stay inside. If a neighbour sees you and then comes into contact with an inquisitive stranger, your location will no longer be a secret.'

'Shit,' I mumbled, stomping up the stairs. I hated that he was right and I hadn't thought of it myself.

I flopped onto the sofa and turned on the television.

MD sat down beside me. 'I'm sorry, it's just, we can't find them,' he said.

'Then you're not looking properly,' I told him.

'Oh, we're looking, but we haven't seen them scouting any of the premium stores, galleries, restaurants, anything.'

'Of course not, that's why they're so good at doing what they do,' I told him, sulkily.

'What's going on? Are you alright?' he asked.

'Yeah, sorry. I'm just bored,' I groaned. 'I can't just sit here doing nothing,' I told him. 'Why don't you let me help? Let me look at some of the footage?'

He thought for a minute, 'Come on then, it can't hurt, I suppose,' he said.

I followed him down the stairs, already feeling better, feeling useful. We walked into his makeshift command centre and he asked someone called Jase to let me watch some video footage with him. I pulled up a chair saying hey to Jase who eyed me warily, which I couldn't blame him for. They all knew who I was, that I was a former criminal, a killer. Just because MD and my friends understood, it didn't mean everyone would.

'So what are we looking at?' I asked.

'It's a premium homewares shop on Hastings Street. Really nice stuff,' he said.

'It's not their kind of place,' I said, watching the monitor.

'Why do you say that?' he asked, doubtfully.

'It's too busy. Look at all the stuff, all the hazards from the counter to the door. It's too busy, as well. There's a constant flow of people and it's unpredictable because it attracts both the serious cashed-up buyer and the bored beachgoer looking for something to do,' I told him.

He nodded. 'Makes sense,' he said, pausing the video.

'What sort of places should we be looking at?' asked Brad from beside us.

'High end. Large transactions, preferably cash or high-end goods, jewellery, art, stuff they can carry out and offload for a high price when they move on. But it needs to have little traffic. Wide open space, isolated staff, one, two at the most.

'The restaurant was a surprise choice. My guess is they were just eating there one night and noticed how careless the staff were around closing and couldn't resist. Depending on how much press was around it, they could definitely try that again if there are any others that lax during closing. Don't rule out the banks either, especially around here. You don't have the security they have in the city or the response times and there's only one or two tellers, maybe a manager. It'll be easy pickings, even better would be their armoured vehicles that transport the money, it's a long way from one bank to the other,' I told them.

'Who has the bank footage?' MD asked.

'I do. Just about to load it up,' said a young blonde guy.

'Alright, Jilly, go watch it with him,' MD said.

I moved over to the young blonde guy.

'You got a sweet deal going on, hey?' he asked casually as he loaded up the video feed.

I glared at him, not sure really what to say.

'What she does or doesn't have going on is none of your business, Robbo,' MD snarled.

'Yes, sir,' Robbo, answered guiltily.

He let the feed play and leant back in his chair, sipping his coffee, watching the monitor.

After about an hour I saw him. The blood in my veins froze. I hadn't known how I'd feel seeing my brother again. It certainly wasn't warm and fuzzy. I barely recognised him. He'd grown up and was now far from the scraggly fourteen, fifteen-year-old boy who'd have done anything to please Aunt Joanne. He'd filled out, become a man, he was bearded, his eyes crinkled. He was hardened and it made me sad what she'd done to him.

I looked at Robbo, surprised he hadn't said anything but he was just continuing to sip his coffee and watch the screen. I wondered if he was even really looking or if he was thinking about where else he'd rather be.

'Are you going to say anything at all about the man who's going to rob the bank?' I asked him.

'What?' he asked, surprised.

'He was just there and you didn't even see him,' I said. 'How many other times have you not seen him?' I asked, my heart pounding.

'Jilly?' asked MD, scooting his chair over. 'Show me, where was he?' he asked.

I got Robbo to rewind the recording. 'There,' I said, pointing to the screen, my finger shaking.

'Are you sure?' asked MD.

'Yes, I'm sure. That is my brother. I'd know him anywhere. There's not enough facial hair to disguise him. And see? See how he's looking around when he speaks? He laughs, like he's enjoying some fun banter, but look at his eyes. He's looking everywhere but at her, making a mental note of every person, everything they're doing or not doing and the teller's too captivated by his charm to notice. Even if she did, she'd probably just think he was nervous about flirting with her.

'Then when he comes back, I bet he'll be clean shaven, dressed in a suit or something smart and she won't even notice it's him. She's probably giving away bank secrets without even knowing it, what time they lunch, who's out the back. He's even better than Peter,' I said, sadly, looking into his eyes as they froze the screen. 'What's nearby? What's out the front? Next door?' I asked.

They pulled up a street view. There was a gift and card shop next door, a cake shop on the other side. 'What's across the road,' I asked.

There was a dentist and a fish and chip shop with a couple of weather worn tables and chairs out the front. 'There,' I said. 'Do you have any footage of those chairs for the same time?' I asked.

Someone found it and put it on the monitor in front of me. They fast forwarded the footage until it reached the same time. 'There, stop. Zoom in,' I said.

They zoomed in and there was a mother and teenage daughter casually eating fish and chips out of a paper bag. The mother had long straight hair. Her face, wrinkled from hard living, looked decades older than she was. She wore a long peasant skirt and tank top like all the other beach visitors. The girl was dressed similarly. To anyone watching they were just a mother and daughter on holidays eating lunch.

'That's them,' I declared as I watched Aunt Joanne laughing, my heart pounding in my chest. 'That laughter's for your benefit by the way,' I told them as my stomach churned.

We continued watching the footage. Neil left the bank, crossed the street and casually pulled up a chair, ruffling the girl's hair as though she were five. He ate a few chips, dipping them into a puddle of sauce on the edge of the paper and then they left, his arm casually draped around Aunt Joanne as though they were a real couple, as though they didn't share blood.

My heart thumped in my chest, my stomach twisted and turned. I thought I'd vomit and braced myself to run to the bathroom.

'It's okay, Jilly, breathe,' MD soothed, his hand on my shoulder, grounding me, reminding me I was safe.

The feeling passed and I nodded.

'We need to see where they go,' demanded MD, putting his hand on mine.

Someone went about finding the footage that would follow them.

'We'll find them,' he whispered to me. 'Are you alright?' he asked.

I nodded. I couldn't speak.

'Found 'em,' called Jase. 'They get into a black sedan down the street. They get stuck behind an armoured vehicle but drive to Noosaville, park and that's it, no sign of them after they go inside.'

'There has to be,' insisted MD. 'Keep watching,' he spat.

'You won't find them,' I said. 'There are hairdressers in there, shops, toilets to change in. They won't be coming out the same. That wouldn't have even be their car. Probably belongs to someone who works in the shopping centre and they will never even know it had left the car park,' I told them, watching Jase's monitor. 'Can you put it at two hours after they went in?' I asked.

He adjusted the footage to the time I asked for and we all watched anxiously.

'There,' I said, pointing at a woman coming out with a short shiny, brown bob wearing a smart, ochre shift dress and sandals with big sunglasses and red lips. 'That's her.'

'Are you sure?' asked MD sceptically.

'Yes, I'm sure. Give it fifteen minutes and the other two will be out,' I told them and sure enough, nineteen minutes later, Neil came out, his hair trimmed and suddenly sun kissed, clean shaven, looking his age, looking handsome with a pair of aviator shades on, wearing board shorts and a t-shirt with his arm draped over a pretty girl with long blonde hair in a short sundress. 'How old's this footage?' I asked, sadly.

'Yesterday,' said Jase quietly.

'Then you don't have long,' I said.

'How do we stop them?' asked MD.

'I don't think they're after the bank, even with the lesser security, it's too risky, I think they're after the truck. But they were definitely scouting the bank and their goings on so it's all connected. I just don't know how.'

Brad interjected. 'The big deposit, the truck brings it once a month but it's never the same schedule.'

'That's it then, that's what he was trying to get out of the teller. He was probably asking about a large withdrawal and she was probably telling him what day he'd have to come back for that amount and he'll piece the rest together. So you can either wait for them to get to the truck somewhere between it's pick up and the bank and hope you guess right or you can cancel all deliveries, close the bank and deter them, but then they'll only find somewhere else,' I told them, getting up and walking dazed up the stairs.

I couldn't believe it. I'd known they were here, but seeing them, it was something else. To see them in action, doing what we did as though no time had passed. Everything came rushing back in one big whoosh. I wasn't sure I could cope with it, with them, the memories and raced for the toilet.

CHAPTER 19

I was sad when I woke up the next day. I should have been at the markets but I wasn't. I was in bed, alone. MD had come to bed late again and was already gone. I'd spent the evening with Sienna setting up a website we both knew there was no point setting up but she'd known about my bad day before she'd gotten to the top of the stairs and I'd welcomed the distraction.

The website had been a lot easier than I'd expected. Perhaps that was because I no longer needed to hide. But I now had an email account, a website and a Facebook page, all under the name of Jilly Cooper, Photographer. Nothing with my actual picture on it. It was nice to exist again. In some way. Be a part of the world. Stamp my place in it. Let the world know I was alive and know that more than just a small market place could see my work. Whatever happened next, a piece of me, of Jilly, would live on.

Catching Aunt Joanne and Neil wasn't going to change anything. It would change the lives of the people in the bank, the men in the armoured vehicle, all the people they would rob and injure in the future. Maybe it would even save the life of my niece, allow her to live a normal life, the life I didn't get. But for me, nothing was going to change. I'd killed a man. Nothing could ever change that.

There was no more hiding, no more running. Everyone would know who I was. Everywhere I went from now on, I'd be that girl who murdered her uncle, that girl who used to help rob people.

'Jilly?' MD called from the doorway.

I wiped my tears and turned to him, forcing a smile. 'Yeah?'

He watched me for a moment then said, 'Can you come look at some footage?' he asked.

'Sure, just give me a few,' I said, throwing back the covers.

I showered, put my hair into a ponytail and went downstairs without even bothering to put on any makeup. What did it matter at this point?

'Hey,' I said, when I saw him at the bottom of the stairs.

'Hey,' he said, leaning in to kiss the top of my head. 'You alright?' he asked.

'Of course,' I said. 'What did you want me to see?'

'Here,' he said, leading me to a computer screen. 'He was in the bank first thing this morning but we couldn't find the other two and he didn't do anything. The truck delivered and moved on, no problems. I wondered if you could figure out what happened?'

I sat down and he pressed play. MD passed me a coffee and I watched the screen until the footage ended.

'So, what do you think?' he asked.

'You spooked him. He knew you were watching. Joanne would have been waiting for his signal and wouldn't have acted without it. He would have been at the bank to make sure everything was still on track but he's not stupid, he saw what was happening, you can see it in his face.' I said, getting up to leave.

'What do you mean?' he asked, stopping me.

'You had plain clothes cops everywhere. The teller was edgy. The manager was hovering. A blind man could see what was going on,' I told him.

'Shit,' he said, throwing the folder he was holding onto the coffee table.

I took my coffee upstairs and lay on the couch to watch daytime TV. I thought about making biscuits. I'd seen the supplies I needed in the pantry the day before but I didn't feel like it. I didn't feel like moving. Soon I'd be on the run again. I mightn't have to hide the fact that I was Sydney Adams anymore, but I'd still be running from her anyway, from her legacy, so I was going to enjoy the safety of Sienna's couch while I could.

'Hey,' Sienna called late in the afternoon when she came home.

'Hey,' I called back.

'Any news?' she asked.

'Nope. Cops spooked 'em,' I told her.

'So Mitch said.'

'What time's your gig?' I asked.

'Gotta be set up before six then we're on at eight,' she said.

'Who even books a band for the middle of the week, anyway?' I asked.

She shrugged. 'Some conference has booked out the surf club. We'll take any gig we can get,' she smiled. 'Wish you could come. You look like you could use a night out,' she said.

'I could. Who knows what's going to happen when all this is over,' I told her flatly.

'Come on Jilly, it's going to be alright. You have to believe it. Brad says you will be okay,' she said, squeezing my hand.

I smiled tightly. Nothing was ever going to be alright again, no matter what Brad said. I couldn't get my hopes up.

Sienna went to get ready and I went back to watching telly.

I called out a see ya and good luck as she was leaving.

I tried distracting myself by uploading some pictures to the website like Sienna had shown me but my heart wasn't in it. I heated up some leftover stir-fry, considered taking some down to MD but I could smell pizza and heard the distinct quiet of men eating, so ate it on the balcony, enjoying the smell of the descending night.

I fell asleep on the couch watching a cop show where they always catch the bad guy. I woke to the sound of a heated discussion coming from the kitchen. I opened my eyes and listened to MD and Sienna arguing.

'I'm sorry, I didn't mean to, Mitch,' Sienna cried.

'What's going on?' I asked them walking into the kitchen and taking in the scene. MD furious. Sienna sobbing.

'Nothing,' snapped MD.

'She has a right to know, Mitch,' shouted Sienna as he tried barging past me.

'Don't put this on her Sienna, she has enough to deal with,' he snapped.

'She is a person and I'm standing right here,' I snapped.

MD's face looked like it might explode. 'Tell me,' I demanded, holding onto his arm, even though I didn't nearly have enough strength to keep him there if he wanted to leave.

'They know where you are,' he whispered.

'What?' I stumbled.

'Sienna told them,' he said, glaring at her.

'I didn't mean to,' she pleaded through a fresh wave of tears.

'It's okay, it's what they do,' I said quietly. 'It was only a matter of time. They would have been in the restaurant the night we were there. They would have tracked me to you eventually,' I told them.

'Well, it doesn't matter because they can't get to you with all of us here,' he said.

'Do they know you're here?' I asked.

'I told them,' Sienna said. 'As I was leaving, your brother tried getting in the car with me, said they'll just come along. I told him there was no point, there were twenty cops camped out at the house. Your brother was furious but they left and I drove straight home.'

'It's okay, they'll wait,' I told them.

'They'll be waiting a long time then,' MD said.

'You can't keep all of those men downstairs indefinitely,' I told him. 'I'm going to bed,' I said, leaving them to argue, no longer having the strength to set people straight about things that should make perfect sense.

MD was still sleeping when I woke up. I watched him breathing, in and out. He had the sheets tucked under his arm. His face was so peaceful, even with the stubble on his jaw, his face was soft and perfect. I'd fallen in love with him, I realised. How could that even happen in such a short period of time? I couldn't say, but I loved him. My heart swelled for him. My hands begged to touch him, to be connected. I couldn't let anything happen to him. Even if that meant walking away. He'd recover from me, surely? Eventually? At least he'd be safe.

Reluctantly, I left MD sleeping and went downstairs where Brad was just getting ready to start his day, a steaming cup of coffee in one hand and a piece of toast smeared with vegemite in the other.

'You're up early,' he said.

'Brad, it's time,' I told him.

'Time for what?' he asked.

'Remember when you promised that if the time came, you'd do what was needed to protect Sienna and Mel?' I asked, purposely leaving MD out of the equation, thinking Sienna and Mel's protection held much more weight.

'Yeah but it's not that time. We'll catch them Jilly, we'll catch them.'

'No, no you won't. They won't make a move while you're here. They'll wait until you move out and then they'll come for me, for their money. We both know it. You can't all live here indefinitely but they can wait that long,' I told him.

'They'll slip up and we'll catch them,' he insisted.

'No, they won't. Not now they know I'm helping you. Their only mission now is me. Their money. Revenge. That's it. That'll be their only job now. They'll be watching the house. Somehow, they'll be watching and we won't even know it,' I said, sadly.

I could see understanding dawning on Brad.

'You know I'm right.'

'Right about what?' asked Mel sleepily.

'Nothing, go back to bed,' Brad snapped.

'No. Right about what?' she demanded.

'I need to leave, Mel, to draw out Neil and Jo, to protect you and Sienna,' I told her, explaining what had happened to Sienna the night before.

'No, you don't. We have Brad and all these guys here,' she said.

'The cops can't stay here forever and Neil and Jo will just wait until the cops are gone.'

She nodded, thoughtfully. 'What were you thinking?'

'That Brad could arrest me or something. That'd draw them out. They'd come for me if they thought they could,' I told her.

'No,' she said.

'No?'

'No, Jilly. There are other ways,' she said, as though she knew.

'Like what?' I asked, expecting her to shrug in defeat.

'We move everyone to the retreat. Or at least a couple, everyone would be too many. We move you and me and Sienna. As though I were going to work in the morning, just you and Sienna would be in the back. Then the cops can all leave, say that they have no leads, something, and then when Neil and Jo think you're home alone, all they'll find is a couple of guys waiting upstairs. Meanwhile, we can go stay in a bungalow at the retreat, watch some movies, eat some good food, do some yoga, whatever,' she suggested.

'That's quite well thought out,' suggested Brad.

Mel smiled and shrugged, clearly pleased with herself.

'Do you think they'd mind?' he asked.

'Eric said it would be fine if we needed it,' she said.

'Eric...' Brad scoffed.

'Not you too?' she asked.

Brad waved her off. 'It sounds like a better plan than what Jilly was thinking, though,' he said.

'We can't just lob up to the retreat and freeload,' I said. 'We should at least pay. I can pay,' I offered.

'No, you can't,' said Brad. 'Not with that stolen money, that stays with us,' he said, with a tougher cop voice than MD.

'I do have other money, you know, money I earnt myself. I'm not a freeloader,' I defended.

'Don't worry about it,' Mel insisted. 'They've offered whatever we need and I get a free week there every year that I never use. Let's just think of it that way. I'm using my staff bonuses for the last three years. Besides, there's loads of empty bungalows right now. It's the middle of the week and we've just hit off season. Don't worry about it Jilly, we've got you covered.'

Covered. I had friends who had me covered. That was new. It was strange but I liked it. I liked it a lot. I liked it too much and it terrified me. I liked them too much and that terrified me more. It was one thing to exist without friends, close friends, when you never knew what you were missing. But once you did, now I did, I wasn't sure I'd ever be able to go back to before.

Having to give up something so precious would break a piece of me and I was afraid I'd never feel whole again. But then I suppose knowing what I know now, I was never whole to begin with. I suppose I would just be irreparably broken. A shadow of a person. But I wasn't sure anymore if I had any say in it. I couldn't walk away. I wanted to stay more than I'd ever wanted anything other than my freedom. But I would do anything to protect them. I would give this idea a chance. I would try, for them, for me.

'Okay,' I said, watching their expectant faces relax with relief. 'But...if anything goes wrong, if it even looks like it's going wrong, you and me, Brad, we have another conversation, alright?'

He nodded.

'No. You promise me, Brad,' I demanded, the words squeezing through my tightening throat.

'I promise,' he said, looking into my eyes, his hands on my shoulders keeping me together. 'I won't let anything happen to them and I won't let anything happen to you either, Jilly,' he smiled.

'Thank you,' I whispered as tears flooded my eyes. I left before the tears overflowed and headed back up the stairs to tell MD. At least he wouldn't flip out at this solution. I could feel Mel behind me but I didn't turn. I walked down the hallway and as I went into my bedroom, she went into Sienna's shouting, 'Wake up, wake up.'

MD opened his eyes sleepily at the commotion. I closed the door to block it out.

'What's going on?' he asked.

I climbed across the bed and fused my lips to his, letting him do the rest. He opened to me too easily, drew me in hungrily and I rode the wave with him. When the kiss was over he pulled away but only a few millimetres, just far enough for me to see him smile. 'Well, good morning.'

'Good morning,' I smiled back.

'What's going on?' he asked.

'Nothing,' I lied.

He raised an eyebrow at me and it was all it took.

'Fine,' I huffed. 'I was talking to Brad. I can't stay here. Not now. Not if it puts everyone in danger.'

'What danger? There's no danger while we're all here,' he said, pulling me to him.

'But that's just it, MD, you won't all be here forever. We need to draw Neil and Jo out but Sienna and Mel need to be safe.'

'You need to be safe,' he growled.

'So everyone keeps saying,' I mumbled.

'So what great plan did you come up with?' he huffed.

'Mel said Eric said the owners have offered us the retreat. We can go there. There's spare bungalows and it should be safe.'

'Eric...' he huffed.

'What is it with all of you and Eric?' I asked, exasperated.

'Nothing, don't worry about it. Just promise me you'll keep your distance from him.'

'Fine, I'll keep my distance,' I said, placating him.

'Thank you,' he smiled. Now,' he said, turning my face to his as his able hands crept under my t-shirt, 'how long do we have?'

'Long enough,' I giggled like a foolish girl before letting him take me however he wanted, savouring our last moments of alone time for who knew how long.

CHAPTER 20

Sienna and I squished onto the back seat of Mel's Prius as she headed off to work, giggling like children. She wouldn't let us sit up until we got to the retreat. 'MD insisted, just in case someone's following me,' she said, enjoying her position of power far too much.

Mel parked her car in its regular spot under the shade of a big tree at the back of the carpark. She waited a moment or three to be sure no one had followed us in.

'Alright, wait here, I'll go get a buggy and drive us out to the bungalows,' she said.

She wasn't gone long before a buggy hummed beside us. She loaded our overnight bags into the carrier bay and then, sure it was safe, Sienna and I unfolded ourselves, donned big floppy hats and big sunglasses. To anyone we passed, we just looked like a couple of regular guests.

'The bungalows are only one bedroom. Jilly, you and MD will

be in one, Rick and me in another and Brad is going to come and room with Sienna,' she instructed.

'Brad, hey?' I asked. 'He's very sexy, you know,' I added.

Sienna raised her eyebrows at me, about to dispute it but gave in. 'He is and yes, he'll be taking the couch because I can't have that much sexy in my bed,' she smiled.

'And why not?' I asked, suddenly thinking they'd be perfect together.

'For so many reasons. But mostly, there's no way Brad would be interested in me. I'm just Mitch's little sister,' she added.

'Really? You know, I don't think any of the men I've seen around since I got here think of you as MD's little sister.'

She was about to protest, when I added, 'they don't *look* at you like you're MD's little sister, anyway,' I smirked.

She had nothing to say to that. But as the first bungalow came into view, added, 'Well, Brad is not like Rick and MD's other friends, he's a whole different breed of man, so that's that and he'll be fine on the couch.'

Mel stopped in front of a small, eco-friendly hut surrounded by lush tropical gardens that looked like something out of a travel magazine. 'The bungalows are scattered throughout the property for maximum privacy, but these three are the closest together. You can't see ours from here, but they're there, buried in the bushes. We'll all hang out in yours mostly, though, that way you won't need to be wandering around, you just stay put, okay?' Mel said, hopping out of the buggy and opening the door for me. She handed me my key and said, 'alright, settle in, we'll just drop off our bags and we'll come back to keep you company.' Then they buzzed off down the trail and into the bushes.

Looking around, all I could see was lush tropical bushland.

You couldn't see or hear another person. Mel said the other two bungalows weren't far but I could no longer hear the buggy. Just the quiet. You would never know that you were a part of a retreat. I'd never hidden quite like this. I'd always hidden in plain sight. This felt isolated and alone. I didn't feel comforted. Instead fear bubbled in my tummy.

Making my way inside the hut, I dropped my duffle bag by the big bed with the triangle canopy over it. There was a bathroom with a corner spa off the bedroom and a small but comfortable sitting room and kitchenette. A bowl of fruit and a welcome note sat on the bench of the kitchenette and herbal teas lined the wall. No coffee tin in sight. I'd have to ask MD to bring me coffee and food. I suspected the restaurant in the main house catered to most visitors' meals. MD had banned me from leaving the bungalow, so I'd have to make do without fancy chef food.

I sent MD a message requesting my necessary supplies.

I opened the plantation shutters that covered the big windows in both rooms and let in the fresh, clean air. Then there was nothing else to do but sit on the poufy couch and wait for Sienna and Mel to return. What the hell was I going to do here all day? There were a few books on the shelves, all self-help or inspirational from the titles I could see. The movie collection was much the same.

I sent MD another message, 'entertainment too, please.'

He replied, 'I have the entertainment covered,' with an added winky face that made my toes tingle.

'How long will you be? I'm already bored,' I replied.

'Where are the others?'

'Dropping their things off.'

'Well, they'll be back before I can get there but don't worry, I'll ravage you before the sun goes down,' he replied.

'Promises, promises,' I smiled as I replied.

'I always keep my promises,' he added as I heard the girls giggling as they approached my door.

'Well, I'll hold you to that, but I now have company,' I told him.

'Good. Be careful. Stay put.'

'Yes sir, Detective.'

'Now that's more like it,' he said with a winky face as the girls let themselves in.

'What are you smiling at?' asked Sienna.

'Nothing,' I said, putting my phone on the armchair beside me. She rolled her eyes.

'Alright,' Mel started, dropping a few yoga mats from under her arms onto the floor then hoisting a big picnic basket onto the coffee table. She began unloading it, 'We have movies, a blender, cocktail supplies, chips and Carmichael sent over lunch,' she said, holding up one of the plastic containers the chef had sent to inspect it.

'They look good,' I said, referring to what looked like some sort of patty.

'Don't get too excited, who knows what's in them,' scoffed Sienna.

'Don't listen to her,' Mel told me. 'Carmichael is famous for his cauliflower fritters, they're delicious,' she added, while Sienna went into the kitchenette to set up the blender.

'Is this cake?' I asked, holding up another container.

'Or some version of,' called Sienna.

'Lemon and almond cake, it's made with almond meal. And if

Sienna keeps mocking the food from over there, she'll be getting none of it,' Mel admonished.

'I have all the lemons I need over here,' Sienna declared, holding up a bag of lemons that were on the bench beside a bottle of tequila.

'Looks like the margarita queen is ready to do her thing,' grinned Mel.

'Then anything will taste like it came from Rico's,' giggled Sienna as she piled ingredients into the blender.

'It's a bit early for margarita's isn't it?' I asked as I remembered I hadn't even had breakfast.

'Well, if you must, there's bread and vegemite in the basket if you need breakfast first, lightweight,' Sienna giggled.

'I like to think of these as extenuating circumstances,' said Mel. 'Pretend we're on holidays. It's never too early for margaritas when you're on holidays,' she said as the blender drowned out her voice.

'Well, I'm not sure I'd know about that, but it sounds fair to me,' I said, laughing. I put some bread in the toaster while Sienna continued the margaritas. I buttered the toast with lots of nut butter Mel had dug up at the restaurant and a small smear of vegemite from Sienna's supplies, just the way I liked it and we ate while Sienna added more ice to the blender.

Sienna ate her toast at the blender and as she shoved the last corner of crust into her mouth, the jugs of margaritas were ready. She hadn't packed any cocktail glasses so she hooked three coffee mugs from the kitchenette over her fingers and brought it all to the coffee table as Mel moved the basket of goodies to the floor and put lunch in the fridge.

Mel had a few sips. 'Mmmmm...' she smiled. 'Now that's how you begin your holidays,' she giggled.

'Already the best holiday I've ever had,' I told them.

'It's only just begun,' Sienna said, clinking her glass with mine.

We each found a spot to sit, Sienna on the chair, me on the couch and Mel on the floor with her legs stretched out and a contented look on her face.

'Eric asked after you,' she said. 'Asked how you were doing, if you were alright, if you needed anything,' she smirked.

'Really? After the other night at the Surf Club?' I asked.

'I suspect he thought things would be over with you and MD by now,' she giggled.

I shook my head. There was just no deterring some men.

'He offered to come and do some yoga with you, bring you some food, keep you company. For as long as it takes, he said,' she giggled.

'Wow, he's keen. I killed a man and he's still being creepy. Guess there's still hope someone will have me,' I half joked.

'MD's not walking away, Jilly. None of us are,' Sienna said, reaching over and squeezing my hand.

'I still don't know why,' I said, taking a long comforting sip of my margarita.

'Because we love you, silly,' Mel said, playfully hitting my leg.

'I can't see why? But thank you,' I told them, more grateful for their kindness than they'd ever know.

'Because you're brave and courageous, wise and lovely,' she said, topping up our glasses.

'You're all too kind for your own good, you know,' I told them. 'Even once this is over it will follow me around for the rest of my

life. I'll always be that girl who killed her uncle and walked away,'
I said sadly. 'How do you ever escape that?'

'I don't know,' Mel said. 'But we'll figure it out. Together. But
if worse comes to worse, my mum said you can stay with the
commune for a while, regroup, wait for the world to forget about
you, reinvent yourself,' she giggled.

'Well, thank your mum for the kind offer. Who knows? I may
need to take her up on it someday,' I smiled tightly.

'As if MD would ever let you disappear with the hippies,'
Sienna giggled.

'If you knew him like we do, Jilly, if you could see how he's
changed, we've never seen him like this. I think he might be in
love with you,' Mel admitted.

'What? Don't be ridiculous. He's a fool if he is,' I said.

'MD is a lot of things, but a fool he is not,' Sienna defended.
'He's an excellent judge of character. He's a good man, a smart
man and Jilly, if you could see the way he's ordering people
around, the way he almost falls to pieces whenever your name is
mentioned, your heart would swell for him,' she said wistfully.

'Or break,' I said, sadly.

'You love him, too, don't you?' she asked.

I shrugged. 'I can't afford to pay too much attention to those
sorts of feelings in my position.'

'You have to stay positive. You protected yourself the only way
you could. You'll get through this and you and MD can go on
being crazy fools in love and we can have more girls' nights with
ice-cream appetisers. You'll see,' she smiled.

'I'm sorry, you know,' Sienna said sadly.

'About what?' I asked, surprised at the change in topic.

'Telling your brother where you were,' she said.

'Oh that. I know,' I assured her.

'They just caught me off guard.'

'I bet they sent the girl and used MD as their lead in. She would have asked who that was with the hot cop and you would have spilled without even thinking. The rest was just child's play for Neil. Once he'd figured out we were housemates, he'd just have assumed you were an easy target to get to me. It's okay, Sienna, I know how they work.'

'Wow, how did you know? That is exactly what they did,' she looked at me surprised I'd know the details.

'It's not a new play, I've used it a few times myself,' I told her sadly.

'Maybe if I'd been paying more attention to what was going on around me instead of drinking and celebrating, I'd have realised what was going on. But I was too many drinks in, there was no way I was paying enough attention,' she apologised.

'It wouldn't have mattered. They're good at what they do. It wasn't your fault. What were you celebrating, anyway?' I asked, assuming it was just a good gig but needing to change the subject, it really wasn't her fault.

'We were offered a recording deal,' she smiled tightly.

'What? When? How?' I squealed.

'The gig, the conference, it was a bunch of musos,' she said.

'Oh my God, and you're only just telling me now? That's fantastic! Congratulations,' I said. 'This deserves a true celebration,' I said, topping up our margaritas.

We were a few sheets to the wind a few hours later when I heard the rumble of a motorbike outside the hut and then the hum of a car and suddenly I realised how stupid it was to be drinking so much when I had so many things to worry about, when I should have been keeping my wits about me.

'Don't worry, Jilly, it's just the boys,' Sienna said, shaking her head.

'No one will find you here,' promised Mel, patting my hand.

The boys let themselves in. MD had a bike helmet in his hand and a tight leather jacket snugly wrapped around him. I never imagined he could be sexier but I was wrong. Rick and Brad followed him in and all three dropped overnight bags by the door.

'You should have that locked, you know,' MD scowled.

'But I was just promised no one would ever find me here,' I said with a giggle.

'How much have you three had?' demanded Brad.

Sienna shrugged.

'It's midday,' admonished Brad.

'So, we're on holidays,' giggled Sienna.

Brad shook his head. 'Come on, let me get you sobered up,' he said, taking Sienna by the arm and leading her out of the hut.

'Come on, you too,' Rick said to Mel, but he was smiling too much to be cross.

'We'll be back,' slurred Sienna. 'We have more girl business to tend to,' she promised as she argued with Brad all the way down the path until I couldn't hear them anymore.

Then it was just MD and me. He took off his leather jacket and draped it over a chair then took of his boots. He had on snug denim jeans, a snug black t-shirt and no shoes. He was unshaven and sexy as hell. I sauntered up to him as best I could with my body swimming with margaritas. He was mine and all I wanted in that moment was what was mine.

He laughed and shook his head. 'No way, Jilly, I like my women coherent,' he laughed.

'I'm not that drunk, geez,' I defended, running my hand over his chest.

'Drunk enough,' he smiled.

'You did promise you'd ravage me before the sun went down.'

'The sun is a long way from setting,' he informed me as he went into the kitchen, filled the kettle and switched in on.

I flopped onto the sofa and sulked.

MD took his overnight bag to the bedroom and returned with a small tin of instant coffee and went about rinsing two of the margarita mugs for coffee.

The next thing I knew he was shaking me awake. 'Here, drink this,' MD insisted, holding out a big glass of water and a coffee.

I looked at his beautiful face, and in that moment, knew that everything, my whole crappy, chaotic, miserable life had led me to this one perfect moment, this one perfect man. I took the water and drank it then wrapped my hands around the coffee he passed me and let MD pull me into the nook of his body while we watched the last half of the midday movie.

'Better?' he asked as I placed my empty coffee cup on the table.

'Much,' I said.

'Good. Look at me,' he asked, turning my face to his.

I tried not to wither under his intense gaze. 'What?' I asked.

'Just trying to gauge your level of intoxication,' he said.

'I'm fine. Much better now. You've no need to worry. We only drank one and a half jugs between us, anyway.'

'Yes, but that's one and a half jugs of my sister's margaritas,' he smiled.

'Well, this is true,' I agreed. 'So what's the verdict? On my inebriation?'

'You look fine enough to me,' he said, with a wicked grin.

'Is that so?' I asked with an eyebrow raised.

'Indeed it is,' he said, pulling my mouth to his.

He kissed me, hard and fast, urgently. I stretched out beneath him on the couch as his hands roamed and searched, little fires erupting all over my body. I wanted him. I wanted him bad. It was a little tequila fuelled I knew but I wanted him anyway. I had that image of him walking in his leather jacket, of him riding up to the retreat on that bike that hummed through the floor and I wanted him more.

'No, no, this won't do,' he said sitting back on the couch, leaving me gasping.

'What?' I demanded, breathless.

He gave me that wicked grin of his. 'I can hardly find you here in this bloody overstuffed couch,' he said. 'Come,' he demanded, grabbing my hand and pulling me up.

My feet were unsteady, more than I'd expected but I covered it by falling into him, my mouth finding his and we stumbled to the bedroom as we ripped at each other's clothes.

He was right about sobering me up first. I wanted to remember this. I wanted to remember him shirtless, lying on the bed waiting for me, his erection pushing against his snug jeans. I set him free, threw his jeans across the room as I crawled up his body. I traced his tattoo. 'It's really beautiful,' I told him as I traced each of the elements, the sun, the sky, the cresting wave.

'It was a bit of a drunken dare, really,' he told me. 'Rick and I got them during that crazy summer when we surfed up and down the coast. His is a big flame. All he ever wanted to be was a fireman.

I wanted to remember what made me happy, the sun, the surf, being one with the ocean,' he told me.

His reasoning was as beautiful as the art and I sank into him, my mouth to his. He rolled me onto my back, covered me with his body as he stripped me bare before making love to me, because that's the only way I can describe what he did, what happened next. I had never in my crazy life experienced anything like it, anything as transcending and beautifully life altering.

We lay fused together, his strong arms wrapped around me, holding me to him as though he, too, had experienced something new. Something incredible and beautiful. Something that changed him as well, altered the cells of his being. Changed the way he breathed. Changed the way his heart beat.

The others burst our bubble, eased of their inebriation but still chattering like monkeys outside the window as they approached the hut.

'Can you move?' MD asked with a salacious, knowing grin.

'Maybe,' I whispered before his mouth took mine, deep and slow.

The others let themselves in but their voices stopped as they must have seen the debris of clothing. 'Sorry guys, we can come back,' giggled Sienna, tequila still coursing through her veins.

'It's okay, we'll be right out,' smirked MD, extricating himself to put on pants and a shirt.

CHAPTER 21

'You guys don't muck about, do you?' teased Sienna as we made coffee and heated lunch.

I looked over to Brad who wore snug jeans like MD but had a white button up shirt on, his hair neatly combed, his eyes, his face, serious, sexy, dangerous. I smirked at Sienna and asked, 'Jealous?'

We both laughed, catching the attention of the others. 'What are you two up to?' asked Rick.

We both shook our heads, MD and Brad watching us curiously.

We took the patties out of the little mini oven and between the bungalows had scrounged up enough plates to serve them on with some salad. We ate scattered around the small living room. There weren't enough seats for everyone, some sat on the floor but it was comfortable and friendly. It felt good.

'So what now?' asked Mel.

'Nothing,' replied MD.

'Nothing? At all?' she asked.

'Nothing,' he replied.

'I could get Eric to do a yoga class for us,' she suggested.

'NO!' shouted all three men at the same time.

'Geez, what is it with you guys and Eric?' she asked, gathering up the empty plates.

They all mumbled their objections incoherently leaving us none the wiser so we chose to ignore them. His sexual prowess was clearly legendary and had all the boys up in arms.

'I could make more margaritas,' offered Sienna.

'No more margaritas,' MD insisted.

'Fine,' she sulked.

'I brought movies,' offered Mel.

'What did you bring?' asked Rick as he started sifting through her supply.

'A movie would be good,' said Brad.

'Pick something half decent would you, mate?' begged MD.

'That's my girl,' declared Rick as he held up a Star Wars Episode One DVD.

'Argh, really?' groaned Sienna, as she whacked Mel in the leg.

'I've never seen them,' I said.

Everyone turned to stare at me. 'Never? None of them?' asked MD.

I shook my head. 'None. Ever.'

'Well then, looks like we're having a Star Wars marathon,' MD declared with a jubilant smile.

Sienna groaned again. 'I hope you at least brought popcorn. And not that hippy stuff you tried passing off as popcorn last time but the good stuff with salt and processed butter,' she demanded.

'Of course,' smiled Mel, dipping into her bag of goods.

She microwaved the three bags of popcorn and handed them out. MD and I had a bag to share on the couch. Mel sat on the end of the couch nearest the armchair Rick was occupying so they could share, and Sienna and Brad made themselves a little camp on the floor, leaning against the wall.

I snuggled up to MD, my legs curled under me on the couch and settled in for hours of movie watching. At some point, Mel and Rick took the buggy over to the restaurant to scour us up some dinner of beetroot burgers and sweet potato fries that didn't at all meet with Sienna's high standards even though she ate every crumb.

Then we settled in for more Star Wars. It was going forever. The last thing I remember after hours of movie was Luke agreeing to go with Obi Wan to Alderaan to become a student of The Force. When I woke, Mel and Rick had made it to the floor to snuggle and Mel had fallen asleep against her man like I had. Rick and MD were still eagerly watching. So was Brad, who had wrapped his arms around a sleeping Sienna, holding her close. No one mentioned it, though. MD didn't seem at all perturbed about his senior officer's arms around his sister.

'You okay?' MD asked quietly.

'Ahuh,' I smiled up at him. 'How much did I miss?' I asked.

'A bit, but I'm sure you'll catch up or we can watch them another time,' he offered.

I hoped there'd be another time, that I'd have forever to re-watch Star Wars movies with MD.

'Everything will be okay,' MD assured me.

I snuggled in deeper, hoping he was right.

It was late when everyone left. Sienna had woken in Brad's arms and had tried to inconspicuously remove herself and pretend something hadn't changed between them. I wondered as they all walked down the dirt path back to their own bungalows, how much exactly would change once they were alone in that small hut.

'What?' asked MD curiously.

'Nothing,' I smiled and followed him inside.

He stripped off in the bedroom as though it was the most natural thing to do, as though we'd been doing it, been that comfortable with each other for years. I smiled to myself. I liked this feeling of comfort and intimacy that was growing between us. I was terrified I'd lose it, lose him, when this was all over. Despite what everyone kept saying, they couldn't be sure what the future held for me.

'How tired are you?' he asked as I climbed into bed beside him.

'Not that much really. I did nap through episodes four and five, so, nope, not very tired at all,' I admitted, hopefully.

'Good,' he said, sliding across the bed and pulling me to him, his mouth to mine.

I gave in and enjoyed every second, enjoyed feeling safe, feeling loved and needed and wanted.

Despite our shenanigans going late into the night, I woke with the sun and the birds. It was that kind of place, I supposed. The air was quiet but for the birds doing their thing. It was peaceful and tranquil and I understood why people would pay a lot of money for a week here. I wished I could mosey up to the restaurant, have some breakfast, take a yoga class. I hoped my friends would do just that, there was nothing stopping them. But for me it was toast and vegemite.

I made myself two pieces and turned on the kettle while I put in some bread for MD, even though, rightly, he could also go to the restaurant but I suspected he wouldn't.

'Good morning,' he whispered, nuzzling my neck as I buttered his toast.

'Good morning,' I replied. 'How do you like your vegemite?' I asked.

He reached around me, held my hand with the knife, dipped it in the jar and smeared his required amount. His hands moved to my hips and his mouth kissed the divot under my ear before he took his toast to the couch.

'It's a beautiful morning,' I declared. 'I don't suppose we could eat outside?' I asked, having seen a beautiful patio with cane, cushioned chairs out the back. 'It's really secluded out there, surely no one could see me,' I told him.

He looked out the window before agreeing as I finished making the coffees. He took his coffee and his toast and I followed him outside with mine. The sun streamed under the veranda and warmed my legs while I ate. We chatted about inane things that new couples chat about. It was nice. He knew who I was now. Nothing was off limits. I didn't have to skirt around my life, my childhood, my thoughts and feelings and where I'd been and what I'd done. I could talk to my boyfriend like a normal person and I appreciated it more than I'd appreciated anything, almost more than his naked body beside me in bed, almost.

'Do you have to go soon?' I asked.

'Nope,' he declared.

'No? Don't you have some criminals to catch so we can get on with our lives?'

'I have people,' he said. 'They're at the house waiting to see what happens. One of the boys took Mel's car home last night. It'll look like you're all just hanging out like normal. We're just waiting and watching for now. So until I hear anything more, I'm spending the day with my girl,' he declared, kissing me.

'Well, I do like the sound of that,' I told him. 'What about the others?' I asked, wondering just how much alone time I had with my man.

'Rick and Brad are under strict instructions to keep those girls away for the morning. I want at least the morning, just us. I doubt my sister will stay away any longer than that, though, never could sit still,' he smiled.

'So,' I started. 'What is it you had in mind for this morning of ours?' I asked.

He grinned, that wicked grin that made my toes curl. 'Before anything else, I need a shower,' he said, putting his plate on the little table beside his empty coffee mug. 'Care to join me?' he asked, almost hopefully.

I shrugged as though I had nothing better to do and put my plate on top of his, my mug beside his. 'I could shower,' I told him as I boldly took off my tank top and dropped it on the ground as I walked into the hut.

I heard him groan as he got up to follow me and smiled to myself. I was really getting the hang of this new feeling of just being me, of letting down my walls. I felt free to be me. To do anything, knowing he was going to stand by me, no matter what I'd done, who'd I'd been. I was allowed to let him in and it was freeing.

I marvelled at his beautiful body, wet from the water of the shower and let him take me to new, incredible places as this thing between us became more, became stronger.

I was starving when I heard the yabber of the others coming along the path.

'I hope they brought food,' I joked as I dressed.

MD had let them in by the time I finished. Sienna and Mel were already unpacking food in the kitchen and I could have hugged them. I'd worked up quite an appetite. A morning alone with MD would do that to a girl.

As I went to help them, they both looked up with the cat-that-ate-the-canary grins and that freshly done over look only a night in the hay can give you.

'Well, well,' I cooed while the boys talked in the living area. 'You, I expected,' I said, pointing to Mel. 'But you?' I said, waggling my finger at Sienna. 'I definitely did not expect,' I smiled.

'I don't know what you're talking about,' she said, squeezing past me to get to the sink.

I moved closer so the boys couldn't hear us gossiping. 'Oh, you know exactly what I'm talking about,' I laughed. 'He wasn't a fan of the couch then?' I asked.

'Don't know,' she smirked. 'He never tried it,' she giggled and Mel and I laughed with her.

The boys looked over and scowled, clearly suspecting we were trading secrets.

'Hungry?' Mel asked them.

They nodded and she set out plates.

'Well, I'm glad to hear it, whatever you got up to, it suits you,' I told Sienna as we scooped food onto the plates.

'Well, it felt pretty darned good, that's for sure,' she smiled.

'What now?' I grumbled, after we'd eaten, not sure I could survive another movie marathon.

One by one the others shrugged.

'There should be board games in the cupboard somewhere,' Mel instructed, going over to rummage through said cupboard.

She returned with Yahtzee and Monopoly.

We started with Yahtzee. It required the least brain power, apparently. One by one they each rolled a single dice but I didn't understand the process and when I didn't roll too, Sienna watched me a moment before asking, 'Have you ever played Yahtzee?'

I shook my head, 'Nope, not much time for games when you're running from the world and the kind of people I spent time with didn't play board games on lazy afternoons,' I smiled.

'You've not played Monopoly either, then?' she asked.

'Nope. I could probably manage my way through blackjack,' I laughed.

'Not even with your brother before your folks died?'

'Nope, we had that Guess Who game and that one with the two coloured circles where you try and get all your colours in a row,'

'Connect Four,' Rick said for me.

'Yeah, that one. But even before Mum and Dad died, my brother and I didn't really spend much time together so we never played.'

'It doesn't matter,' Sienna said. 'Mel didn't know either when she left the commune, but we taught her,' she added.

MD shook his head. 'I'll teach you.'

We spent the afternoon with me learning to play board games. Bowls of chips appeared, Sienna whined there were no beers. MD lectured her on the importance of staying sober in such a situation and it was perfect. A perfect afternoon.

After Mel suspiciously beat everyone at Yahtzee, we moved on to Monopoly, which I was no better at but didn't care because I was spending time with my friends. We were laughing and telling stories. I was involved. I could ask questions without being afraid they'd ask them in return. I shared and I trusted and I laughed without the weight of the world sitting on my shoulders. MD's arm was casually draped over my shoulders as he bickered with his sister and blushed from the secrets shared by his best friend and his boss, and I didn't think life could get any more perfect. I was me and even though I clearly sucked at board games, I was having more fun than I could ever remember having.

We kept playing into the night until all the properties had been acquired, traded, houses built and upgraded to hotels. We played until there were no more deals to make, until everyone's money dwindled except for Mel's, whose piles grew fat. Eventually everyone conceded defeat.

There may have been a few grumbles of cheating but no one really minded.

'I think that might have been the most fun I've ever had,' I declared as MD locked the door after our friends had left.

'Really?' he asked suspiciously. 'Does that mean my prowess has slipped and I have some work to do?' he asked with a mischievous glint in his eye.

'No,' I laughed. 'That's a whole different kind of fun. But, I'm not entirely against you trying to outdo yourself,' I added, feeling a little naughty myself.

'Is that so?' he asked, cocking an eyebrow. Then he scooped me up. 'We'll have to see if we can turn things up a notch, then,' and my tummy fluttered. I suddenly wasn't sure if I was ready for what I'd just instigated.

CHAPTER 22

M&D's phone hummed on the bedside table. We were hungry, but not hungry enough to move, too eager to hear each other's stories and secrets as we whiled away the morning, laughing. He let his phone buzz a minute but aware of the reality of our world, eventually gave in and picked it up.

'Yeah,' he answered. 'Yep. Sure,' he responded before hanging up. 'Looks like we might have something,' he said. 'Stay here. The girls will be over soon,' he said, kissing me then getting up and rummaging through the debris on the floor for his pants.

I waited, lay there watching him dress as each of his body parts were concealed, bit by bit. Then he gave me one of those toe curling, wicked grins before walking out.

I managed to dress in shorts and a tank top in time to wave him goodbye and lock the door as he instructed, just in case.

The girls came chattering down the path not much later. I met them at the door. They were both grinning from ear to ear and their skin tone had more of that smoothed, pink, freshly fucked

240

look about it. Seems this hiding business was working out for everyone.

'Where's Rick?' I asked Mel as Sienna made herself at home, rummaging around in the kitchen.

'Still sleeping, he'll be over later,' she said as Sienna continued hunting in cupboards and slamming doors.

'What are you looking for?' I asked.

'The blender, what did you do with it?' she asked.

'Nothing,' I told her. 'It was right there on the sink last night.'

'Bloody Mitch,' she groaned.

'Seriously? He took our blender?' I asked.

'Well, someone did and he's the only OCD control freak I know,' she said.

I pulled my phone out of my pocket and messaged him, 'where's our blender?'

'Gone,' he replied.

'Gone where?'

'Just gone.'

'But we're bored, how are we going to make margaritas?'

'You're not. That's the point. I told you, no more margaritas. Stay alert, just in case,' he replied.

'Argh,' I groaned and the girls smiled knowingly at me.

'Are we at least allowed to go find some food?' asked Mel. 'I'm bloody starved,' she declared.

'I have bread and vegemite,' I said, holding up what was left of the loaf of bread.

'I need way more than bloody toast,' she smirked. 'You guys stay here. I'll take the buggy up to the restaurant and see what I can scrounge up from Carmichael,' she said, letting herself out.

Sienna made herself a coffee and then started patting her pants.

'What's the matter? Did Brad have you rolling in a swarm of ants this morning?' I asked.

'Shut up, no,' she laughed. 'I've left my phone behind. Will you be right while I go back and get it?' she asked.

'A bit distracted, were you?' I asked, smugly.

She smirked. 'A bit,' she admitted.

'You happy?' I asked her.

'Deliriously,' she smiled.

'Good. Go, get your phone, I'll be fine,' I told her.

Once the girls were gone, I let myself indulge in my bubble of happiness. Despite everything that was going on, everything that was my life, it had somehow become more perfect than I could have ever imagined. I thanked the universe, or whatever governing body oversaw our meagre existence and drank Sienna's coffee. It'd be cold by the time she returned anyway, so I'd make her another one then.

I was just finishing her coffee, staring into space and smiling at myself when I heard the buggy stopping out the front. Mel must have brought back a lot of food if she needed to deliver it to my door. She'd been parking the buggy down by her hut because regular guests didn't have buggies at their disposal. But if anyone saw Mel with one, or Mel in a hut, they wouldn't even think twice because she belonged here and a staff member spending a night in a hut was a perfectly reasonable thing to do.

I was about to go and let Mel in when someone pounded on the door. 'Jilly! Jilly! Are you in there? It's me, Eric,' he called, sounding frantic.

What the hell was Eric doing here?

I opened the door but not far enough to let him in. 'What's up?' I asked sceptically.

'We gotta go,' he declared.

'Go where?' I asked.

'Anywhere. But I know somewhere. I'll keep you safe,' he said.

'What's going on? Where's Mel and Sienna?' I asked.

'They're fine, they're safe,' he insisted.

'Why are you here?' I asked.

'MD asked me to come and get you. He thinks you're in trouble,' he said.

'What?' I questioned as I pulled my phone out of the pocket of my shorts. 'I don't have a message. If there was trouble, MD would have messaged me,' I told him.

'What do you want me to say? Maybe you had no reception? Maybe he just thought I could protect you? I don't know,' he said, getting frustrated.

'Why would MD message you, anyway? He doesn't even like you,' I said.

'I don't know Jilly. But I do know the last thing I need is bloody MD chopping my balls off for letting something happen to you. Would you just come on?' he demanded.

'Fine,' I said, exasperated, not knowing what else to do and putting my phone in my pocket.

'No, leave it here. They can track it,' he said.

'Who? My brother? My brother who just got out of gaol? My brother who has been locked up since before GPS was invented?' I questioned.

'I don't know. Maybe. Or maybe your niece or your perverted fucking aunt, I don't know,' he said, exasperated.

'It's not a smart phone anyway, no one can track it,' I told him.

'Who knows what they can do these days, just leave the fucking phone and come on before I'm scraping you out of the fucking bushes,' he demanded.

I quickly tried MD but I got an out of service message so I agreed, because I didn't know enough about technology and he was freaking me out. There was always the possibility Neil and Aunt Joanne actually knew what they were doing and I didn't want to die. It made sense. If the bush blocked my phone reception, MD would call the retreat. Who else would he have sent to rescue me? Carmichael? He hated Eric, but not enough to risk my life. I was sure of that.

I checked my phone again, I had a couple of bars, so I sent MD a message saying 'Eric made it. I'm okay. I love you.' then threw it on the couch and followed Eric to the golf buggy.

We hadn't actually said the 'L' word to each other but no matter what happened with me and Neil and Aunt Joanne, I wanted him to know I loved him. I wanted him to know that I was safe, that Eric had come for me like he'd asked and that I was grateful. But mostly, I just wanted him to know, in case when this was all over, I didn't get another chance to say it to him.

I should have told him before he'd raced out the door. I should have told him in the shower, over breakfast, last night in bed. But I hadn't. Now I had. Now he'd know. No matter what happened, he'd know and it was comforting.

I glanced over my shoulder, they could be anywhere, watching, waiting. There was too much vegetation. Anyone or anything could be hiding in the bushes. A shiver ran up my spine. I didn't like this hiding in isolation business. Hiding in plain sight was easier, smarter. There was always somewhere to run, somewhere to hide, somewhere to blend in. Here, there was no safety anywhere. So I had to go with Eric to the place he knew, because

I didn't want to die alone. I didn't want MD to have to live with that. I had to trust that if MD had sent Eric, he had a good reason and I trusted MD with my life, my heart, my entire existence.

I held on tight as Eric swung the buggy around and went in the opposite direction to Sienna's hut. She must have gotten a message from Brad or she'd have come back by now. I hoped she hadn't run into Neil or Joanne. I prayed for it, even though it had been a long time since I'd believed in a God. Believing in anything other than myself wasn't a luxury I could afford in my life and after so much tragedy and so much pain, God made no sense at all. But then I thought of MD and I believed, in something, what I couldn't be sure. But he was my something good and I was glad that everything was coming to a head and that all of this would be over soon. That MD would sort out whatever we were leaving behind and when it was over MD would come to me and everything would be okay.

Eric drove the buggy towards the back of the property, over jagged pathways the guests didn't use, between bushy trees, behind storage buildings, past the orchards and the vegetable gardens, down a rugged hill and through some more bushes with big and bushy branches that whacked me in the face as he squeezed the buggy between them.

Finally, he stopped, suddenly breaking in front of a shed made out of rusted tin and partly concealed in overgrowth. 'You'll be safe here,' he said, his voice hoarse from the wind and the bugs. 'Come on,' he said, getting out.

I followed him into the shed. How on earth would anyone find it? They wouldn't. Which was the point, I supposed. He'd done well to find something so well hidden. You'd have to know the area, know the land to hope to find it. Neil and Aunt Joanne would never find me here, I thought gratefully.

The inside of the shed was just dirt, a few forgotten planks of wood and old tyres covered in cobwebs piled in the corners. He led me to the back wall where he pushed a pane of tin behind a rotting workbench aside. He climbed under the bench, over the footrest and squeezed through the gap he'd made in the tin, his flexible body bending without any trouble. Holding out his hand, he helped me through. I took his hand and followed him in a little less gracefully. This bloke understood hiding better than me, I thought as I squished through and he let the tin fall back into place.

It was dark. Pitch dark. I couldn't see a thing. I couldn't see my finger in front of my face. 'Where are we?' I asked, nervously.

'You're fine. You're safe. I promise,' Eric insisted, lighting a small gas lantern.

I'd feel safer if I could see the room, the way out. I didn't like being confined. I didn't do well when I felt trapped. But the light from the lantern only lit the immediate area. There were a couple of chairs leftover from the '70's, clean, upholstered in an orange red, timber arms, a coffee table and that was all I could see.

'Sit, please,' he insisted kindly as though I were a guest in his home.

I sat, cautiously. I'd expected an inconspicuous shed at the back of the property used for storing stuff and hiding in a corner of it until MD could come for me. I had the sneaking suspicion MD would never find me here. The furniture looked too well cared for, too carefully placed for it to be any kind of store room. I looked around but my eyes were lost in the infinite darkness so I watched Eric instead, trying to gauge, I don't know, something.

He took the lantern over to a workbench with a gas stove. He poured a tin of baked beans into a small, dented pot and hummed as he stirred. 'You must be hungry. Mel had gone to get food,' he said, conversationally.

'You saw her?' I asked.

'Sure, she was with Carmichael. She'll be safe with him. You've no need to worry,' he said again, before humming happily.

He toasted some bread over the open flame of the second burner and smeared the toast with butter before pouring half the baked beans onto each plate with toast.

He brought one of the plates over, carrying the lantern in his spare hand. I had a sudden thought that if I wanted to, I could incapacitate him at that moment. I couldn't put my finger on why I'd need to though. He was being kind. Helpful. But something made me nervous. Looking around left me feeling utterly disorientated. I couldn't remember from which way we'd come, which panel it was that moved. How long would it take me to find it? How long would it take him to regain his senses and his footing? But again, why would I need to run? He was helping me.

I had no reason to suspect Eric of anything. He'd been kind and friendly and flirtatious. Then I remembered that one night at the surf club when he'd manhandled me and wouldn't take no for an answer, even when I'd told him about MD. Then there was MD, Brad and Rick and their incessant grumbling and cursing every time we mentioned Eric's name. But why? He was a good, kind man. He worked at the retreat. He was a yogi and didn't they all believe in peace and kindness? I had no reason not to trust him. Other than this something in the pit of my stomach. This something I'd trusted for a long time, this sixth sense that had kept me safe all these years.

So what if he had some slightly creepy shed buried in the bush to hide in. I bet all country people did. I bet Mel had some secret place she liked to hide in growing up in her commune. Everyone needed a place, a quiet, special place of their own, didn't they? I had no place. I'd had the old lady's house, I supposed. Even though it only existed in my head now, I'd gone there when times were tough at home. When Peter and Jo were giving me too much grief, I'd hide in her bushes. I'd even slept in the bushes once, in a little ditch when I was too afraid to go home. Eric probably did the same growing up. Why wouldn't he? Everyone had some kind of trouble they needed to be free of for a few hours. So I took the beans and toast Eric offered me and began eating as he walked back to the bench to get his own.

As he returned with his plate, something began scratching about deep in the dark. Eric held up the lantern to see what it was and a marsupial of some sort scurried away but as he lowered the lantern, I glimpsed a wrought iron bed in the corner and I broke out into a sweat but the lantern was back to his front before I could see anything more.

'It's just a quiet place I come to think and work. I've been coming here since I was a kid,' Eric offered without my having asked as he sat and began eating his beans.

See, just as I thought, I tried telling myself. I was just overreacting because of everything that was going on. He was just being helpful. This was his quiet place and he'd shared it with me to keep me safe. I should be grateful not suspicious.

We ate our beans quietly then we tried to talk but there wasn't much to say. I was finding the dark overwhelming. I hated not being able to see around me. Even outside, in the middle of the night, in the middle of the bush, there were the stars and the moon. In here there was nothing and despite the assurances I kept telling myself, my stomach twitched and turned. But with the stress and the nothingness and the dark and my long night and morning of lovely shenanigans with MD, I was too tired to think anymore. There was nothing I could do anyway. It was Eric. I was safe. I had to trust in that. Mel trusted him, so could I. So I did and I let the dark claim me and I fell asleep in the chair.

CHAPTER 23

W aking, slowly, I didn't feel right. I felt queasy, my head hazy, fuzzy, slightly incoherent. My body was heavy, as though weighted with lead, so heavy, I couldn't feel my muscles or my bones. I felt numb. My eyelids scraped like sandpaper as I forced them to open over my eyeballs.

It was dark, too dark, and I remembered I was in Eric's secret shed. I tried to sit up but I was stuck. My heavy body wouldn't move. I pulled my arms, my legs, trying to get them to work, confused as to why they wouldn't but I could barely feel them and they wouldn't move. I pulled and pulled my arm and the bed rattled. I realised then my shoulders were stretched, uncomfortable, forced into an odd angle and slowly, recognition dawned. Handcuffs shackled me to that wrought iron bed.

I looked down at my body but it was too dark, I couldn't see anything in the dark.

'You're okay. Stop pulling or you'll hurt yourself,' Eric called from somewhere in that dark.

'What have you done?' I asked, unsure the raspy, shaky voice that came out was even mine.

'I'm keeping you safe,' he insisted. 'I'm protecting you from yourself. From those around you. You'll see. You'll thank me when this is all over. I can keep you safe like no one else. I told you that. I promised you,' he told me.

'MD never sent you to get me, did he?' I asked, feeling stupid.

'MD wouldn't give me the time of day. MD doesn't deserve you, Jilly. MD doesn't deserve anyone. I don't know how you could go to bed with him. The only explanation is that he has coerced you, has some sort of hold over you. You needed saving from him, protecting from him.'

'You're protecting me from MD?'

'Of course.'

'You're not worried about my brother? My aunt?'

He laughed. 'Absolutely not. Those fools haven't got a clue. They'll never find you here. No one will find you here,' he said, proudly.

My blood went cold. Ice pumped through my veins. I'd rather face Jo and Neil than this deluded psycho. MD had warned me. Warned all of us and I'd ignored him. Laughed with the others thinking it was just stupid male pride. Did MD know about this place? Know who Eric was, that he was a psycho? I doubted it. It was probably just a suspicion, which is why no one ever said anything concrete.

'Why me?' I asked, desperately wanting to know what it was about me that attracted psychos. What had I done to encourage Eric? Nothing that I could think of. I'd been clear that I wasn't interested and he had to have heard about my past, who I was, that I'd killed a man and walked away. That had to matter.

'Why not you?' he asked as though none of that mattered. 'You're beautiful and fuckable. Why not you?' he asked.

'Fair enough,' I said, thinking if I agreed with his deluded reasoning, didn't piss him off, there might still be a way out. I couldn't face a Peter scenario again. I couldn't. His face haunted me every day, no matter that he was scum. I'd killed him. I'd seen life leave his eyes, his face go slack and all the blood pouring out of his body and it haunted me. I closed my eyes to the images but only saw them clearer. I couldn't do it again. I couldn't fight again.

How would I defend myself, anyway? I was cuffed to a bed. I now knew they were cuffs as feeling slowly came back to my arms and I felt the cold of the metal against my skin. He'd drugged me with my beans. That was clear now too.

I couldn't sense if I had my clothes on. If he'd already raped me. My body hadn't yet regained all of its feeling, which was probably a good thing. But if he hadn't and he tried, I couldn't fight him, even if I could somehow get free. I couldn't. He was stronger than I was and all that yoga and muscle strengthening would overpower me in an instant. I'd only survived Peter because of Jo's gun obsession.

I should have taken my chance when Eric had had his hands full, when he held the lantern in one hand and the beans in the other. But still, how would I have found the one single panel of tin that moved in amongst all the others, in the dark so dark I couldn't see my own nose, before he'd regained his footing?

I had no idea how long I'd slept but I could feel the cold of night seeping through the tin, coming up through the dirt. MD would be looking for me. I'd sent him that text. I'd sent it to thank him, to tell him something I'd desperately wanted him to know but he would have received it and been confused. It would have set off an alarm.

Mel and Sienna would have called him, told him I was gone. He'd be looking for me in the cool night but he wouldn't find me here, buried in the back of a forgotten, rusted shed hidden in the bush. Even if they opened the shed, all they'd see was a wasteland of rusting tin and a couple of old tyres covered in cobwebs. There'd be nothing to suggest there was a secret panel in the tin, a secret room hidden at the back. The bushes outside would make sure the extra space was concealed. No one would think to look any further than what they could see. Why would they? Decades of bush growth veiled it all. He'd probably planted the trees himself. He seemed mad enough.

As the cold air seeped, as it crept over my body, I felt it snake around parts of my body it shouldn't have been able to reach, parts I only ever wanted MD to be touching and I knew he'd taken my clothes, that he'd stripped me bare. Was it for his pleasure or practicalities? To keep me from running naked into the bush, into the night? Did he think that would keep me here? It wouldn't. If he thought it would then he was seriously underestimating my survival instincts. I'd happily run into bush naked but I couldn't run anywhere while I was shackled to the bloody bed.

At the reminder, fear raced through my body, hot, cold while my heart pounded in my chest. I was trapped. I didn't like being trapped. My body, my instincts wanted to run, but I was stuck and I couldn't breathe. I had to breathe. I had to focus, think, figure something out.

I focussed on my breathing, calmed myself. Are you okay, Jilly? Check that first, I told myself. I focussed on each of my body parts, everything appeared to still be connected, immobile, but in working order. I was afraid to mentally check my most vulnerable parts but I had to, I had to know. I didn't hurt, in my lady parts. They felt intact and untouched. That was a relief. It was something. I could have coped with a broken arm, a broken face, anything but that, not again, not without my knowing.

I felt him move before I heard him. Just soft scuffs in the dirt. I felt him looming over me, heard the long, slow, intake of breath and the careful exhalation. I waited for him to do something but he did nothing. He inhaled again, exhaled again. Then, unexpectedly, his icy cold finger touched the instep of my foot, then he began trailing that cold finger up the soft inside of my leg, the cold of it burning the path it took.

I contracted all my muscles so tight I thought they'd snap, preparing for the inevitable. The inevitable I had no control over, that I couldn't stop. I couldn't run. I couldn't scream. I couldn't fight. I shivered with fear.

'Relax, shhhh...' he soothed.

My eyes filled with tears. Hot tears rolled down my face. I couldn't see him. He hadn't brought the lantern with him. I could only feel him and it was more terrifying than anything I'd known. More terrifying than Peter. I'd had a chance against him. I'd fought him. I stood no chance against Eric.

His hand inched close to my lady parts and the fear was too much. I felt the warmth of my urination pool around me, smelt it as it wafted around us. Shame filled my body but still, there was nothing I could do.

'Shhh...' He soothed again, gently pushing some stray hair off my face before leaving me.

He returned with a towel, warm and wet and wiped me clean,

placed a dry towel under me. I turned my head to the side, closed my eyes, even though I couldn't see him.

He rested his hand on my pubic bone, his fingers flayed as he sucked in air through his teeth as though it was taking every ounce of his being to restrain himself.

My insides shook, they rattled as ice cold blood pumped ferociously through my veins. I couldn't tell if the rest of my body was shaking, I was losing feeling. I was losing cognitive thought. I was drifting, off to my happy place. It was the only way I knew how to survive.

I drifted to the room with pale pink wallpaper with tiny white flowers. It was coming off at the corners and some patches were more faded than others. You could see where there'd once been a bigger bed, where now there was just a single white Queen Anne bed. The bed covers had been dusty when I moved in but that hadn't taken much to fix. I'd even washed them while the old lady had been away. It was a nice room. White Queen Anne furniture held empty drawers and coat hangers and sat under layers of protective dust. I never saw the furniture taken away. I hoped someone had taken it, maybe whoever it was she visited at the other end of her Greyhound voyage, perhaps a cherished granddaughter who'd never had the pleasure of visiting the mansion and staying in the lovely room with the pink wallpaper with tiny white flowers.

I jumped with fright as tin crashed to the floor, male voices shouted and Eric's weight fell suddenly across my legs and it ripped me away from my happy place.

I heard scuffing in the dirt and lots of harsh whispers but I couldn't see anything. Then a torch shone in my eyes. It was bright, too bright after so much darkness. I turned my head away, wishing I had a free arm to cover my face and protect my eyes.

'Jilly,' the familiar voice begged.

I turned, the light was no longer in my eyes but it lit my surroundings and right there in front of me was MD. His eyes were full of tears as he slowly came over to me, held my face in his hands. 'Are you okay? Please, be okay,' he whispered.

I found my voice, 'I'm okay,' I said quietly. 'I'm okay,' I assured him.

Someone undid the cuff around my wrists and ankles at the same time someone lit a lantern.

'Shit,' spat MD as he noticed my naked body. He ripped his t-shirt off and gently, carefully put it over my head.

'Should you really be doing that, MD?' asked Brad. 'You'll contaminate any evidence, mate,' he insisted.

'He didn't touch me,' I told them. 'I don't think. Not yet. He was just starting.'

MD finished covering me, his movements careful. He scooped me up in his arms and walked out through a panel someone had removed in the side of the shed, carrying me through the bushes to a nearby buggy and sat me in it.

'Are you okay?' he asked me again, trying to look me over for evidence to the contrary.

'Yes. I think so,' I told him.

He kissed my forehead and held me to his bare chest. 'Good. Because I couldn't breathe if anything happened to you,' he said.

'How did you find me?' I asked.

'The buggy. Brad put trackers on them all when we arrived,' he told me.

'Is he...?' I asked unable to say the words.

'No,' he told me. 'Incapacitated. He's lucky Jase was in first or he would have been,' he grumbled.

I was relieved. I couldn't have that image in my head, not with Peter's already there. 'Why? Why did he do this to me? I thought he was helping me.'

'Baby, I don't know. But we've suspected him of things, we just didn't have any proof. But I didn't know this, I promise. I'm just sorry I took so long. I'd been following your brother's breadcrumbs all morning, he had me halfway down the coast when I got your message, but I swear, I'd have locked Eric up a long time ago if I'd known any of this,' he insisted.

'Well, I'm glad I could help,' I said, trying to smile.

He held me to him so tightly, I thought my bones might crumble. 'Come on, let me take you home.'

'Home?' I asked hopefully.

'Well, that hut we're calling a home. It should still be safe. I lost your brother when I got your SMS it took me a while to get back, track down Brad and get a trace on the buggy,' he rambled. 'I love you too, by the way.'

I grinned stupidly as he drove up the rugged hill and headed for our temporary home.

CHAPTER 24

———

By the time we reached the bungalow, the adrenalin had worn off and I was numb. I felt heavy and hazy, incoherent, as though my brain had totally vacated my head and gone somewhere else.

'You okay?' MD asked when I didn't move.

I'd forgotten him. 'Ahuh,' I said, trying to smile.

I stepped out of the buggy but my legs gave way.

'Hey, hey,' soothed MD as he caught me. 'It's alright, I've got you,' he said, scooping me into his arms.

My head lolled against his shoulder. I could feel it but I couldn't move it. I'd lost all capability to control my own body. What did that mean? I wanted to ask but I could feel a lump in my throat and knew that as soon as I spoke, it would be all over.

A white-haired gentleman, because he looked every bit the gentleman, sat on the couch in our hut. Sienna and Mel hovered in the kitchen fussing around and I could hear Rick and Brad talking somewhere, more mumbling quietly but I couldn't see them, not without moving my head and it wouldn't move.

The gentleman stood to make space for me on the couch and I noticed a stethoscope swinging around his neck.

Sienna placed a hot cup of sweet tea in my hands but they shook and the hot tea slopped over the sides, so she took it away and mopped the spilt tea with a tissue. She held the mug to my mouth instead and I took a few soothing sips before she put it on the coffee table. 'This is Dr Price. He's the retreat's doctor. He's going to have a look at you, okay,' she said.

I tried to nod, but my head still wouldn't work. I could feel the panic building in my tummy. Fear. Why couldn't I speak? Why wouldn't my body work? I tried sucking in air, one, two, three, it was too much, too fast. My eyes found MD's and I felt better. I could breathe.

'Hey, easy,' he said, squatting before me, placing a calming hand on my shoulder. 'Easy,' he whispered.

'Shall I get started?' asked Dr Price.

'Can we get some space?' asked MD.

Everyone quietly went out the front door and it was just the three of us.

'I'm going to give Dr Price some room, but I'm right here, okay?' MD insisted as he went to stand by my feet.

Dr Price attached his blood pressure cuff to my arm and inflated it, noting the results. Then flashed his light in my eyes and throat. 'I need to take the shirt off,' he said quietly and kindly.

MD helped him take it off and I felt the panic rising up again. I was naked and vulnerable, again. Tears spilled over. I couldn't stop them. I couldn't stop anything.

'Shhhhh...' MD whispered, holding my hand.

'I'll be as quick as I can, dear,' assured Dr Price, kindly.

He ran his flashlight over my body. I could feel more tears

pricking at the back of my eyes. I wasn't going to be able to hold them off much longer. I turned my head to the side and found enough strength to grip MD's hands. I knew I was safe but it didn't matter, I felt the fear all over again, felt the dark, felt Eric's cold hands on my body.

Dr Price finished his search. 'Did he...?' he asked.

I shook my head as best I could, but I still couldn't speak. The lump in my throat was too big, it felt like a dam was about to burst and whatever happened once it did, I'd be powerless to stop. He checked anyway as part of his exam and I just kept my eyes on MD.

'Well, she looks okay,' Dr Price told MD. 'But she appears to be in shock. I'll give her something to help her sleep and I'll stop by tomorrow morning. She may experience some depression as well so just go easy on her for the next couple of days, let her set the pace of what feels okay but don't let her sink too deep if you can, you call me if you need.'

Dr Price injected me with something then left. MD laid his discarded t-shirt over my naked body, scooped me up and carried me to bed.

I heard the lock clicking into place and the others leaving. MD took off his jeans then he was in the bed beside me. He held me to him, held me so tightly, I could no longer hold back the bursting dam and I sobbed. Hot tears soaked my face, soaked MD's chest.

'It's okay, let it out,' he whispered. 'You're okay now. You're safe,' he promised.

I wanted to grip onto him and never let go. I'd never felt so safe. I felt, for the first time since my parents died, that nothing could touch me, that nothing could destroy me as long as MD was beside me.

I eventually fell into a medicated sleep to the soothing shhhh...of MD's voice. Whatever Dr Price had given me blocked out all the dreams I'd expected to haunt my sleep. But there was nothing and when I woke, sun steamed in around the curtains. MD still held me tightly, as though too terrified to even roll over.

He stirred as I stirred. 'You okay?' he asked, his voice heavy with sleep.

'Mmm...' I mumbled, because I still wasn't exactly sure if I was or not.

'Do you need anything?' he asked. 'Water? Food? You must be starving,' he said.

'Water?' I asked.

He left the bed to get it and I wished I hadn't asked for anything. I wished he had stayed in the bed. Fear rumbled in my tummy and it wasn't until he returned that it stopped. This wasn't good. I couldn't be this dependent on him. But I was and I couldn't stop it. Not now.

He helped me to sit up and I drank the whole glass.

'Better?' he asked.

'Better,' I smiled.

'Anything else?' he asked.

'Clean. I need to be clean,' I mumbled, suddenly feeling disgusting and filthy now that I had my cognitive senses back.

I tried to stand, but my legs wouldn't hold my weight.

'It's okay,' he said, lowering me back onto the bed.

He left me for a moment and I heard the taps in the bathroom turn on. He came back for me, held me up, his arm around me, taking my weight as he led me to the bathroom. The bath was filling, bubbles forming. He held my elbow with one hand and my waist with another as I stepped over the lip of the bath and he lowered me into the water. He did away with his trunks and lowered himself in behind me, his arms under mine to keep me from sinking.

He squirted some body wash onto a puff and limb by limb, he cleaned me as I quietly sobbed, sobbed for the position I was in, that I was incapable of washing myself, because finally, after everything, I had MD who was cleaning me without question, without me asking. He was caring for me like I was a broken baby bird and he hadn't questioned it, he didn't baulk at the task, he just stepped up.

MD dried me when we were done and dressed me in track pants and a hoodie Mel had brought over from the retreat gift shop. He carried me to the sofa, laid me on it. 'I'm just going to make some toast, okay? You want tea? Coffee?' he asked.

'Coffee,' I whispered.

I stared at the black television screen while I listened to MD moving around in the kitchen. I was numb. My brain was silent. I had nothing, no brain power or energy to make my body do anything other than stare at the blank screen.

I felt like one of those people with those diseases where they can see and hear what's going on around them but they can't move, they can't speak. That's how I felt and I wondered if it would ever pass. If I would ever feel like a person again. If I'd ever be able to be alone again, afraid I would trust the untrustworthy. If I'd ever be able to look at myself in the mirror with anything other than revulsion and disgust.

Sure, none of it was my fault. Not Peter, not Eric. But still, I was a person who'd been broken down to nothing too many times. I didn't know if I'd be able to rebuild myself again. If I'd ever look at myself again and see me, or if I'd always see what they'd tried to do, who they thought I was, who they wanted me to be. A victim. A nothingness victim. A thing with no soul. A person with nothing more to offer than the appropriate body parts.

Would I ever be able to be touched again without thinking of Eric's cold fingers on my instep? The next time MD touched the soft skin of my inner thigh, would I shudder with revulsion?

'Stop thinking,' he told me, putting my coffee on the table and making me look at him.

He wiped some stray tears from my cheek. 'It wasn't your fault, Jilly,' he told me.

'You told me. About Eric,' I whispered. 'I didn't listen,' I sobbed quietly.

'Shhhh...' he soothed. 'I should have said more. It doesn't matter. None of it was your fault. Or mine or anyone's. He's good at what he does. We thought he was just a dick that went too far, got a bit too obsessive. There was never any proof and the girls always went somewhere else. A couple disappeared but their social media remained active. We had no proof other than a couple of detectives with a gut feeling.'

'I should have known better. My guards were down,' I said, realising that's what had happened. 'I'd gotten too comfortable. I'd forgotten to protect myself. And bloody hell he was convincing.'

'It's okay, Jilly. You don't ever have to put your guards up again. I'm here. I've got you,' he said, pulling me to him and letting me cry.

'Come, eat, drink, before it all gets cold,' he said, when I'd stopped sobbing.

He put some pillows behind me and made me sit while I ate toast and sipped coffee. The coffee went down like a healing potion and the toast with vegemite was familiar and comforting and slowly I felt myself coming back, feeling in my limbs, in my fingertips, my voice and sight returning to normal.

'Thank you,' I told MD.

'For what?' he asked.

'For being here. For everything. For saving me,' I told him.

He smiled. 'Always.'

When I'd finished my toast, MD allowed me to sleep. He covered me with a blanket and sat in the armchair with his laptop, working. I drifted in and out for I don't know how long but he was still there every time I stirred.

He woke me sometime late in the afternoon and made me drink some water and eat some soup Carmichael had sent over before carrying me to the bed and letting me sleep some more.

He was beside me, sleeping when I woke with the sun. I watched him, wondering how that perfect man could love me. Me. But he'd said it and he'd shown me and still I couldn't believe it. Would he still love me when he couldn't touch me? The thought of being touched, even by MD, cooled the blood in my veins, sending shivers of fear along my skin.

I closed my eyes on another wave of hot tears. No matter what I did, my life just kept fucking up. I thought once killing Peter was out, once that life was out and done I could move forward. But I wondered if I'd ever be free, if there would always be something, some psycho waiting to destroy me?

MD pulled me close. I could feel his hot skin against my cheek, his beating heart. 'It's okay, I've got you. I'm not going anywhere,' he whispered.

'But MD, what if...'

'What if what, Jilly? No what ifs,' he said.

'I don't know if I can ever be touched, MD,' I whispered.

'Hey,' he said, tilting my face to his. 'I would wait forever for you, and even then some. Don't you go worrying about it. I'm here. I've got you. I'm not leaving,' he insisted, kissing my forehead.

I gripped on to him as though he were the only thing that was keeping me together and I breathed.

'Come, you need to shower and eat,' he said.

'No. I'm just going to sleep a little more,' I said, rolling over.

'No, Jilly. Shower, eat, then you can sleep on the couch.'

'Why can't I just sleep now?' I begged.

'Because it's not good for you. I promise, a quick shower, some toast and you can sleep until lunch time.'

I nodded. I didn't have the energy to fight him. I had no fight left, so I let him lead me to the shower.

He turned on the taps, checked the temperature. He took off the t-shirt I'd slept in, my knickers and held my hand as I stepped into the shower.

'Do you need me?' he asked.

I shook my head but I didn't move, I couldn't move. I couldn't lift my arms to pick up the puff or the body wash or the shampoo. I just stood under the hot running water. Was it shock or something else? Everything just felt too heavy, my brain too fuzzy and nothing was working right.

'Let me help you,' he said, taking off his boxers and stepping into the shower.

He squirted soap onto the puff and washed me. Shampoo into his palm and lathered my hair and then conditioner.

I stepped into the towel he offered when we were done and let him dry me. I had to find some strength. I couldn't keep needing him to wash me. But my arms just wouldn't work. They wouldn't do as I asked, so I let him dress me in the track pants and hoodie from the day before.

He draped his arm across my shoulder and helped me walk to the sofa. My legs were working, that had to be a start, right?

He turned the television on while he went to make coffee and toast. I watched the cheery presenters of a morning show laughing about something I didn't hear. Tears filled my eyes as I wondered if I'd ever laugh again.

I took a breath and calmed myself as the toast popped. I didn't want MD seeing me cry again. I had to start pulling myself together.

'Here,' he said, sitting me up and putting the plate of toast in my lap and the steaming coffee on the coffee table.

The rest of the day was a repeat of the day before. Me sleeping on the couch, MD working in the chair keeping watch over me.

I woke to a soft knock with the dark creeping in through the door. I heard MD's mumbled voice and the door close.

He sat at the end of the sofa and I sat up, the most movement I'd felt able to do in days. 'Who was it?' I asked, pleased I'd been able to form a question, have a cognitive thought, even though I'd asked it quietly.

'Mel, she brought us food,' he said, unpacking the containers from the paper bag she'd given him.

'What is it?' I asked, feeling hungrier than I had in days and suddenly hoping it was those patties or that sweet potato soup.

'Patties, mash potato, maybe, with Carmichael you can never tell,' he joked.

I smiled.

'Well, hello there,' he smiled back. 'I'll get some plates,' he said, patting my leg tenderly.

I scoffed the food. I couldn't help it. I'd eaten nothing but toast and soup for days. And Eric's beans before that. I didn't think I'd ever eat beans again but I was glad my appetite had returned. Perhaps there was hope for some normality after all.

'Slow down, you'll make yourself sick,' MD smiled, clearly as happy as me at my returning appetite.

'What else is there?' I asked when I'd finished.

'You're still hungry?' he asked, surprised.

'I'm not sure, depends on what else there is,' I said, not feeling particularly hungry but still, not entirely satisfied.

'There's a thermos of something,' he said, picking it up. 'It could be more soup,' he warned as he opened it, smelt it. 'Nope, not soup. Here,' he said, letting me smell it.

'Hot chocolate?' I asked, not trusting my own sense of smell or perhaps not trusting that Carmichael would really have hot chocolate in his kitchen.

He nodded. 'Want some?'

'I do,' I said, again, happy that I really did.

I snuggled against him as we sipped our hot chocolates, made with almond milk, not real milk. It was Carmichael, after all, and slowly, bit by bit, I began to feel like a person again.

MD turned the telly on and we watched *Friends* reruns and MD talked, and I felt the smallest bubble of happiness lurking somewhere deep in my belly. I was going to be okay. Because of MD, I was going to be okay.

I was falling asleep against him when he said, 'Come on, bed,' and I followed him to our bed without even needing him to hold me up.

He took my hoodie off and helped me with my pants but I knew it wouldn't be long and I'd have enough strength to do it myself. Hope, that's what was taking up residence inside me.

He pulled me to him after he'd turned out the light and I slept with that hope filling me.

CHAPTER 25

I showered alone in the morning having found some strength in my limbs, rediscovered the ability to make them move as I wanted.

We were on the couch, sipping coffee, my legs stretched across MD's lap, for long enough that the sun no longer streamed through windows. There was a quiet knock on the door. MD got up to open it and let in Sienna.

'Mitch, we have a problem,' she said in an attempted whisper standing in the doorway.

I could see Brad hovering protectively just outside the door. 'What's going on?' I asked Sienna as she stood in front of us hopping anxiously from one foot to the other.

'Oh hey, Jilly, how are you feeling?' she asked.

I shrugged. 'Better, I suppose. What's going on?' I asked again.

'Nothing,' she insisted, stepping outside.

MD followed her out but left the door open. I could still hear Sienna even though she was still attempting a whisper. 'You have to see this,' she told him and I heard the rustling of a newspaper as it switched hands.

A moment or two passed before MD muttered, 'Shit,'

'Can you just come inside and tell me?' I begged. 'No more secrets, MD,' I insisted.

'She's right,' he said as he led Brad and Sienna inside.

He handed me the newspaper. I read the headline, 'Sydney Adams found at last.' I read on and it told the world that I, Sydney Adams, wanted for the murder of Peter Roberts, had been found in the shed of yogi, Eric Murray and had been carried away by the police and was being kept under guard by local detective, MD Harris, in a bungalow at the retreat.

I handed the newspaper back to MD and lay down on the couch.

'Are you okay?' he asked.

I shrugged. 'They're just words. Not even correct words at that. But just words. I don't care about them. I care that Neil now knows where I am. If he didn't already.'

MD squatted before me. 'I'll keep you safe, Jilly. I promise. I'm not going to let anything happen to you,' he insisted, holding my hands for emphasis.

I smiled because I knew he meant it. I knew he'd try. He'd do anything he could to protect me. But at the end of the day, it wouldn't be enough. I knew it wouldn't be enough. Not for me. Not for Sienna and Mel. Not for anyone. And I couldn't bear the thought of any of them getting hurt. Of MD getting hurt protecting me because I knew he'd do anything, risk anything to protect me and I couldn't let him. I couldn't let it get that far.

Despite Sienna begging to stay, Brad sent her, Mel and Rick to a hotel. Sienna knew it was the right thing to do. That they would be safer and Brad and MD could concentrate, but she protested anyway because she was a good person, a good friend. Even though Brad and MD were staying behind, she didn't want to leave me. It was sweet. It was nice. Mel had insisted on organising some food on her way out but then they were gone and it was quiet.

After serving us up lunch sent over by Carmichael, there wasn't much else to do but watch television in companionable silence.

The three of us were watching television in the afternoon, pretending everything was okay as we stared at the pictures of retro reruns with a young Ted Danson when a commotion outside interrupted our silence.

Brad went over to the window, peeking out of the curtains as he said something into his walkie talkie. I couldn't understand the staticky response. I don't know how they communicated with those things.

Brad nodded at MD who then threw my legs off his lap and said, 'Stay here. Don't move,' as he followed Brad to the door.

They closed the door behind them but I could still hear a lot of shouting and wondered what the hell was going on. It couldn't be Neil because there'd be bullets flying by now.

I disobeyed MD and went to the door and looked out through the peephole. When I recognised the poor bugger at the centre of the commotion, I opened the door.

'Guys, come on, leave him be,' I begged.

'Jilly? Jilly, are you okay?' Michael begged, rushing to me, holding my shoulders as he looked me over.

MD closed in, his face thunderous as he gently took Michael's hands off me.

'You should probably come inside,' I said, trying not to smirk at MD's jealous protectiveness.

'Jilly...' growled MD.

'You want me to do this out here, in front of all of them?' I asked, indicating all the police in front of our hut.

'Fine,' he conceded, storming into the hut with Brad.

I followed and Michael followed.

'What's going on, Jilly? Are you okay? You know they can't keep you like this. I'll fly up the best lawyer in Sydney,' he said, pulling me to him.

'Hey, hey, no manhandling,' insisted MD, offering Michael the armchair while MD and Brad sat either side of me on the couch.

'It's not like that Michael, they're protecting me.'

'Right, from your brother. So it's true? You really are this, Sydney Adams?' he asked heartbroken.

'I'm sorry, Michael. I never meant to hurt you. If any of this comes down on you, affects your career, I'll never forgive myself. I know how hard you've worked for it.'

'I don't give a fuck about my career, Jilly. I care about you,' he said. 'Why didn't you just tell me? I would have protected you from all of it.'

'I couldn't take that risk,' I told him.

'How did they find you?'

'I was at the same restaurant my brother robbed. They found my prints. MD recognised me in the photo,' I told him.

MD looked at me sadly, apologetically and put his hand on my knee.

Michael looked from MD's hand to my face and I watched as realisation dawned on him that I was no longer his.

'Jilly...what's going on? Are you with him? That cop. How long?'

'Michael I'm so sorry. I didn't plan to move on this fast. I didn't plan to be romantically involved with anyone for a long time after I left you. It just happened.'

'But what about us?' he asked, hopefully.

I shook my head. 'I'm sorry. I really never meant to hurt you. I love MD. He's the love of my life,' I told him, trying not to smile too much when I said it because it felt so good to say it out loud.

'You don't love me?' he asked, sadly. 'Did you ever love me or was I just a means to an end?' he asked, getting angry.

'It wasn't like that. I liked you, Michael. You're a good person. But you and me, we're not meant for each other.'

'We were perfect for each other,' he disputed.

'No, we weren't. It was just our secrets that made us perfect together. I accepted things I wouldn't have ordinarily. It was only because of who I am that I let it go for as long as I did.'

'You know?' he asked.

I nodded with a tight smile. 'I know.'

He nodded sadly.

'You should see someone about it, Michael. You don't have to live the way you do. See someone and then when you're better, you should ask Sarah to dinner, she's hopelessly in love with you, she won't mind you're a little broken,' I told him.

'Sarah? My assistant?'

'She'd be good for you if you let her, if you didn't have to hide who you were anymore. Trust me, it's liberating,' I smiled.

He smiled. 'I bet. It must have been hard not letting anyone in. Not letting me in. I really had no idea you weren't who you said you were. What made you leave when you did? I was worried bloody sick, by the way,' he said.

'I know. I knew you would be and I'm really sorry. I found the ring.'

'How?' then it dawned. 'You knew about that, too?' he asked surprised.

I laughed. 'Sorry, I hated snooping. I found the false bottom quite by accident one day when I was putting away your washing.

He nodded and shook his head. 'Yet you stayed anyway. It wasn't all about hiding, was it?' he asked.

'Of course not. You're a good man. You were good to me and we had a great life together. But you have to be true to yourself for a relationship to work and neither of us was being true about anything.'

'Clean up and get real you say?'

'You'll feel like a whole new man,' I promised him. 'And that Sarah might just surprise you,' I smiled knowingly. Sarah had confided after a few cocktails her penchant for the naughty.

'Right, then. Well I suppose I should go if you're sure you're okay?'

'I am. I really am sorry you came all the way up here. And I'm sorry…about everything.'

He nodded and smiled tightly. 'It's okay. I'm glad I got some closure. I really was worried. Call me, if you need anything at all, won't you?'

'I will, thank you,' I said, getting up and hugging him goodbye.

After he'd left, we went back to being quiet. We watched television quietly and we ate quietly. I suspected they were thinking the same thing I was. If Michael found me that quickly, then Neil and Jo wouldn't be far behind.

I watched MD sleep beside me. His face beautiful and soft in sleep and my heart swelled in ways I never thought humanly possible. I would do anything for him. I'd give my life for his. I loved him. I had to protect him.

I slipped out of the bed as easily as I could and put on my track pants and hoodie with the retreat's fluorescent logo on it and went into the other room. Brad was lying on the couch under a blanket.

Brad had the television on, the sound so low it was just a whisper.

'Brad, it's time,' I told him.

'For what?' he asked.

'Something drastic,' I told him. 'It's time to use me to draw them out, get this over with. I need it to be over Brad.'

'MD will never allow it,' he said. 'There's no way MD's leaving this bungalow without you.'

'Don't you outrank him?' I asked.

He laughed. 'You've met MD, right?' he joked.

'I don't care, it's for his own good.'

'It doesn't matter. I won't go against MD on this. If anything happened to you after Eric, it would kill him. No, Jilly. No.'

'We have to do something, Brad, I can't just sit here and do nothing. The waiting is killing me, doesn't that matter to anyone?' I asked, tears filling my eyes.

'Hey,' he said, jumping off the couch and wrapping me in his arms. 'It's going to be okay. We won't let anyone hurt you. You have to trust us, Jilly. We've got this. We've got you. It's easier for us to manage it here, get it done rather than move you and risk involving the public. Trust us.'

I nodded into his chest.

'Okay, now just go back to bed, alright? We'll figure it out tomorrow. Just get some sleep.'

'What's going on?' MD asked when I tried slipping silently back into bed.

'Nothing,' I lied, kissing him.

'Hmmm...,' he mumbled, knowing better.

MD woke me in the morning. 'Here,' he said, handing me a computer.

'What's this?' I asked.

'It's Mel's. Carmichael brought it over.'

'Carmichael's been?' I asked, wondering what treats he'd brought us.

MD smiled. 'Yes, there's food when you're ready.'

'So, what's the computer for?' I asked as I joined MD and Brad in the kitchenette where Brad had laid out the scrambled eggs, grilled mushrooms and tomatoes, turkey bacon and make-believe sausages. I saw a puddle of beans in tomato sauce in the bin.

'He didn't know,' MD said, following my eyes.

'You can still eat beans, you know,' I told him.

He kissed my forehead and handed me a plate of food.

'The computer?' I asked again, seeing as he'd closed the beans debate.

'Oh, Mel wanted you to use it so she can Skype you. They're worried about you and the only way we could keep them away was this,' he said.

I smiled. I missed them. 'I've never Skyped,' I admitted.

'It's okay, I'll show you. After. Eat,' he insisted.

MD showed me the basics I needed and connected me to the computer the girls were using.

'Hey!' they cried when they answered.

It was so good to see their faces cramped together on the computer screen I wanted to cry.

MD smiled, 'I'll leave you to it.'

'Hey,' I said back. 'How are you guys? I miss you,' I said, wishing they were in the room with me.

'What? Us? We're fine. How are you?' Mel demanded.

'I'm doing okay. I think. Much better, anyway,' I told them.

'Good. We've been so bloody worried about you,' Sienna added.

'Sorry I stole your man,' I told her.

'Ah, don't worry about,' she laughed waving me away.

'Really?' I asked, not believing her.

'Well, you know, make sure he's in one piece when he's done but really it's okay. I'm glad you've got the best of Noosa looking out for you,' she said.

'I just want it all over with,' I told them. 'I tried getting Brad to do something but he was having none of it,' I said frustrated.

'Good. Just listen to them, would you?' added Rick from the background. He stuck his face between Mel and Sienna's, 'Hey Jilly, you okay?' he asked.

'Yeah, I'm okay,' I told him.

'Good. You look better. Just keep resting and do as they say, would you?' he insisted.

'Yes, Boss,' I laughed.

'Now that's more like it,' he smiled. 'You ladies could learn a bit of something from Jilly here,' he joked.

Sienna pushed him away and he was gone.

'I'm really sorry about Eric,' said Mel sadly. 'I really didn't know,' she added.

'I know, Mel. Don't be sorry. It's fine. Well it's not your fault, anyway. None of us saw it. Saw who he was.'

'That's what I keep saying but she won't listen to me,' said Sienna.

'The boys did,' Mel said. 'I feel so stupid pushing him on you, talking about you with him.'

'Don't you dare let him steal your niceness, Mel. The boys could have said more. But still, they didn't even really know how bad he was. It's nobody's fault, Mel. It's definitely not yours. I should never have gone with him. MD told me not to be alone with him. I should have known he'd never have sent him.'

'It's not your fault either, Jilly,' said Sienna.

'I know. It's no one's fault but Eric's. But it's over with now. He didn't even touch me, just scared the crappers out of me. I'm doing okay. You have to let it go, Mel. Please. Promise me.'

She nodded, tears filling her eyes.

'Sienna can you hug her for me,' I asked, wishing I was there to hug her myself. Soon, I thought. It would have to be over soon, surely. 'Are they at least letting you guys out now and again?' I asked, trying to change the subject.

'No!' they both groaned.

'Rick practically has us under lock and key,' moaned Sienna.

'I'm sorry,' I told them.

'For what? Making my man go all caveman protective? Are you kidding? It's as sexy as hell,' Mel winked as Sienna rolled her eyes.

I laughed. 'Are you as bloody bored as I am?' I asked.

'At least we have each other,' Mel said. 'We wanted to stay there with you but MD said no. Said it would be too many people to worry about.'

'He's right,' I told them. 'But it doesn't stop me from being bored. Luckily I've slept for most of the last few days but now I'm feeling better the boredom's really kicking in.'

'You've slept that much?' asked Mel.

I nodded.

'Then we should stretch you out, do some yoga,' she suggested.

'That would be great,' I said.

'Alright. Give me a minute to set the computer up here. I left one of the mats in the cupboard in the hallway,' she said as the computer started moving.

I went and found the mat rolled up in the cupboard and came back. I moved the computer to the edge of the bed facing out so I could lay the mat on the floor and still see them.

'You're surprisingly flexible for someone who disputes the validity of all things hippy, you know,' I commented as Sienna kept up with Mel.

'That's because she does it all in secret,' giggled Mel.

'Well, I have to be ready for when hot men climb into my bed,' she smirked as we stood on one leg and reached for the sky.

I fell out of my pose I laughed so much. I don't know how Mel didn't. Practice, she tried telling me. 'God it feels good to laugh,' I told them.

'Oh Jilly, I wish we were there,' said Mel wishfully.

'We can hang out some more though, can't we?' I asked.

'Of course,' she said and we rearranged our computers again.

They both lay on their couch, their heads meeting in the middle so they both faced the computer. I lay on the bed and we chatted.

'So, how'd you get the name Jilly, anyway?' Sienna asked.

'I stole it. The old lady with the mansion had the biggest library you've ever seen. Crammed full of books, it was. Lots of romance, too and boy, did I learn some things,' I laughed. 'Anyway, Jilly Cooper was one of the authors and I liked the sound of it, so I stole it.'

'It really suits you,' Sienna said.

'Did you get really lonely?' asked Mel sadly.

'For a while. I didn't speak to anyone for a long time. Perhaps a couple of years. Sometimes I wanted to say hello to a bus driver or a check out chic but I knew I couldn't. I couldn't be remembered. I just had to be silent and invisible. It was hard,' I told them.

'That sounds so sad,' Mel said.

'I guess looking back it was, but at the time, it was just about survival and I was too busy looking over my shoulder to worry about friends. I think I was just glad for the quiet. To not have to live the life they'd made me live anymore. But after a while it got easier. After the old lady died, I had no choice about returning to the world. By then everyone had forgotten about Sydney Adams. I'd grown, I'd filled out, I didn't even recognise myself when I looked in the mirror. Me and my new identity jumped on a truck heading north and Jilly Cooper was born.'

'I wish I'd known you then,' said Mel. 'I wish I could have helped you,' she said.

'Thanks. I wish I'd known you too.'

'Although,' said Sienna with a smile. 'If you'd known Mel back then, you'd have been dragged into the commune and you'd be wearing homemade cotton smocks and farming your own vegetables.'

'You know, that doesn't sound too bad. It actually sounds a lot better than where I've been. And I wouldn't have had to sleep with men I hardly liked for a roof over my head,' I laughed.

'Oh no,' groaned Sienna. 'Were they really awful?' she asked.

'No, they weren't that bad,' I laughed. 'I do have some standards, you know.'

'It was survival, Jilly,' Mel reminded me.

'I know. I just wonder, how grossed out do you think MD will be by my past?'

'Pft,' scoffed Sienna. 'Like he can judge. You should see some of the filthy skanks he's gone home with.'

We all laughed and I felt better. They made me better.

We talked for a while longer but then we signed off. 'You look tired, Jilly,' said Mel. 'Go get some sleep and we'll call back later,' she said.

I was tired, but MD said it was too early to sleep. 'You need fresh air and something to eat first,' he insisted so I let him lead me out to the back courtyard that was secluded and private. Our own little piece of paradise.

CHAPTER 26

———

Feeling the sunshine was just what I needed, smelling the fresh air filled my soul.

'See, I told you,' MD smiled.

I smiled back because he was right and I felt like smiling.

'How about a cup of tea and some toast?' he offered.

'Mmmm... perfect,' I said, closing my eyes and breathing in deep.

The sun stroked my hands and a chill ran through my body and the shiver it brought startled me. I blinked into the sunshine. There was a rustling in the lush bush growth, 'It's an animal, stop it,' I told myself but then someone stepped out into the sunshine.

He stepped forward. 'Neil,' I gasped. He'd changed his look again. He'd coloured his hair brown, styled it like a yuppie, put on thick, black-rimmed glasses. The look suited him. But then, that's why he was so good at this, any look suited him.

'Hey, Neil. That's it?' he asked making sure I saw the gun on his hip.

'I'm supposed to say more?' I asked, trying to keep my voice even and quiet before MD came back and did something stupid.

'You're supposed to say, hey bro, good to see you. Here's your money. Sorry I ran off with it, it was just for safe keeping, I promise. Sorry I left you with a public defender to rot in gaol. Not hey Neil from some plush bed in some fucking overpriced bungalow after you've been helping the cops hunt us down, ruining a job we'd planned for bloody weeks,' he scoffed.

'Sorry about that,' I said with a smile to annoy him. Neil I could handle, he just wanted the money, Jo was a whole other pile of crazy.

'Sorry? Sorry? Jesus, DiDi, what the hell happened to you?' he asked keeping his voice low.

'Self-preservation,' I told him. 'And don't call me DiDi, you know I hate it.'

'Self-preservation? Is that why you killed Uncle Pete?' he asked, taking a step forward.

I shrugged to annoy him.

'Tell me, damn it,' he said, exploding forward and gripping my neck as though he wished he could pull my head off my shoulders.

'What does it matter to you?' I asked barely able to speak.

'It doesn't but Jo's pissed. You know she wants to kill you?'

'Let her try. I don't care anymore.'

I heard the toilet flush inside the bungalow. 'You want peppermint or one of these fancy blends?' MD called.

Neil held his finger to his mouth, moved to the side so MD couldn't see him through the window and pulled a knife out of his pocket.

'Peppermint's fine,' I called back and listened as he went about making tea.

'I don't care about you, anyway. I just want our money and I'll leave you be. Where is it?' he asked.

'The cops have it. I had no choice when they found my fingerprints in that restaurant you robbed. What the fuck were you doing there? You nearly killed that bloke. Anyway, they knew me and they came before I could leave and they took the money.'

'Jesus, DiDi,' he groaned, smashing his hand against the wall. He swore then he left before MD came to see what was going on.

I sat shaking, blinking away the tears and then MD was squatting before me.

'What's going on? What happened?' he demanded.

I burst into tears before I could tell him. He scooped me into his arms and sat beside me. 'What happened Jilly?' he asked again.

'He was here,' I whispered.

'Who was here?' he asked, even though I suspected he knew who I meant, he just couldn't believe it.

'Neil. He stood right there and spoke to me. He came out of the bushes. He grabbed my neck,' I said, demonstrating.

'Come inside,' MD insisted before storming out.

I could hear him shouting at people outside, shouting instructions to search every inch of bush. It wasn't their fault. Neil could blend in with the shadows and creep around like a cat.

Brad came in, his face full of thunder, but still he had nothing on MD when he was mad. 'Are you alright?' he asked.

I nodded.

'I can't believe it. He must have been sitting in those bushes for ages. There's guys all over the property. I don't know how he slipped through,' he said, completely stunned.

'It's what he does,' I told him. 'He's changed his look again. He could have checked in at the retreat, asked questions over appetisers in the restaurant and no one would have thought anything of it,' I said.

'I get a haircut and no one notices,' he said. 'He gets a haircut and he's completely unrecognisable,' he said, shaking his head.

I smiled.

'What now?' he asked MD as he came back. 'Any ideas?'

'We get her out of here, Brad. We fucking get her out and we find them,' shouted MD.

Brad shook his head. 'Take a walk, MD.'

'Hell no, I'm not leaving her,' he spat.

'I'm still in charge. You're no good to anyone worked up like this, take a walk, I'll sit right here until you get back,' Brad said, rising to his full height which was more than imposing.

MD grumbled. 'Don't do anything stupid,' he said, pointing at me before walking out.

'So, any ideas?' asked Brad.

I shrugged. 'Maybe one,' I smiled.

He shook his head. 'Go on, tell me,' he said.

'You let me go. Say you don't have enough evidence. No proof the money's not mine. Disgraced, nowhere to go and make sure it's on the news. I go to the beach. You, MD, the whole force nearby. They'll come. They won't come back here again. Neil knows I don't have the money and that's all he wants. He didn't bring Jo. He knows she wants to kill me, so I guess that's something. The best of his brotherly love, I suppose. We'll have to draw them out some other way.'

'MD won't let it happen and I won't go against him,' he said.

'MD won't let what happen?' MD asked re-joining us, looking much calmer.

I repeated my idea and he huffed, running his hand through his hair in frustration.

'Not happening Jilly. Your brother will know we're never giving you that money back. And that woman, your Aunt, she's going to get desperate. A woman like that, with that much anger, she's not going to be patient for long. She'll come. Especially as she thinks it's just us. She doesn't know Brad is sleeping on the couch. We've kept that low key for a reason, Jilly. We know what we're doing and what we're dealing with now, you won't be alone, not for a second. We'll get our chance.'

I wasn't getting my way so I grumbled, made something to eat then caught up on the missed Star Wars scenes.

The day passed in an interminable fog. My brain was numb but still I was anxious. MD was in and out, here and there, checking on things, calling in, checking with the people outside.

'Why do you just get to sit here and watch Star Wars movies while MD can't sit still?' I asked Brad.

'Everyone thinks I'm hanging out at the hotel with Sienna.'

'You're hoping she comes for me, aren't you?'

He shrugged. 'We're prepared for it if she does.'

'Come on, you're more than prepared, Brad.'

He smiled. 'Okay, we're more than prepared, we're hoping she does. We're counting on it. MD's driving us all bloody nuts, we need it over.'

'And you have other work to do, I'm sure?'

He shrugged. 'We all need it over Jilly.'

I nodded. 'What's going to happen to me Brad? When it's all over. What's going to happen to him?' I asked ask MD paced the little kitchenette on the phone.

'You're both going to be fine, Jilly. I told you. You were just a kid. No one wants to prosecute you. You're a victim.'

'Is it really that easy? I killed someone, Brad, I walked away and left him to die.'

Brad's hand covered mine. 'No one is prosecuting you, Jilly.'

I was about to argue but smelt something. Smoke. 'Do you smell that?' I asked as the breeze blew it inside.

Brad looked at MD and they shared some kind of nonverbal cop talk. MD nodded reluctantly, knocked on the back door, waited for the two cops that had been placed out there to come inside, then came to kneel in front of me.

'I have to go Jilly. Please, please, stay with Brad. Do not do anything he doesn't ask you to do. Okay? Promise me, Jilly. I need to know you're going to do what he says,' MD begged.

'I'll do whatever Brad says, I promise. Why? What's going on?'

'There's a fire at the main house.'

'What? Is everyone okay?'

'Everyone will be fine. But we think it's a diversion.'

'You think it's Joanne?'

He nodded.

'Then why are you going?' I asked, suddenly worried.

'Because they'll be watching. If she sees me leave, she'll think you're alone.'

'You're using me as bait?'

He looked sad.

'It's okay, I told Brad he could. It's okay MD. Brad's here, I'll be fine. Go.'

He looked like he wasn't going to go.

'MD,' Brad said quietly.

MD nodded. 'I know. Take care of her. Please.'

Brad nodded. 'I've got her, MD, it's okay.'

MD pulled me to him, then he was gone.

Brad reached for my hand. 'It's going to be okay Jilly. I've got you.'

Then he went to the kitchen, spoke to the cops there, sent them to the bedroom before arming himself then he sat in the armchair facing the door and we waited.

And waited.

And waited.

The smell of smoke grew stronger. I was surprised I couldn't see a blaze when I looked out the window.

'Are there cops out there?' I asked as we both watched the door.

'Nope. They went to the main house with MD.'

'It really is just us?'

He nodded.

'Then why isn't she coming for me? Where are they?'

'I don't know. Maybe they're just giving it some time, making sure MD's not coming back?'

'Is he okay? How do we know he's okay?'

'He'll be fine. Don't worry about MD.'

I sighed, it'd been hours. I got up to empty my bladder.

'Where are you going?' asked Brad, his voice on edge.

'Bathroom. I'm allowed to pee alone, right?'

He nodded with a smirk.

I opened the bathroom door, closed it behind me and sighed. The waiting was too much. It was like I'd been holding my breath for the last two hours. Then I turned around.

Joanne smirked at me. My brother stood behind her holding a young girl tight, a gun hanging in his hand. He saw me as my eyes caught it, smirked, shook his head making it clear I wasn't to do anything, her life was at stake.

'I told you, I don't have the money. They're never giving it back to me.'

'I don't care about the money,' spat Joanne.

'Then what do you want?'

She smirked, her teeth showing the signs of too much smoking and whatever else she'd indulged in while locked up. 'You know the rules, Sydney. No one in this family lives for free. There are consequences for every action,' she reminded me.

'I'm not a part of this family anymore.'

'What, you think these people are your new family? You're a fool if you think they're hanging around when this is all over. If you think that cop is sharing your bed when this is all done and dusted, you're an idiot. They're using you Sydney. This is a career making case for them, that's all they care about.'

'You're not getting in my head this time Joanne. You may be able to wrap my brother around your finger, but I'm not falling for it. Not anymore. I'm not a kid anymore.'

'What, now you think you're smarter than me?' she laughed, a nasty laugh that made my stomach turn.

'What do you want then?'

'It's simple, Jilly, a life for a life.'

My blood ran cold.

'Jo...' questioned Neil, clearly not on board with wherever this was headed.

I took a deep breath, trying to make a plan, to work out how long it would take Brad and the other cops to come if I screamed. Could I dive on Neil to protect the kid he was holding onto, the kid whose eyes were so frightened, my stomach twisted. I looked over Jo's body, trying to assess if she had her own weapon, if I screamed, dove for Neil, what did she have on her?

'Don't even think about it,' Joanne smirked. 'Neil will have that kid's throat cut before you can blink. We learnt things in gaol, see? While you were out here, living it up, spending our money, we were locked up learning how to survive and we did, as you can see, but there was a price. We had to do things. But not you. No, not you,' she smiled.

'I had to do things, too. I had to survive the only way I knew how. I didn't like it. I didn't like myself. I haven't been out here having a fucking party, you know.'

She took the gun out of Neil's hand, lined it up with my face. 'Nothing could have been close to what we went through. Nothing could have been close to what my Pete went through when you fucking shot him and left him to fucking die,' she shouted, no longer caring if anyone heard her. She must have known Brad was in the living room, the cops in the bedroom, otherwise she'd have come for me, not waited in the bathroom but she was losing her cool, her control. She clicked the safety off the gun and I fell to my knees. I was here again. Someone's victim again and I had no way out, no way to protect myself. My head fell to my hands as I cried. MD was never going to forgive himself. His face filled my mind and that was all I saw as the gunshot exploded.

'Jilly, Jilly, come on, open your eyes,' begged Brad.

Slowly I could feel his arms around me as his voice sank in.

'Jilly? Jilly?' MD called.

I slowly opened my eyes, not sure what was happening but there was MD, his hands holding my face as he looked at me, then he pulled me close.

'Oh Jilly, are you okay?' he asked, looking me over.

'What happened? I heard the shot,' I said.

'That was me,' Brad said. 'Through the door.'

'How?'

'You took too long to pee and by the time I came to check on you, the guys already had the infrared imaging in place. We couldn't get a clear shot through the door though until you went down to your knees.'

'Where's Neil? The girl?'

'They're outside. It's fine, it's over,' MD soothed.

'I want to see them.'

'Jilly...'

'Please, he's still my brother. She's my niece or cousin, or something.

MD nodded and guided me outside where Joanne was in a bag being loaded into an ambulance. Neil was cuffed, on his knees sobbing like a baby. The girl stood stunned to the side.

'Are you okay?' I asked her.

She nodded. 'I think so. Can I go home now?'

I pulled her in for a hug. 'You can go home.'

Someone led her away. Neil howled as they shut the door on the ambulance containing Joanne.

I knelt beside him, pulled him to me while he cried. 'I'm so sorry DiDi, I'm so sorry,' he cried. 'It wasn't supposed to turn out like this. DiDi, we were supposed to just start over.'

'She had this pull over you Neil, you could never see straight. It's not your fault,' I soothed while he kept saying sorry until someone hoisted him up and loaded him into the back of a car.

As he drove away, I fell into MD and sobbed.

'Jilly?' Brad said.

I looked up. 'It's not over, is it?' I knew everything he'd said was too good to be true. You can't kill a man, walk away, leave him to die after everything I'd done as part of Jo and Peter's team and just walk away scot free.

'Hey, no, it's not that. I just need you to speak to some people and then MD can take you home. It's okay Jilly, I promise,' Brad smiled.

I spoke to Brad's people, gave a long statement about everything that had happened. Then, like Brad promised, I was free to go.

CHAPTER 27

'Jilly,' called Brad. 'I just got word that there's a few people and a jug of margaritas waiting for you over at The Beach House,' he smiled.

'Really?'

'We just need to finish up here but Jase will give you a lift and we'll meet you there,' MD smiled. 'Are you okay?'

'I'm okay,' I said, kissing him, letting our mouths mould together in a way I never thought they would again. Perhaps there was hope that I wasn't ruined, after all?

'Go,' he nodded towards the car with a smile.

When Jase pulled up to the kerb, I flung the door open and almost ran. I needed to see my friends. My good, perfect, kind, beautiful friends. I saw them from across the street sitting by the big open window. Sienna, Mel and Rick sitting around a table by the window and a jug of margaritas and a bunch of glasses in front of them. They were waiting for me and I couldn't help but smile. It was really over. I had friends. A life. I could finally breathe.

'Jilly!' they cried as the saw me crossing the street.

Sienna jumped out of the big open window and ran to me, smacking into me and hugging me so tightly I lost my breath but I laughed. We both laughed.

'Come, come, we've been waiting for you,' she said dragging me into the bar.

I hugged Mel and Rick before sitting down beside Sienna as Rick filled my glass.

We 'cheers'd' and clinked our glasses.

'How long have you all been here?'

This is where we've been staying. Brad called us about 15 minutes ago and we came straight down here to wait for you.

'Did you hear they're not charging me with anything?'

'Brad mentioned it, yes,' smiled Sienna.

'I feel guilty. Especially being here, drinking margaritas with my friends,' I said.

'Why?' Sienna asked.

'I killed a man,' I whispered, choking up, still not believing it was all over.

'In self-defence when you were a child,' said Rick. 'It's okay, Jilly,' he said, reaching across and holding my hand. 'This is right. This is how it should be,' he insisted.

'Well, I hope the rest of the world agrees with you,' I said as I saw the journos starting to gather but being held off by Jase.

'Don't worry about them,' insisted Mel. 'MD won't let them crucify you.'

I looked across the road and I saw MD talking to a journalist. Our eyes locked across the street and I smiled. He smiled. He politely excused himself from the journalist and ran across the road.

I stood as he came in. 'You okay?' he asked.

I nodded.

He smiled. He kissed me and Sienna went around the bar for more glasses as Brad came in and kissed her like he meant it, catching her off guard and rendering her speechless.

'So, what happens now?' I asked.

'You finally get to have a life,' Mel said, raising her glass.

'I suppose I do,' I smiled.

'What do you want to do? With your life, how do you want to live now you don't have to run?' asked Sienna.

'I don't know,' I said. 'I've never thought about how else I'd like to live. I never thought I'd have a choice,' I said.

'Well you don't have to decide anything right now,' MD said.

'What's the matter, Mitch, afraid she won't choose you?' teased Sienna, knowing full well I'd never choose anyone else.

MD huffed and I realised perhaps Sienna had hit a nerve.

'You know that no matter what else I do, I'll always choose you. You'll always be the centre of everything else,' I said to him.

'Would it be too soon for you to move in with me, then?' he asked, hopefully.

'Or you could move in with us,' Sienna offered. 'I might be out a bit more than usual,' she smirked, looking at Brad. 'And we'll be recording in Sydney soon and with Rick away so much of the time, I don't think it would be nice to leave Mel in that big house all by herself.'

'I'd appreciate it, mate,' said Rick.

'Me too,' said Mel.

'You're there all the time anyway and it's as much your house as it is mine,' Sienna said.

'Then I guess that's that decided,' he smiled, shaking his head.

'I know, they're a bossy bunch, right?' I laughed.

'Like he's not. You wait, Jilly, you don't know what you've just signed up for,' Sienna laughed.

MD threw a peanut at his sister and we all laughed.

Sienna went behind the bar and made another jug of margaritas and for the first time in my life, I drank with my friends without worrying about what I'd let slip if I drank too much. I was me. Just me. Entirely me and they loved me. We laughed and we talked and I counted every single blessing.

When the second jug was empty we took our party home. Inside the door, Mel and Rick went to their room. Upstairs we lost Sienna and Brad to Sienna's room and it was just MD and me.

'Do you want to eat?' he suggested.

I shrugged. 'There's probably no food here, anyway.'

'I could order a pizza,' he suggested, leaning against the doorframe of the kitchen.

'In a bit, maybe,' I said. I took a couple of steps toward him, placed my hand on his chest. He watched me, cautiously. 'You know what I think I'd like?' I asked.

'What's that?' he asked, as though he had no idea where I was going.

I pulled his shirt up, pulled it over his head, letting it fall to the floor. He didn't stop me but warily he said, 'Jilly...you know you don't have to,' he said.

'I know,' I told him.

'Why don't we wait, sleep on it. You've had a few drinks. I don't want you pushing yourself too far too soon and regretting it.'

'I won't regret it. Not with you. I'm sick of living my life under the clouds of other people's shit. I'm not their victim, not anymore. This is my life. I'm not going to be afraid anymore, MD. I'm not going to let the Eric's and Peter's of this world stop me from living my life, from loving you.'

'I know you love me,' he said.

'I do,' I agreed. I ran my hands over his bare chest and he just stood there, letting me, watching me. 'I have had a few drinks, yes. I still have a little adrenalin running through my body. But I also have something else. After Eric, I never thought I'd be able to stand being touched again. But right now, I don't think I could stand it one more minute if you don't touch me. I need you, MD. I want you. I want to celebrate my new life with you. I want to be with you,' I said, looking into his eyes, hoping he understood.

He smiled. 'Well, I would like nothing more than to celebrate with you,' he smiled, tipping my chin so our mouths met in one of those toe-curling, heart-stopping kisses he was so good at. 'But with a house full of people, I'm not celebrating with you out here,' he winked. 'Come,' he said, leading me to our bedroom.

'Are you sure?' he asked quietly after he'd closed the door.

I nodded. 'I'm sure.'

'You tell me if I need to stop, if I'm hitting any triggers. Promise me?'

'I promise,' I agreed.

'Okay, then,' he smirked, ambling into my personal space and reaching for the bottom of my tank top and edging me onto the bed.

Everything he did, he did carefully and slowly and sweetly. He avoided touching my inner thigh but I don't think it'd have mattered. His hands were warm and beautiful. Everything he did was perfect and electrifying. Those hands did things that made me wish we'd gone to his place, after all.

A Harrington Family Story

Alexandra
DEEN

TAMARA
MARTIN

Alexandra Deen

Beside me, the River Seine bubbled like a witch's brew. Fat raindrops soaked my clothes, chilling me right through to the bone. Tears streaked what remained of my make up and I was glad I couldn't see my own face. I'd become a version of myself I no longer recognised. Not just in the last couple of hours, but the last few years if I were honest. If I were brave enough to face the reality of who I'd become, who I'd allowed myself to become because it would be easier. It was expected.

The streets of the most romantic city in the world were suspiciously quiet, as though it were ashamed it hadn't lived up to the hype. My feet hurt, from the cold, from the wet, from poorly chosen pretty ballet flats. I shivered, unable to stop the quivering of my lip.

A car horn blared, my heart near leapt from my chest.

I stepped back onto the kerb. 'Pay attention, Lexi,' I scolded myself. Billy bloody McCrae certainly wasn't worth getting run down on a dark Parisian street. So my life was officially in the gutter, it wasn't reason enough to die. Or worse, end up in a

Parisian hospital all alone and having to call my mother to come and get me.

Catching my breath, I wiped my tear-stained face, checked the street for traffic and trundled across the road towards the music, the laughter, the dry roof of the hostel matching the map on the now bedraggled pamphlet in my hand.

I was angry and sad and so disappointed the weight of it crushed my lungs, stealing my breath as I stood before the big blue doors, the rain falling in sheets around me, my clothes soaked and heavy. I watched a piece of peeling paint flapping in the breeze, resisting the urge to pull at it and wondered if I should I knock on the door or should I just walk in? I'd never stayed in such a place before, somewhere without a doorman to direct me. Was there an etiquette I should have been aware of? The paint chipped doors suggested etiquette didn't rule this little corner of Paris.

Looking for guidance, for something, I spotted a girl with wild black curls sitting on the balustrade of a small verandah heaving with jovial young people, drinking beer from bottles, unaware the world was full of misery and cheating bastard boyfriends. She laughed, her whole body shaking from the happiness. I wondered if it would feel as good as it looked, to laugh that way, to be that happy. I wondered if I'd ever been that happy. If I'd ever laughed that freely. I couldn't remember.

The girl looked over her sun-kissed shoulder, smiled and nodded towards the door. I turned away, embarrassed. What was wrong with me? I don't stand on streets in the middle of the night, lurking, staring at strangers. I was losing my bloody mind.

I sucked in a deep, fortifying breath. It wasn't a palatial hotel with marble floors, but it would do until I could get the hell out of Paris, I reminded myself and pulled open the door.

The foyer was sparse but clean and dry. A worn timber chair sat beneath a phone attached to the wall. A staircase opposite wound its way up into the hidden heart of the hostel. The well-worn reception desk was directly in front. Behind the desk, sat a girl with red hair so bright it almost glowed, framing a face as perfect as porcelain. The girl chuckled at something Homer Simpson said in French on the television beside her, completely oblivious or perhaps purposely ignoring the fact that I'd just stumbled in and was dripping all over the streaked timber floor.

I walked towards the desk, my shoes squelching loudly in the quiet, my insides cringing from embarrassment. She finally looked up from the television as I reached the counter, raising her eyebrows, trying not to smile at the makeup streaked all over my face and hair stuck to my head like paint and dripping all over her counter.

'Dorm or single, hon?' she asked with a poetic French accent.

'Whatever's cheapest?' I stammered, tears choking my vocal chords as I pulled scrunched, damp euros from my handbag.

'Dorm it is, then. Room two, bunk three.' She put a key attached to a block of wood atop a pile of linen and a towel and handed the pile over the counter as though I were an army recruit reporting for duty. She sent me up the stairs with no further question, as though I'd stood before her in a sundress in the middle of the afternoon instead of a drowned, miserable version of a person in the middle of the night. But maybe that's what happened in places like this? Vagrants, society's misfits and those spat out by the world, appeared at all hours so often, it was accepted as the norm?

Four bunk beds had been crammed into the room she sent me to, each flanked at the foot with a metal locker. Flimsy curtains covered the long, short, rectangular windows that were too high up to see out of. The dull light from the bulb hidden under the white plastic shade on the ceiling wasn't dull enough to hide the worn timber floor covered with the debris of the room's missing inhabitants; a discarded towel, a pair of thongs, backpacks, socks and a navy blue hoodie.

They had squeezed the tiniest bathroom I'd ever seen into the far corner, just big enough for a toilet, basin and shower. It was a far cry from the fancy hotel I'd woken in with its giant bathtub and shiny white tiles and luxury complimentary bath products, but it didn't matter. Not much mattered right now other than getting through the night and thinking about tomorrow when tomorrow showed up.

As I organised my things, my mind flashed to the morning when I'd strolled the streets of Paris, the bridges that arched over the Seine, hand in hand, happy, in love. I'd seen the Eiffel Tower rising above the trees in the distance, wondered if it would be there that Billy would sink to one knee on the grass and ask me to be his wife. I'd have said yes, too. I'd been a fool. Of course I'd been a fool. I'd been a fool for years. Now I had to find the strength to go home and face my family, my friends. What friends? They'd all known, I'd seen it on their faces in the fancy Parisian restaurant where we were dining, when my life had unravelled at my feet. They'd eaten dinner in my home, eaten my food and drunk my wine laughing in my face, laughing behind my back.

No, they were Billy's friends and he could keep them. I didn't want them. Friends don't allow you to be blindsided in foreign countries. Friends save you, they protect you, they look out for you. They don't just sit back and watch your life crumble. No, I had no friends. I didn't have much of anything now. Perhaps just the scrap of dignity I'd held onto when I'd told Billy to go to hell and walked out of the fancy restaurant where he'd sat with that woman draped across his lap and the revelations had unfolded, piece by piece in seconds but what had felt like hours. I'd walked out with nothing, no friends, no savings, nowhere to go, nothing.

I dug around in my suitcase for something to wear to bed but almost everything was damp. I knew I should have bought the one with the hard shell case, I thought to myself as I began pulling things out. After hanging my wet clothes over the edges of my bed, over my suitcase, from the open locker door, I squeezed between the bunks to the bathroom. The cubicle was small but the water was hot and I thawed, movement returning to my fingertips and toes. I leant on the wall, letting the hot water beat on my body, glad to be feeling something other than devastation or misery or self hatred.

Careful not to overuse the hot water, I reluctantly stepped out of the shower, my bones finally warmed, my skin red, raw, and shiny new. I threw on an almost dry t-shirt and undies, already imagining the sweet perfection of the warm bed and the desperate bout of indulgent wallowing that waited.

With my towel and wet clothes gathered in my arms, I squeezed between the bunks and found the girl with the wild black curls sitting on my bed, absently picking at a hang nail and swinging her leg as though to a tune only she could hear.

She looked up as I dropped my loot onto my suitcase.

'Hey,' she said in an Australian accent, holding out a bottle of beer.

'Hello,' I replied as though in question, but taking the beer she offered anyway.

'You alright?' she asked.

I shrugged.

'Wanna talk about it?' she asked.

'Not really.'

'That means you really should. It'd be better than wallowing or letting it eat you up all night. It might help you sleep at least,' she offered.

I shrugged. She had some good points and really, what did I have to lose? Pride? I couldn't lose much more and maybe once I hit bottom I could start building myself back up. Somehow.

'I got duped, that's all. Utterly blindsided. The man I loved wasn't who I thought he was. My friends let me down, let me fall. I just, I don't know, my head's still spinning.'

'Are there actual details in there? Come on, sit, spit them out, otherwise you'll keep seeing them every time you close your eyes.'

'I sure as hell don't need that,' I laughed, surprising myself. 'We came for a wedding. We were at dinner with some of our friends. I went to the toilet, stopped to take a phone call from mum. I'd called her earlier but forgot the time difference. Anyway, we only talked for a few minutes. When I came back into the restaurant, there was this girl, I'd seen her a couple of times at the footy, never paid her any attention, knew she knew some of our friends but had no idea her and Billy knew each other as anything more than passing acquaintances. I'll never forget her, tall, lanky, all arms and legs, Kardashian hair and a laugh like a strangled hyena. She was draped all over my boyfriend. His hands were all over her and his face was buried in her hair. I don't know what he was doing, kissing her neck, whispering something. I don't know. I just froze and when he saw me he just laughed. He was drunk I guess, just enough to not care what I saw or what he said. Suggested a ménage a trois. Said it'd be very French of us.'

'What did your friends do?'

'They just sat there. Fuckers,' I laughed, taking a long sip of cold beer.

'Fuckers,' agreed my new friend, tapping her bottle to mine.

'She wasn't the only one. She laughed when I thought she was. Then it all began falling into place, the late nights, the 2am showers, the unanswered calls and I asked the questions. Turns out he's been all over the place with anyone who'd take him for years. None of it was real. We weren't real and I just don't know who I am now without him. Everything has been him. Everything I'd planned for the rest of my life had been with him. Now it's just me and I don't know what to do. He chose everything, decided everything and I let him because he was usually right and it was easier than hearing I told you so. So I let him and now I feel so stupid and lost.'

'Did you notice you never said you loved him or that your heart was broken? You've just been humiliated and horribly inconvenienced,' she smiled.

'Really? Huh,' I mumbled, realising she was exactly right. I was pissed off. I was annoyed. I was afraid and utterly humiliated. But I wasn't sad. I wasn't brokenhearted. How was that possible? I'd loved him, didn't I? We shared a home, a bed, a future. I'd planned babies and old age with him. I had to have loved him. But this bringer of beer and kind shoulders was right, my heart didn't feel broken. I wanted to wallow but I didn't feel the need to cry for him. I'd cried from the surprise, the devastation, for who I'd become, but the thought of never seeing Billy again, never having to listen to his obnoxious lectures or be bossed around, left me with nothing but relief.

As I finished my beer, my new friend said, 'Come on, plenty

more of those downstairs. Your new life starts now. A new life where you're in charge,' she smiled.

I liked the sound of that.

'We'll be gentle, I promise,' she offered, holding her hand out to me.

I took her hand and let her pull me up.

'I'm Lydia,' she said, finally introducing herself.

'Alexandra.'

'Come on Alex, let's go see if you're in there somewhere.'

I laughed, forgiving her for the choice of nickname. I hated Alex, it was a boy's name. My friends and family call me Lexi, but for one night, what did it matter? For one night I could be anyone and at that moment I was pretty done with Lexi the lovely doormat.

I followed Lydia onto the verandah and into the throng of people still enjoying the night and thanked my beer buzz when she called everyone to attention, commanding the spotlight.

'Alex, this is everyone. Everyone, this is Alex. She needs beer and kindness and it's our duty as fellow travelers, to provide her with both,' she insisted as I tried smiling.

Mumbles of agreement followed sympathetic nods. Beers were passed forward through the crowd of people with words of sympathy and welcome. Lydia draped a kind, friendly, comforting arm around me and led me to the balustrade she'd occupied earlier.

'What a bastard. Forget him,' Lydia said. 'Everything will be better now you've left him, you'll see. You'll pick yourself back up and find a new way now you've found the strength to stand up for yourself.'

'He has to be a real asshole to bring you all this way and then do that,' claimed a bright, bubbly girl with blonde dreadlocks when Lydia told her my boyfriend had turned out to be an ass. She was another Aussie. In fact, they mostly seemed to be Aussies, like the hostel was a magnet for lost Aussie souls, although I seemed to be the only one truly lost.

'Thanks,' I said, taking deep breaths, waiting for the tears welling in my eyes to evaporate. It would take some getting used to, figuring out who I was without him, thinking of how I would move forward alone, it had all happened so suddenly it was a lot to comprehend. Six years with the same man was a long time. He's all I knew, we'd been together my entire adult life.

A few beers in and I couldn't believe the world I'd landed in. These people spoke of adventures and places that sounded too good to be true, surfing in places I'd never heard of, finding treasure in small European towns where no one spoke English, cycling along the coastline in remote villages, the sun kissing their skin, falling in love, eating incredible food. They laughed loud, they wore simple cotton summer dresses and crazy board shorts, the men with permanent five o'clock shadows, living in a world so far removed from my grey cubicle and suburban life back home that I could hardly comprehend any of it and now here they were, welcoming me into their fold, commiserating with me over beers as though we were old friends.

I leant on the balustrade, looking out over the dark road, slick and wet under the moon's bright rays now the clouds had moved on. Had I really stood out there on the footpath in the rain? Now I was dry and warm and comforted, sipping cold beer amongst the laughter and camaraderie, I couldn't believe that had been me. Who was that person? In fact, who was that person I'd become over the last six years? Not someone I recognised. Not someone

I particularly liked and I hadn't even realised it was happening. Somewhere it'd just been easier to give me up and go with the flow, abide by everyone else's expectations, my boss, my mother, Billy. I didn't even know which bits were me and which were Billy. All I knew was Lydia was right. It was time to find out who I was.

'What's with all the thinking?' asked Lydia, twisting the top off another beer.

'Oh, nothing,' I half smiled. 'Just thinking how different the day's ended to how I'd expected.'

'Yeah, life does that,' she smiled.

'I've been here one bloody day and my life's been turned upside down. How does that even happen? This trip was not supposed to go this way.'

'Maybe it was and you just didn't realise it. The universe has a way of kicking us up the behind when we don't pay attention.'

I laughed a huffy laugh because she was probably right. 'It was easy to ignore it all.'

'Isn't it always,' she grinned. 'Until the kicking comes and you have no choice.'

'So, what are your plans from here?' a man asked, joining us at the balustrade.

I turned away from the rain soaked street, looked up and our eyes locked. It was him. My knight, my saviour who'd given me the pamphlet that had led me here. The waiter with the sun bleached shaggy hair, broad shoulders, wide smile and laughing grey green eyes that knew things, that loved things, that loved life. He wore a loose fitting, faded yellow tank top with bright, multi-coloured board shorts and blue thongs on his sun drenched feet.

The sun had soaked his body, from his biceps to his beautiful broad shoulders. I tried not to look but my eyes wanted to linger, to drink him in. Where did men that beautiful even come from? What was I even doing noticing? I was supposed to be crying into my beer not admiring handsome strangers that help damsels in distress find refuge. But for just one second, everything stood still and my breath caught in my chest.

'You?' I asked softly.

He smiled.

'You know each other?' Lydia asked.

I wanted to laugh, as if I know men that look like him. Billy was alright, handsome enough, a good catch even, so everyone kept telling me, but Billy had nothing on this bloke. This bloke was tall, slightly rugged, his strong jaw covered lightly in stubble, everything about him was strong, then there was his lovely mouth and puppy dog eyes that smiled without trying. I mentally shook my head clear to stop from staring.

'It was my restaurant she was at earlier,' he told Lydia. 'Well not mine,' he said to me, 'the one where I was working. Just filling in actually, not really my thing waiting tables, prefer pouring beers, but a mate needed a favour, they were short and needed a hand.'

'Well, thanks,' I said. 'I've no idea where I'd have gone without the pamphlet you gave me.'

'Oh a regular knight, huh,' joked Lydia.

'I'm Tom by the way,' he smiled, his whole face lighting up as though lit from the inside by his own personal sun. Then, his right bicep flexed beautifully as he stretched his arm around Lydia's shoulders, draping it there casually, as though he'd done it a thousand times. I felt my heart sink all the way down to my toes.

Don't be ridiculous, I told myself. Of course he has a girlfriend. What was wrong with me? What was wrong with my brain? I'd just left Billy, the supposed love of my life, the man I'd shared intimate moments with, cared for when he was sick, gone to birthday parties with, hosted barbeques with, told all my deepest secrets and wishes to, the man I'd expected a bloody proposal from under the Eiffel Tower. My head was still spinning with everything that had happened, where I'd ended up, what lay ahead. I couldn't fancy someone else already. My traumatised brain was just confused, that was all.

'Um, I'll see if I can get a flight home in the morning, I suppose,' I said, answering Tom's question

'Home? No!' cried Lydia. 'You're in Paris, Alex. You've only been here a day. You can't go yet. This is one of the most beautiful cities you'll ever see.'

I shrugged. She was right. But I was short on funds now I had a life to rebuild and really, no inclination to wander the streets alone.

'You know what you should do,' Tom said, looking at Lydia as though he'd solved the most intricate puzzles of the universe.

'Absolutely!' she cried, reading his mind.

I watched them, waiting for an explanation.

'Come down the coast with us, Alex. Oh you have to. It's just what you need, a bit of sun and sand, the ocean will heal all those wounds and you'll be good as new in no time. France is incredible, you can't miss out now that you're here. Please. Please say *oui*,' Lydia begged, gripping my arm in anticipation.

'What? No, no. We just met. You don't want me imposing on your trip,' I insisted, despite how nice the prospect of forgetting my life and laying on a beach in a foreign country sounded.

'Don't be ridiculous, the more the merrier. We'd love you to come with us. I promise, we're relatively normal, non murdering types, you have to come and balance out all the testosterone,' she insisted with a smile that left me both nervous and more excited than I could remember ever being.

'We have a car,' Tom added proudly.

'That's so nice, really it is but I don't think my failing funds will allow me to stay much longer than tonight anyway, I'm afraid. This was Billy's trip. He paid for the flights, the accommodation. I've just got a little spending money for bits and bobs, souvenirs, snacks, maybe a dinner or two, that sort of thing,' I admitted sadly.

'That doesn't matter,' Lydia said, waving my worries away. 'None of us have any money, but we get by, that's half the fun.'

'Really?' I couldn't believe it. They were all so happy. They didn't look hungry and the travel stories they'd shared in the last hour were so mind blowing they didn't even seem real; how could they all have no money? Living the life they lived cost money, surely? Billy and I had spent nights planning and budgeting for this trip. But what if all this time I'd had it backwards? 'But how?' I had to ask.

'Ah, you have to come for us to share all our secrets,' Lydia winked, laughing.

'C'mon, Alex, it'll be fun. You need some fun. We leave first thing tomorrow and it's just for a few days. It will cost next to nothing, I promise. We have a spare bed in the villa, and I am pretty sure it has your name on it,' Tom insisted.

'You can't go home yet, you have to come,' begged Lydia.

All the usual thoughts ran through my head again as though on repeat. Blah, blah, blah. What I really wanted to do was blow off my life and go to the bloody beach with this group of the coolest, most amazing people I'd ever met. To have the much needed fun Tom spoke of. To lay in the sun and pretend none of it had happened, that I hadn't been so humiliated I was afraid to look people in the eye. Forget it all and laugh. It'd been so long since I'd just let go and laughed, I'd forgotten what it felt like. These people were reminding me and I wasn't ready to let it go, to go back.

So, after taking a long sip of beer for courage, I ignored that annoying voice in my head, the one that had led me down this path in the first place. 'Fine, fine, okay, *oui*,' I agreed, panicking as soon as the words were out despite my newfound courage and resolution.

I couldn't drive to some French coast with these people. I'd just met them. It was crazy. Lydia was crazy. Tom was crazy. They were all crazy. But it did seem silly to waste the airfare Billy had paid for and they were right, I was in Paris, anything was possible in Paris, right?

*
*
*
*